"Victor really was a very good man."

Why then did someone brutally murder Victor Whyte, an elderly man chiefly known for his dedication to helping the gay community?

Inspector Claire Summerskill and Sergeant Dave Lyon investigate and are drawn into the world of the Hereford and Worcester Lesbian and Gay Switchboard, a telephone helpline for LGBQT+ people. Operatives and callers help piece together a picture of the murdered man, and gradually a surprising picture of Victor emerges with the possibility of a murderer in the very last place Summerskill and Lyon would have thought of.

Even as they deal with this latest case, the two officers are forced to deal with turning points in their personal lives. Can Claire balance the demands of her position as an inspector with those of her husband and children? Is Dave ready to settle into a relationship with earnest young police officer Joe Jones or will he opt instead for the excitement of an almost certainly shorter fling with charismatic MP Sean Cullen? And what exactly is Sean's real motivation?

Crossed Lines is the fourth in the series of Summerskill and Lyon police procedural novels.

GW00401035

CROSSED LINES

Summerskill and Lyon, Book Four

Steve Burford

A NineStar Press Publication

www.ninestarpress.com

Crossed Lines

Printed in the USA

ISBN: 978-1-64890-429-5

First Edition, November, 2021

Also available in eBook, ISBN: 978-1-64890-428-8

CONTENT WARNING:
This book contains depictions of violence, and references to domestic abuse, homophobia, and cheating.

For Robert.

Good friend. Good opponent.

Chapter One

Dave Lyon examined the muscular, naked man smiling up at him from the sheepskin rug. "I'm a Power Bottom," read the caption beneath him, "And I Always Have Safer Sex." Dave sighed.

"Wishing you were curled up with him?" his immediate boss, DI Claire Summerskill, asked as she entered the cramped office. "Or is there only room on your rug for one other now?"

"You know you get very camp when you take the piss. Ma'am."

Claire shrugged. "That was quite a longing look there. Love's young dream isn't fading already, is it?"

"Love's young dream is, at this moment, on hold while Love's young dreamers investigate a murder." Dave indicated the poster they had been considering. "And actually, I was wondering why gay men have to be in such a rush to label themselves. 'Top'. 'Bottom'. 'Passive'. 'Submissive'. It's more confusing than quantum physics." He gave one last look at the happy stud on the rug, particularly at his magnificently rounded arse. "Still, this was in a good cause, I suppose."

"Eyes back in your head and on me, Sergeant. Let's have a look at what we've got here. Could you give us a moment, please, Maggie?"

The SOCO officer in whites put down her camera and stepped away from what she was photographing, revealing the figure of a man slumped in a chair in front of a desk. His face was distorted and blackened. Around his neck was a length of telephone cord wrapped several times and pulled tightly into the flesh.

"I've only seen one other person killed like this," Claire said quietly.

"Bill Kilby."

"Yeah. But he was a big man, prime of his life." She grimaced. "Bit of a shit, too, as you'll recall. But this. An old man. On his own." She scanned the cramped room. "Surely there wasn't anything of value here?"

"I wouldn't have thought so," Dave said. "We'll find out soon enough, I suppose."

Claire took a moment to imprint the unpleasant scene on her memory. She hated it, bitterly resented filling her mind with such vile imagery. But it was her job, and the only way to exorcise the picture was to find the bastard responsible for it, and if that meant sitting on any squeamishness she had till it was done, then that was what she would do. "All right, Maggie," she said finally, gesturing for the SOCO officer to return to her work. She turned to Dave. "Let's go and talk to these witnesses Chris has got for us and see if we can't begin piecing together what's gone down here."

Summerskill and Lyon stepped out of the office and into a large, incongruously ornate hall. On three sides was a series of doors, all presumably leading to small offices or rooms similar to the one they had come out of. Above them, there was a mezzanine, with more doors all around that. White columns, presumably wooden but carved like something out of a Greek temple, reared up around the space, topped with gilded wreaths of what Claire assumed were meant to be laurel leaves. "What is this place?"

"How long have you lived in this city?" Dave reached for his notebook.

Claire scowled but couldn't deny the implied criticism. The building they were in stood on the very edge of the city's high street, its worn brick and wood exterior a sharp contrast to the clean-cut brightness of the metal and glass shop fronts surrounding it. Over the years she had lived in Worcester, Claire must have passed it several hundred times, either while on duty or when out shopping, but beyond its name, which was carved in stone over the impressive main double-door entrance, she realised she didn't know anything about it at all.

"The Halo Centre," Dave read from his pad. "Grade Two listed building. Built 1887 by the Congressional Church as a Sunday school. Repurposed as Vagabonds Nightclub, 1974. Repurposed again in 1990 as a centre for various arts and charity groups." He flipped his notebook shut and slipped it back into his jacket pocket. "Including the Worcester and Hereford Gay and Lesbian Switchboard."

"And what's that when it's at home? Some kind of hook-up operation?"

"It's a telephone helpline. The sort of place you can turn to in the face of all too prevalent homophobia. And microaggression." He gave his boss a look that he would have described as "jaundiced" and she would have dismissed as "sarky". "The Centre is noted as having an unusual plan with offices in rows around a central two-storey hall with a gallery on columns in polygonal plan.'"

"You had time to look up and memorise all that, and you still got here before me?"

"Other way round, ma'am. I got here first and then had time to learn it. While I waited."

Claire scowled at him again and strode out across the hall towards the small group of people gathered at the far end. "I might be slow in traffic, but you'd be amazed how fast I can bust mardy sergeants. Chris!" she called out.

Sergeant Chris McNeil looked up from the seated person he was dealing with. "Inspector. Sergeant."

"What have we got?"

"Will you excuse me for a minute, please?" Sergeant McNeil stepped away from the man he'd been talking to and moved to one side so he could speak to Claire and Dave in a low voice. "You've seen the victim? Name is Victor Whyte. Midseventies. Was working for the Worcester and Hereford Lesbian and Gay Switchboard. That's their office where you saw him. The Switchboard is for—"

"I know what the Switchboard is for," Claire said. Dave coughed. She ignored him. "And these people are witnesses?" She indicated the man McNeil had been talking to and the woman across the hall who was also seated and being attended by a pair of paramedics.

"Kind of. Both that bit too late to stop the killer, and neither able to detain him. He was long gone before we got here, ma'am."

Claire looked across to the seated woman. "Is she okay?"

"Slight bump on the head and a small amount of bleeding from a cut on her cheek. Nothing major. Bit shook up though."

"Not surprising. And what were these two doing here at this time of night? Do they both work for the Switchboard?"

"The man does. He's another Switchboard volunteer. The current chairman in fact. The woman is a cleaner for the Halo Centre. Works in all the offices."

"Right. Pad out again, Sergeant," she said to Dave. "Let's go and talk to these people."

They began with the man McNeil had been interviewing. "This is Mr. Clive Grover, ma'am," the sergeant said, stepping back to let the detectives take over.

Claire made the introductions for herself and Dave, and the two of them drew up a couple of old, wooden fold-up chairs that McNeil had brought over from the corner of the hall. She reckoned Clive Grover must have been in his early fifties.

He was stocky, his hair thinning and silver at the temples but very fashionably cut for a man his age, and he had those little round glasses she always associated with accountants but which were also inexplicably trendy at the moment. Somewhat at odds with the hair and glasses was the tweedy though not inexpensive jacket he was wearing. Right now, he had that look: the dazed expression of someone shocked by the sight of something he had never dreamed he would ever see.

With an unexpected bitterness, she remembered when she'd been that un-spoiled. "I know Sergeant McNeil has already asked you to explain what happened to you, Mr. Grover, but if you could, I'd be very grateful if you'd run through it again, for Sergeant Lyon and myself." She watched as Grover made a visible effort to compose himself before speaking.

"Of course, Inspector." Grover glanced up at an ormolu clock over the entrance to the hall behind the officers. "It must have been forty, fifty minutes ago now, when I called in on the office. Most of the hall was in darkness which it usually is at this time of night unless one of the other groups that uses it is holding an evening meeting or event. That was how I could see the light from our office coming through the gap at the bottom of the door. As I was walking towards it, I heard someone talking. At first, I thought it was one of our operators on the phone but then I realised whoever it was was shouting, which is definitely not normal practice."

"Did you recognise the voice?"

"No. I'm sorry. Anyway, I thought something must be wrong, maybe one of our operators was having a really rough call, so I made my way over to the office pretty quickly. But as I reached the door, it flew open in my face and a man barrelled past me and sent me flying. I fell back against one of the pillars there. It fair knocked the breath out of me, I can tell you. I could hear him running across the hall, and then I heard the door thrown open. I suppose I should have got up and run after him, but as I was getting up again, I heard Karen screaming."

"Karen?"

Grover nodded towards the woman with the paramedics. "Our cleaner. I say 'our'—she works for the Centre as a whole. As I said, she was screaming—" He paused. "—shouting I suppose would be more accurate, so instead of following the man I ran into the office to see what was wrong. And that was when…" He stopped, and they saw again that effort to compose himself. "That was when I saw him. Victor. He was…" He looked down at his hands clasped in his lap, unable to go on.

"It's all right, Mr. Grover. We know. You don't have to say it."

"I…I don't think I could believe it. It was so horrible. Karen flung herself at me and clung to me. It was several minutes before I could get her to let go. Then I called the police. On my mobile. I have to say, it didn't take them long to get here."

"The station is very close by, sir."

"Of course. Anyway, they got here, and then they called the paramedics, and then you, and now…here we are." In under a minute, Clive Grover had summed up what would probably prove to be the most traumatic event in his entire life.

"The man who pushed past you," Dave said. "Did you manage to get a look at him? Could you describe him?"

"I'm sorry, Sergeant. I don't think I can. It all happened so fast. Plus, as I said, most of the hall was in darkness. When the office door burst open in my face, the sudden light in my eyes made everything else seem even darker, and it was coming from behind the man, so he was just a giant shadow to me. All I got was an impression of this hulking black outline."

"Hulking? And giant you say. Definitely a big man, then?"

"Yes. No." Grover's face twisted in anguish as he struggled to answer the question. "I'm not sure. I'd like to say yes, but it all happened so quickly, and for most of it I was on the floor on my back looking up." He gave a mirthless, disparaging laugh. "And I'm not a big man myself. Most people look large to me. It could have been that he was wearing a heavy coat. I'm afraid I can't say with any degree of confidence. I really am very sorry."

"There's no need to apologise, sir," Dave said. "We know how hard it is to take everything in under circumstances like that."

Over the months she and Lyon had been working together, Claire had grown increasingly grateful for her partner's patient handling of the public. She knew he was right in what he had said to Grover, but that didn't stop it being bloody irritating when someone who could have been a prime witness turned out to be of such little use. To prevent her feelings showing, Claire looked up into the dark oak rafters of the restored hall. She quickly found what she had hoped she would. At least two CCTV cameras that she could see straight away. Pretty standard for a public space like this. One of them looked like it would cover the Switchboard office door, and the other most definitely covered the main hall exit.

"Thank you for your help, Mr. Grover," she said, hopeful now that the little he had been able to offer might yet prove unnecessary. "I'm afraid we will have to interview you again within the next couple of days to make a formal statement, but what you've told us has been very useful. My advice now would be to go home and try to put as much of it out of your mind as you can. Would you like one of our officers to drive you to your house?"

The look on Grover's face made it clear he didn't have much hope of putting the evening's events out of his mind. "No. Thank you. That's very kind, but my car's only parked round the corner." He went to rise from his chair.

"One more question, Mr. Grover," Dave said, "if I may? You say you arrived at about nine fifteen, I think that's correct? May I ask why you had come to the Halo Centre tonight, at such a late time?"

"I came to talk to Victor."

"Any particular reason?"

"Victor was like me, on the Switchboard Committee. We'd had a meeting a couple of nights ago and he hadn't turned up. That was very unusual for him. I thought I'd drop in to see that he was all right. I was passing by anyway."

"I see."

Grover took off his glasses and polished them furiously with a cloth pulled from his jacket pocket. "If I'd been earlier. Five minutes even. I could have… I might have been able…"

"There really is no point in thinking like that, sir," Dave said. "Go home, have a drink maybe, but do as Inspector Summerskill said, and try to get a good night's rest."

Grover nodded, jammed his glasses back on, muttered his goodbyes, and left. Summerskill and Lyon watched as he walked, head bowed, from the Centre. They waited until he had gone before turning to the second witness of the night's crime.

The paramedics who had been attending her were leaving as they approached. "Is she okay?" Claire asked.

"Well, she's fairly shook up of course," said one of the paramedics, a young man Claire was pretty sure she'd met at some other incident in the not-too-distant past. She hoped he wouldn't expect her to remember his name. "We've given her something to help her sleep tonight if she wants it, but other than that, yes, she'll be okay. She hit her head on a wall or door, she's not sure which, and at some point, got a scratch on her face, but it really is only that, a scratch. Nothing to worry about."

Claire thanked him and moved on to the woman who was, she now saw, in good hands. *Well done, PC Joe Jones.* With the apparent ability to rustle up a hot drink in any situation, the rookie constable had brought a cup of tea to the woman and was now squatting by the side of her chair, chatting quietly. At least, Joe was chatting. The woman was sitting silently, the mug in both hands in her lap. *In shock like Grover?* Claire wondered.

Before beginning her questioning, Claire snuck a look at Dave. When Joe Jones had started at Foregate Street, only a few weeks previously, she'd taken great pleasure in teasing her sergeant about the inevitability of a romance with the only other (openly) gay officer in the station. He'd responded, as she'd known he would, scathingly to the idea that he and Joe would have to fall for each other simply because they were both gay, and his annoyance had been half the fun for her. But lately, she'd had the feeling that her predictions were, excusing the expression, bearing fruit. Dave must have known she was hinting not so subtly at Joe with her "Love's young dream" crack earlier. And he hadn't exactly denied it, had he? Had he known that Joe would be at the scene tonight? *Of course. Memorises duty shifts at the start of every bloody day.* She watched as he acknowledged Joe with the briefest of nods. Well, what had she expected? A full-on snog, before they went on to deal with the murder at hand? Still, there was something, wasn't there? A softening? The hint of a smile? *And I thought gay guys were supposed to be flamboyant. Dave Lyon's about as flamboyant as a brick.*

"Evening Constable Jones," she said out loud. *Professionalism, Summerskill.*

"Inspector. Sergeant." Joe gave them both his customary cheery smile. If there was any more warmth in it for Dave, Claire couldn't see it. "This is Miss Haines. She's been put through the wringer a bit tonight."

"So I hear. Hello, Miss Haines. How are you feeling?"

"All right I suppose. I kept telling this one there was no need to be making such a fuss. It's a bump, that's all."

Claire was going to suggest that PC Jones was more concerned about the psychological effects of discovering a brutally murdered man than the physical knocks she might have suffered, but a closer look at the woman in front of her made her change her mind. Karen Haines had one of those faces that could have belonged to anyone from thirty to sixty, with not a scrap of makeup used to persuade an onlooker one way or the other. A solid-looking woman, if one was being generous, she was still in the acid-yellow cleaner's jacket the Centre provided, though she had a coat over her shoulders. Claire guessed that Joe had put it there and insisted she keep it on to stay warm in case of shock. She saw no sign of shock. If anything, Karen Haines looked annoyed at having to sit and answer questions, and practically glowered up at them.

"Could you tell us, please, what happened?" Claire asked, sitting down on one of the chairs she and Dave had brought over. "I know you'll already have told the constable, but if you could go through what happened with us again now, it really would be very helpful."

The cleaner looked unconvinced but, with obvious reluctance, began. "I was doing my rounds. Cleaning. I heard a noise in the office. I went to see what it was, and there was a man in there with Mr. Whyte. It looked like they were fighting. He pushed his way past me, knocked me to the floor, and was gone. Next thing I knew, Mr. Grover was picking me up."

Claire nodded and tried to look as if she really was grateful for every word the woman had spoken. Inside, she was fuming. Haines was one of those supremely unhelpful witnesses, the kind who described everyone as "normal" or "average". She leaned back and let Dave take over.

"Mrs. Haines," he began, pencil, as yet unused, poised over his notebook.

"Miss."

"Sorry. Miss Haines. When did you start work tonight?"

"Eight o'clock."

"That's a late start, isn't it?"

"Suppose. It's the time we always start. Up until then there can be all sorts still in here, getting in the way."

"Ah. Of course. You say 'we'. Was there anyone else working with you tonight?"

Haines snorted. "Should have been. Veronica Whatsername. Can't tell you her last name. Polish. I think. Should have been on duty with me but didn't turn up. You know what Poles are like. All…"

"All sorts, you say," Dave interrupted, not wanting to hear Karen Haines's views on Worcester's Polish community.

Haines eyed him, obviously not unaware of what he had done. "Yeah. There's about twenty of 'em, different groups, that use this place. Most of 'em goes on till about six. Thursdays there's two of 'em goes on till half seven, sometimes later. No use starting till they've gone." Her expression made it clear she wasn't impressed by any extra hours the charity workers might be putting in for their various good causes.

"The Switchboard operators would normally be here, though, wouldn't they? They start at seven thirty I think, and go on until ten?"

"The gay phone people? Yes. They're always here late. Well, on the days when they are in. They always stays in their office, though, so they're not a nuisance."

"Right. So, you started work at eight. You were on time, I presume."

"Course."

"Of course. And Mr. Whyte was already here?"

"Suppose so. The light was coming from their office. I supposed someone was there. Didn't know who."

"And you heard this noise about quarter past nine?"

"Don't know. Think so."

"Did you see anyone between when you started work and when you heard the noise?"

"No."

"And what exactly was the noise? How would you describe it?"

The cleaner's face scrunched up in thought. *If she says a 'normal' noise,* Claire thought, *I may scream.*

"It was like a crash. Like people fighting."

"Did you hear voices? Were people shouting? Did you hear any words?"

The scrunched expression became more pronounced. "No."

"So, you went to see?"

"Yes. It didn't sound right."

"Now, I'm sorry to have to ask you to do this, and I know that you've already done it once tonight, but could you tell us *exactly* what you saw?"

"Like I already said," Haines began pointedly, "I saw two men fighting. And then…"

"One minute. Please. Two men. Were they both standing up?"

"I suppose so. I couldn't see Mr. Whyte."

"Why not?"

"The other man was standing in front of him."

"So, you got a good look at the other man?"

"No."

"But—"

"He had his back to me. And look, it was all really quick, right? I walked in, and the man turned round really fast and pushed past me. I went flying into the wall and fell down. I didn't get a chance to see his face because he put his arm up in front of it, like this." She demonstrated. "I was just glad when he ran off. It was only when I got up that I saw what he'd done." She looked Dave straight in the eyes. "It was horrible," she said flatly.

Claire doubted they'd have to worry too much about this one losing any sleep that night. "How about his clothes, Miss Haines? Can you tell us anything about what he was wearing?"

"A coat."

It's a cold November night. Of course, he was wearing a coat.

Dave nodded encouragingly as if this was an invaluable clue. "Colour?" he prompted.

"Black. Blue. Sort of a bluey black."

"Nothing that stood out?" Claire asked. "No badges or logos or flashes of colour, anything like that?"

"Nothin'."

Dave flipped his notebook shut. "Thank you, Miss Haines. You've been very helpful. If you like, I can get a police car to take you back home."

Karen Haines stood up. "I haven't finished my cleaning yet."

Diligent or thick-skinned? "I'm afraid this building is now a crime scene," Claire said. "There can't be any more cleaning, any more anything for that matter, until after we've had a good look round."

Haines sniffed. "Long as I get paid." She picked up a plastic carrier bag. "I don't need a car. I don't live far away."

"Did you know Mr. Whyte?" Claire asked, as much because she was irritated by the woman's callousness as for any need to know.

"I seen him every now and again. When he was on duty, I suppose. Didn't have anything to do with him. Didn't have anything to do with any of them really. Not like I would, is it?"

"No. I don't suppose you would. Well, thank you so much. I'm afraid we will have to be in touch with you again at some point for an official statement but you're free to go home now."

Karen Haines grunted, turned, and left.

Claire watched her go, looking up to the CCTV camera over the exit door as she passed through. *Please let there be some good video footage.*

Chapter Two

Why, thought Dave, as he strode up the steps into Foregate Street police station, *are gay relationships so complicated?*

He liked his job. In fact, he loved his job. He liked Joe. In fact…he *really* liked him. Joe was good-looking and funny. Joe had the same job as him and worked in the same place as him. All these things should have made Dave really happy. And they did. And yet…

It had been in the aftermath of a previous case, the first in which Joe had had any substantial involvement, that the two men had finally acknowledged their mutual attraction after a decided reluctance to get "involved"—at least on Dave's part. It had been a further four days after that before they had been able to meet up again in their own time, mainly down to the demands of their job and their different shifts. It had to be at Dave's again as Joe was sharing a flat with Baz South, one of Foregate's other "babies", and Dave had made it very clear that he didn't want their relationship to be the talk of the station, what Summerskill called "scuttlebutt".

"Why not?" Joe had asked. "Who cares?"

"C'mon, Joe. You really think everyone is going to put out the rainbow flags for us? Dodgy enough for straight officers to have relationships within a station. Especially, when one of them…"

"Is black and one of them is white?"

"That's not…"

Joe had grinned and kissed him. "Lord, you are so easy to wind up, y'know?"

"I know. I have a DI who reminds me of that constantly. And what I was going to say was, when one of them is a constable and one of them is a sergeant."

"I'll have to get promoted real quick then, won't I?" Joe had kissed him again.

"Or," said Dave, unable to help responding to Joe's enthusiasm, "we could do this in Foregate canteen and I could be busted back to constable again."

"What? And shock Eileen? We'd never get one of her world-famous bacon butties again."

Dave could have given his opinion on the station cook's sandwiches but was much happier to be kissing the man in his arms.

It had been three days after that before they could manage another evening together. It had been considerably less constrained than the first, with Joe in particular making it very plain he was more than ready to jump into bed with Dave there and then. But Dave had held back.

"It's Richard, isn't it?" Joe had said. "No, it's all right," he went on with a smile as Dave looked as if he was going to protest. "I get it. You've not long broken up. It can be a bit strange, getting together with another guy. It's cool. I can wait"— and he had pulled Dave in closer—"a bit longer."

Dave had felt bad for keeping Joe at arm's length. And for letting him believe the lie about Richard.

It was four days after that when they finally had made it into the bedroom. Any of the inevitable, if faintly held, doubts or reservations about compatibility were enthusiastically dismissed, several times. But, because it was obviously what Dave had wanted, Joe had still gone back to his own flat at the end of the evening.

That next day, Dave had been as twitchy as a meerkat at work, nervous that Joe wouldn't be able to keep a lid on things as he had requested. When he and Summerskill had walked into the station, Joe had already been there, discussing his day's duties with the desk sergeant. He'd turned, greeted them with a cheery smile and a call of "Good morning." Dave had completely overcompensated, and responded with a silent, curt nod. He'd known he'd got it wrong when he'd caught Claire's thoughtful look out of the corner of his eye.

"Cheerful soul, isn't he, our new recruit?" she'd said as they made their way to their office. Dave had made a noncommittal sound in reply. Once in the office, he'd presented her with a pile of time dockets to sign as soon as he could to forestall any further fishing.

As the days had passed, though, Dave had grown easier as it became clear that Joe was perfectly capable of being discreet. In fact, he felt guilty at having underestimated Joe's good sense. He should have felt on top of the world. And yet...

Are straight relationships this involved? he wondered as he settled himself at his desk and prepared for the arrival of his boss. *Or is it the job situation rather than us being gay? Or is it...?* Dave focused on the humdrum task of clearing his emails, rather than dwelling on the other possible reason, the one he was reluctant to admit even to himself.

"Yes, I'm late. Sue me," Claire snapped as she swept into the room. "And if I don't get a coffee within the next five minutes, everyone is in for a really shitty day."

No, Dave decided, as he rose to fix the coffee, if his boss's marital situation was anything to go by, then straight relationships definitely weren't any easier. And if any of them were to survive the morning, he'd better put his personal life on the back burner and concentrate on the job at hand. As always.

Within two hours, Dave had assembled a manila folder of information which he dropped onto Claire's desk. She gave it a sour look. It was a thin folder. "Victor Charles Whyte," he said. "Age seventy-two. Retired chemist. That's the aspirin and prophylactic kind, not the mad scientist kind. He had a small shop in Malvern but retired from that about ten years ago. Small bungalow on the outskirts of Worcester. Lived alone. Not a great deal of money by the looks of it, but far from the breadline. Probably on a reasonably comfy pension. No criminal record. I've sent uniforms to interview neighbours."

"Which didn't take very long at all," said a voice from the office door.

"Hi, Jen," said Claire. "What'd you find?"

WPC Jenny Trent nodded at Claire. "Inspector. We had a chat with the neighbours on either side. Professional couple and a retired couple. Both said Whyte was a really nice guy. Friendly. Helpful. Gave some extra science tuition to the daughter of one of them when she was doing her GCSEs. On his own most of the time. Occasional visitors, men and women. Both sets really shocked and saddened to hear what had happened."

"In short…"

"No leads."

"Great. Thanks, Jen."

Trent nodded again and left the office. *Things still frosty there, then?* Dave wondered. He'd noted the cooling of the friendship between the two women in recent weeks and knew there had been some kind of defining "difference of opinion". He didn't know the details. Or if he was a significant part of it.

"No immediate personal motive emerging so far, then," said Claire.

"Seems not. But if this wasn't personal, what was it? No one in their right mind would break into the Halo Centre looking for anything valuable to steal. There are shops on either side with more money and goods for the taking. Even if we're talking about someone dumb enough to look to a charity centre for rich pickings, with all the offices they could have gone through looking for cash or valuables, why go to the only one that had a light on and was obviously occupied? And even then, if you're drawn to the light like some kind of thieving moth, and you get caught out by the guy who was in there, you don't strangle him with a telephone cord. Hit him with your fist or handy heavy object maybe. Stab him if you're a kid with a blade, but not strangle him. No, I think this was someone setting out to murder from the start which means there's got to be a motive." Dave made a disparaging gesture at the folder. "It's just not in there."

"Perhaps. But if you were setting out to murder, wouldn't you have taken a weapon with you rather than relying on there being a handy length of telephone cord available?" Claire leaned back in her chair and ran her fingers through her hair. "What about the CCTV cameras? I'm guessing by the way you didn't start with them that there's nothing there."

"Would you believe, they still use videotape? I refer you back to my comment about charity centres not being money pits. They can't afford to update their systems. The cost of tapes and upkeep of the CCTV system at the Halo Centre is shared by all the various concerns that use the building. The overall building manager—" Dave consulted his notebook. "—a Mr. Duncan Lewis, said that nine times out of ten the system isn't even running, either because they haven't sorted out who's supposed to be in charge of it that week or because they've run out of tapes. 'More of a deterrent,' he said."

"Didn't deter our killer," Claire pointed out. "All right. What have we got? Victor Whyte is murdered while on duty at the Switchboard. I'm thinking that if he was the predetermined target rather than collateral damage, our killer, if he isn't a complete moron, would have realised it would have been much easier to have gone for him in his home rather than in a place like the Centre with the possibility of other people being present. Therefore, there's a reason it was done where it was, so there must be some kind of link with the Switchboard."

Dave looked doubtful. "Or we're looking at this arse forwards."

"Is that a gay thing?"

"It's something my dad says. It means, we're looking at something the wrong way round. You're right; the killer didn't take a weapon along with him, or her, which would suggest it wasn't premeditated."

"Thank you."

"But what if," Dave went on, ignoring Claire's sarcasm, "the target wasn't the man but was the organisation, Switchboard itself? What if someone wanted to kill, or even just attack a member of the group, any member, and Victor Whyte was the unfortunate guy on duty that night?"

"A hate crime? Shit! So instead of looking for a suspect from a relatively small pool of friends, relatives, and people known to Whyte, we have to widen the scope to include any one of the hundreds of thousands of homophobic psychopaths out there."

"Thanks for making me feel safe in my city."

"You know what I mean. It could be anyone."

"Not helping my sense of unease."

"Damn it! Why the hell didn't these people sort their security?"

"You can't plan for blind hatred."

Claire gave a determined shake of her head. "No. We are not going there. Not to begin with. Not just because it's horrible to think about but because it gives us nothing to work with. We start with the Switchboard. He's not going to be happy, but we need to talk to Mr. Grover again. We need to know what actually goes on there, and we need the names of the other operators. Who knows, maybe it's a hotbed of bitter rivalries and petty jealousies."

"A bunch of bitter, vicious queens you mean?"

"Isn't every workplace? And you said it, not me. What I was thinking was this might be more to do with someone who's called in on their phones rather than with someone who works there. Who knows? Maybe Whyte had said something on a call that had really pissed someone off. I don't know, do I?" she snapped in the face of Dave's obvious lack of conviction. "But at the least, we need to interview the other operators and take a look at who's called in recently. I hope to God their record keeping is better than their security system." Claire got up from behind her desk. "C'mon. You took Grover's address, didn't you?"

"Of course. But I…" Dave was brought up short by a knock on the office door followed by the entrance of an imposing figure, unwelcome to both of them, though for widely differing reasons. "Good morning, Inspector. David. May I come in?"

"Good morning, Mr. Cullen," said Claire. "And it seems you already have. To what do we owe this unexpected pleasure?"

Sean Cullen, the Conservative MP for Worcester, stood in the doorway and gave what Dave thought of as his trademark lopsided smile, as ambiguous as the Mona Lisa's and probably as artificial. There could be no doubt he had registered Claire's coldness, but Dave knew it wouldn't have bothered him a jot. One didn't become as apparently invulnerable a politician as Cullen was without a thick skin.

Dave noted again how the tall, powerfully built Cullen effortlessly dominated whatever space he walked into, seemingly reducing their office's already limited dimensions. At the same time, his exquisite tailoring and grooming brought out, by contrast, the shabbiness of their place of work. Dave wasn't sure if this was a natural talent Cullen had or something that was taught by the more exclusive public schools.

He also wished to hell and back that Cullen hadn't addressed him as "David" in front of his boss. The man was an arch manipulator and never did anything without a reason. Dave wondered uneasily what game he was playing now.

Claire stood, arms folded, waiting for an answer. Her dealings with Cullen had been limited and not cordial. For a short time, he had been the main suspect in a series of murders of young men centred around local gyms. He'd quickly been cleared of any involvement in that crime, but not before his questionable relationship with a woman who had a much closer link to the murders had come to light. There was, Claire had admitted, absolutely nothing he had done that had ever been against the law, but everything he had done had been carried through with an urbane air of entitlement and a clear belief in his own superiority that had set every single one of her teeth on edge.

She was also unaware that, since the last time she had seen him, Sean Cullen had slept with her sergeant four times. Dave was anxious that should remain the case.

"Ask not what you can do for me, Inspector, but what I can do for you."

Claire looked him straight in the eye. "I don't think there's a great deal you can do for me, Mr. Cullen."

"I think you'd genuinely be surprised, inspector. However"—Cullen held out his arms in a giving gesture—"today I talk of business, not pleasure, although the two are not inextricably linked. I come to offer once again a most attractive package should your station sign up for my Fitness First Initiative. You know it's a cause close to my heart."

A former rower and Oxford Blue, Cullen was something of a local celebrity for his sporting achievements, and he'd parlayed this expertise into a political policy that did a great deal to further boost his popularity amongst the Worcester electorate. Initially sceptical, even Dave had finally had to admit that his Fitness First Initiative was something Cullen genuinely believed in, and his work in this area, encouraging sports and an active lifestyle, really did a great deal to support the disadvantaged from all walks of life. Even so, Dave doubted that was the real reason for Cullen's appearance now.

"I'm afraid we haven't had a great deal of time lately to think about gym memberships and keeping fit. Rather a lot to do." Claire's tone made it clear what her opinion of the fitness industry was, and that there was always going to be a lot to do.

"Yes, so I hear," Cullen said. "Nasty business at the Switchboard."

How the hell had he known about that? There hadn't been time for it to hit the papers. What kind of social media connections had Cullen tapped into to find out about the murder so soon?

Momentarily nettled by this suggestion of a leak, Claire looked to Dave who mouthed one word: *Madden*. Of course. It wasn't what you knew, or even which tweets you read. It was *who* you knew. And Cullen knew their chief superintendent well, if not in a biblical sense then in a masonic way, or so the rumours went. "Yes, it is," she said tightly. "Though you will understand that I cannot at the moment say anything about it."

"Of course, of course." Cullen's smile dropped and his tone of voice softened. "Victor really was a very good man. I will miss him."

That was one of the many problems with politicians, Dave thought. It was impossible to tell when they were faking sincerity and when they were telling the truth.

"You knew him?"

"Of course. You have heard of the gay mafia, Inspector? We know everyone."

Dave caught the flicker of outrage in Claire's eyes, before the re-emergence of that twisted smile made it clear Cullen was joking. Mostly. "Ah, I thought perhaps he might have been a fellow photography enthusiast."

Well done, ma'am. Claire had gone straight for the only known chink in the armour of Cullen's public persona, his fondness for photographing attractive young men. That *peccadillo* had got him mixed up in the previous murder case. Dave looked for some reaction to the barb, guiltily aware he hoped it had stung. Cullen's smile only grew more pronounced. His "vice" wasn't criminal, and he knew it. He'd been open about it from the start and had made it clear he would admit no shame for something that harmed no one. In anyone else that might almost have been admirable. In Cullen's case, it was bloody annoying.

"No. Dear old Victor was a lot more hidebound than yours truly. I would have said straitlaced but that hardly seems appropriate, does it? No, I knew him and several other members of the Switchboard from a while back when certain bigoted local councillors were determined to withhold funding from them. They came to me for support, and I was more than happy to give it to them. It may be a bit of a dinosaur these days, but in its time, the Worcester and Hereford Gay and Lesbian Switchboard was an important institution for our community. I even did a few stints myself as an operator." He looked across at Dave. "You should have a go, Sergeant. I can see you as a source of great solace to distressed, needy gay men."

Claire figuratively stood back, giving Dave the space to respond with a put-down of his own. She appeared mildly surprised when he didn't. She would have been even more surprised if she had been able to see beyond his carefully main-tained, impassive expression to the anger beneath.

"If there is anything at all I can do to help you in your investigations, please don't hesitate to get in touch," Cullen continued. "And, if I may, I would appreciate your keeping me in the loop with this particular case. I really did admire Victor quite a lot."

"I'm not sure how you could help us, Mr. Cullen."

"Well, I did know Victor for some years. I do have to say, though, that I cannot think of a single person who would want to harm him. The man was a complete gentleman, in every sense of the word. Perhaps I could help you to build up a picture of him. Profiling, I believe it's called."

"Only when applied to criminals."

"Well, let's call it constructive background information, then." He turned his smile towards Dave. "Perhaps you and I could work together again, Sergeant. Bring your notebook and you can take down whatever you want."

Dave kept his expression neutral. "The last time we worked together was when you were a suspect in a murder case. For this, I think we can send along a junior officer."

"Excellent idea," said an unfazed Cullen. "Perhaps Constable Jones. Let my secretary know when and I promise you I'll make an opening."

"I really don't think that will be necessary, Mr. Cullen," Claire said. "Thank you for your offer of assistance though. It is appreciated, and your character refer-ence for Mr. Whyte is duly noted. However, for the moment, I think that is about all you have to offer us here, so if you'll excuse us, we will press on. And I assure you, when we have any information, you will find it available. Through the appro-priate channels. Goodbye."

Dave scrutinised Cullen. Not a flicker of a reaction. His smile didn't slip by a fraction. "Thank you. That is very much appreciated. Goodbye for now, Inspector. Sergeant." He went to leave but turned back in the doorway. "And please don't forget the Fitness First discount offer which can be used in a number of local gyms and sports halls. A healthy mind does need a healthy body." He smiled at Dave. "And I'm afraid, like all offers of good things, it doesn't last forever. *Ciao.*"

"Was he suggesting I'm fat?" Claire said the instant he had closed the door behind him. "Was that what that healthy body, healthy mind crap was about?"

"Yes." Dave was still wondering about the implications of Cullen's parting shot. "But you're not," he added quickly, when his mind caught up with what his boss was saying. "It's what he does. What *they* do. Politicians. They needle."

"And how did he know," Claire fumed on, "about Joe? I mean, of all the new recruits, he knows the name of the only gay one? Shit, he must be further up Madden's arse than I thought. And not in a good way." She looked to her sergeant for a response.

"Yeah."

"There's snappy. What's up?"

"Nothing. Cullen. He…winds me up."

Claire tilted her head to one side. "So I saw. Not like you to let a smarmy git like that get one over you. God knows how he ever got enough votes to be elected. You might like to have a word with young Joe about him."

"What do you mean?"

"Well, he's obviously on Cullen's radar. Wouldn't want him snatching Joe from under your nose, would we?"

"For Pete's sake! Joe's not exactly a kid, is he? He's a police officer."

"Probationary."

"He can still look after himself. I hardly think Cullen's going to be breaking out the Rohypnol and rope."

"If you say so." Mildly surprised by how far Cullen seemed to have rattled Dave, but obviously believing that she mostly understood why, Claire showed rare diplomacy when dealing with her sergeant and dropped the subject. "C'mon. We need to see Mr. Grover again."

Dave picked up his coat and followed his boss out of the office, inwardly fuming. How dare Cullen waltz into the station, trading on his position as the local MP to wind him up in front of Summerskill? What was he after? There was no avoiding it: Dave would have to go and see him and find out what game he was playing this time. Except, wasn't that probably what he was angling for anyway?

Why are gay relationships so complicated?

Chapter Three

If she'd been asked beforehand to picture the kind of house Clive Grover lived in, Claire would have come pretty close to the reality: a neat townhouse, not too far from the cricket ground and racecourse; manicured lawn, well-tended flower beds, and sturdy fences. She'd have done a good job of imagining the interior too: olde-worlde oak and leather, a real fire, a whiff of polish and tobacco, and a discreet selection of hardback books on the shelves, mostly about antiques from what she could make out. She would, however, have been way off about Trevor.

Grover greeted them and showed them into the living room. He still seemed a little dazed, and Claire wondered if that was the aftereffects of the shock and a bad night's sleep, or whether he was a naturally fretful man. Looking at the waistcoat, bow tie, and polished shoes he was wearing, Claire wondered if he had dressed in the expectation of their coming to see him. She suspected not.

He showed them to a pair of deep leather chairs, and as she sat down, Claire realised this might be the most comfortable chair she had ever sat on in her life. Correction: the most comfortable she had ever sat *in*. "This is my partner, Trevor," Grover said as another man walked into the room. Trevor smiled shyly at both of them and said nothing.

Grover, in his early twentieth-century public school teacher getup, looked so right in this setting. Almost everything about Trevor looked so wrong. Tall and heavyset, he was dressed in frayed jeans and a faded T-shirt with some children's cartoon character still faintly visible on it. He had to be a good twenty years younger than Grover, and his thinning blond hair was shaved close. Claire didn't want to be uncharitable or to jump to inaccurate conclusions, but something about Trevor's vaguely genial face didn't suggest to her the kind of man who would curl up next to that real fire with any of those antiques books. Whatever these two got up to with each other, she doubted it was meaningful conversation.

"Get us some tea, will you, please, Trevor?"

Trevor nodded and scuttled off to the kitchen.

"Does your partner work for Switchboard?" Claire asked.

"Good God, no." Grover appeared genuinely amused at the idea. "That would definitely not be up Trevor's street."

"What does he do?" The question had no relevance, and she could tell that Grover obviously thought so, too, but she was curious.

"If you mean what is his job, he doesn't really have one. I suppose you could say he's a kind of house husband."

"A husband who looks after the house? Sounds wonderful." Claire brought herself back to the more serious business at hand. "Thank you for meeting with us again so soon, Mr. Grover. We've started our investigation, collected some background information, and carried out a few interviews. What we'd like to know now is a bit more about your Switchboard. What it does, and what Victor did as part of it."

Grover nodded, obviously having expected this, sat himself down in another of the magnificent chairs and began. His answers were clear and concise, and he was perfectly happy to go back and explain any points either of the officers asked him to clarify. Although he provided no new evidence as to who might have killed Whyte or even who might have had a motive, he did give Summerskill and Lyon an outline of the Switchboard's work.

They learned that the Board manned its phonelines from seven thirty in the evening until ten, three days a week, Tuesdays, Wednesdays, and Thursdays. This was down from its heyday some years past of four days a week and alternate Saturdays. The ideal was to have at least two operators on call at any one time, preferably a man and a woman in case callers requested a specific gender. "Men prefer talking to men but tend not to object if there's only a woman available," Grover said, "but women frequently feel more comfortable talking to other women, and if one isn't available when they call, they will wait and call back another time when one is."

"I have to say, I feel the same way about doctors," said Claire.

"Quite. Sadly, due to the falloff in the number of volunteers in recent years, it's not uncommon for there to be only one operator on duty. Or even sometimes none. Events happen, as the politician said, and sometimes an operator can't do his or her duty and can't find someone to stand in at short notice." He sighed. "And as our relevance has waned so, too, has the commitment of some of our volunteers. I'm afraid I have to admit, one or two do have a reputation for being, shall we say, lax."

"It was possible, then, that no one might have been on duty that night?"

"Oh no. Not that night. Victor never let us down. In all the years we've been operating, I don't think he missed a single duty."

"Who would have known he was on duty that night?" Dave asked.

"Well, anyone really. The rota is sent to all our operators, of course, but it's also posted on the Halo Centre's communal noticeboard by the entrance to the Hall."

At that point Trevor re-entered with a large silver tray from which he served them tea and a quite excellent fruit cake before leaving them to carry on with their conversation. He spoke only to ask if they wanted sugar, his soft voice a contrast to his large frame. Grover didn't say a word to him. *He's like a butler.* Claire abandoned yet again all vague intentions of a diet in the face of the cake. *No,* she corrected herself as he served her a slice, bending over to pass it to her. *More like a geisha.*

"What happens when someone calls up. What's the usual procedure?" Dave asked.

"Well, it depends on the nature of the call of course. It might be a simple request for information. It might be a more complicated call from someone struggling with aspects of their sexuality or from some difficulty at home or in the workplace because they're gay."

"Are the calls recorded?" Claire asked.

Grover's lips thinned in what might almost have been a disapproving look. "No. Confidence is guaranteed. It's a cornerstone of what we do."

"Many companies these days begin their calls by saying they're being recorded for training purposes. I thought maybe…"

"Switchboard isn't exactly a company, Inspector. I doubt we could persuade callers to relax and open up if they thought their confidences were being taped."

"Confidences and confessions?" Claire said. Grover stiffened. She noted that Dave did too.

"It's been a while since people talked about confessing to being gay, Inspector. And that's about the extent of the confidences. I certainly can't think of a caller who has ever told me about anything illegal." Grover took a sip from his tea, possibly to recover his ruffled composure. "All members are required to attend regular training sessions to keep them up to date with legality as well as making sure they have the latest news about medical matters. For a long time, particularly back in the eighties, we were one of the very few reliable sources of information gay men could turn to about HIV/AIDS. Nowadays of course, there's the internet." He put his cup back down and gazed at it sadly. "Although we hear that even so, the rate of infection is on the rise again. Those who don't learn history's lessons, eh?"

"Are doomed to repeat them," Dave said softly.

"Quite." Grover looked a little surprised, perhaps by Dave's recognising the quotation, perhaps by his obvious sadness at what he had said.

Claire was annoyed with herself for having used the word "confession", particularly in front of Dave. She really hadn't intended anything by it, but it was done now so she moved on, admitting to herself as she did that she'd been wrong, too, in underestimating the degree of Switchboard's professionalism. She noted the beat of sympathy between Grover and her sergeant and sat back with her teacup and sipped thoughtfully. She knew Dave would recognise the hint and take over the interview.

"If your calls aren't recorded, sir," Dave said, "are any notes taken? Is there any way of knowing who called and what was said?"

"Of course. A written log of all calls is kept. Date. Length of call. A summary of what the call was about. And, if appropriate, recommendations to other operators on how to deal with a caller if he or she calls again."

"Written? Your records aren't kept on a computer?" Dave gave a small smile to show that he wasn't being critical.

"We set Switchboard up long before computers became so commonplace. I suppose we fell into a habit of writing up and filing call sheets, and never got round to updating. There is something so much more satisfying, though, isn't there, about using pen and paper? And," he conceded, "not all of our volunteers are as computer literate as others."

"I understand," Dave said. "That can make things difficult." He didn't have to look at Claire for her to know that he was referring to her. "Perhaps after we're through here you wouldn't mind accompanying Inspector Summerskill and me back to the Switchboard office to pick up these records. It really would be very much appreciated."

Grover looked uncomfortable at the idea. "We do guarantee our callers a measure of confidentiality," he reminded them.

"I think they'd understand if they knew a murder was involved." Dave waited, knowing full well that someone as well-versed in the law as Grover had suggested he was would understand he had absolutely no choice in the matter.

"Of course. Though I must say, I'm not sure how it can help."

"We'd like to see who Victor had been talking to recently. How far back do your records go?"

"We start a new folder each year, so in the latest you'll find a sheet for every call Victor took since January. If you want to go back any further, I can show you where all the other folders are kept."

"Thank you, Mr. Grover. We really do appreciate the concession you're making for us here. Can I also ask, where can people find Switchboard's number?"

"It's in the national gay press, the big four—*Gay Times, Attitude, Campaign,* and *Diva*—and in all the local freebies you can pick up in specialist shops and gay pubs and clubs. I can give you a list if you like, but it really does get out to a large number of people." He gave a small, bitter laugh. "Would you believe that when we started, we weren't allowed to put our number in public lists? People thought we were a 'mucky' chatline. It was years before we made it into the *Yellow Pages*. And now no one uses that anymore. Oh, and of course it's on our website. Yes, we have dragged ourselves far enough into the twenty-first century to have one of those. It's put together and run by one of our younger members. Actually, I'm pretty sure he is the youngest, certainly the most computer literate of all of us."

"I have to say, Mr. Grover, your Switchboard does seem very well-organised and thorough in its approach," Dave said.

"Thank you." Grover took his glasses off and polished them, probably, Claire thought, to cover his embarrassment though he was also clearly delighted. "Oh, I nearly forgot," he said as he resettled his glasses, "we also offer a befriending service."

"Befriending? What's that?"

"Another facet of Switchboard that may be fading away, I'm afraid. Befriendings are face-to-face meetings."

"What, like hook-ups?"

Grover's lips thinned. "No, Inspector."

"For people with really serious problems?" she suggested.

Grover winced. "Befriendings are for men and women who, for whatever reason, are finding it hard to come out, to engage with what we'll call the gay world in a real rather than a virtual way. The typical case would be that someone will call up, talk to one or more of our operators over the course of a few weeks, sometimes even months, getting comfortable with the probably first openly gay people they have actually spoken to, and then, when they feel they are ready for it, we arrange a time and place for them to meet up with two of us for a face-to-face chat. You can't imagine how lonely it can be as a closeted gay person, especially in a largely rural area like Worcestershire." Claire noted that Grover addressed this last comment to her rather than to Dave. She wondered if that was a reaction to her perceived lack of sympathy, or maybe because he'd twigged that with Dave he was preaching to the converted.

"It's always been easy to meet with other gay people in the big cities," he went on. "Not so easy when you're living in a comparatively small city like Worcester, a small town like Malvern, or any of the tiny villages scattered around the county. Many of the people we've befriended have described it as literally life-saving."

"People who go along to these befriendings of yours must be very vulnerable," Claire suggested.

"Indeed." Grover's clipped tone made it clear she had offended him again. "That is why our protocols are strict and thorough. No one arranges a befriending without having first attended a training programme that is designed for the protection of our clients and ourselves. Meetings always take place in public places and there are always at least two operators at any meeting, preferably a man and a woman. Needless to say, all these meetings are also recorded in our folders."

"I'm sorry. I didn't mean to imply that anything inappropriate might happen. You'll understand, we have to consider every angle in cases like this."

"Yet you say befriendings are fading away," Dave said. "Why's that?"

"For better or worse, the world is shrinking. The internet connects us. Gay people, or people who are beginning to accept they are gay, can find others like themselves at the click of a mouse."

"I presume Victor Whyte had been involved in these befriendings?" Claire said. "Had he done any recently? Within, say, the last year?"

"He may have done. I must admit, I'd have to check the book myself to see." Grover sighed. "Again, in his time, Victor was probably one of our best at them. In fact, I think as time went on, he got better and better. To be blunt, his age probably helped. One can empathise so much more when one has that depth of life experience. And older people do tend to be less threatening as well. He did have that whole silver fox thing going on." Grover drifted away for a moment, bringing himself back to the moment with a sad shake of the head. "I'm really going to miss him."

"Thank you so much for all your help, Mr. Grover." Claire replaced her teacup on the silver tray and rose from her armchair. "It really has been so useful. Now, if you are free and could possibly come along with Sergeant Lyon and myself to the Switchboard office, we'd very much like to have a look at these call sheets of yours."

"Of course, Inspector. Trevor!"

Claire jumped. Grover had barked his partner's name out in a very different tone from the mild one he had used in their conversation. Trevor appeared almost immediately, as meek and silent as before.

"I'm going out," Grover said. "Have tea ready for when I get back. Shall we go, then?" He modulated his voice to its more normal softness as he turned back to Summerskill and Lyon. "Ladies first."

"Well, that was a minefield," Claire muttered as she and Dave got into their car.

"Really? And yet, you went stomping around it quite heavily. Ma'am." Dave kept his eyes fixed on the road as he pulled out to follow Grover's car.

"What d'you mean?"

"Well, apart from suggesting that the operation he was chairman of wasn't really very well run, you also implied that it was some sort of knocking shop cum confessional. Oh, and that its operators were preying on the vulnerable."

Claire shrugged. "I liked the cake. Did I say I liked the cake? And what was it with that Trevor guy? Odd couple or what? I thought he was Grover's son at first."

"Not his son, ma'am, though I think Grover is his daddy." Dave sat behind the wheel, looking straight ahead, as if his entire concentration was needed for the short drive to the Halo Centre.

Claire knew she had annoyed him. She sat back and resigned herself to a silent ride.

"This won't have pleased the other charities and groups," Grover said as he, Claire, and Dave stood in front of the Halo Centre. Garish yellow-and-black police tape had been strung across the entrance, barring entrance to the public.

"It hasn't," Claire said. "We've had three calls of complaint already. The Mother and Toddlers group was particularly vocal."

"Yes. They do tend to be a bit strident."

"Well, that's their problem." Claire ducked under the tape and held it up for Grover to follow her into the hall. "The place is a crime scene so I'm not having a bunch of yummy mummies and their sticky-fingered sprogs traipsing all over it." The three of them came to a halt in front of the Switchboard office door. "Having said that, we're pretty sure now that nothing happened outside this room and its immediate vicinity, so the rest of the building should be up and running again to-morrow. Your office probably the day after."

Grover stood in front of the door, looking at it.

"It's okay," Dave said quietly. "There's nothing in there. It's all been…cleaned up."

Grover gave him a grateful look and went to take a key from his pocket.

"It's already open," Claire said.

They walked in, and Grover stood, taking in the sight of the cramped space. "I thought…I thought we'd be able to see something of what had happened."

"From what we can tell, there was actually very little disturbance to the room and its contents," Dave said. Claire and he had already conjectured that this was because seventy-something Whyte had been overpowered in very short order by a younger, larger, more powerful man. He didn't share this thought with Grover. The man already had enough horrific images in his head of his friend's last moments.

Now, Grover was standing, staring at the chair in which Whyte had died, as if drawn to it by some awful magnetism. "Mr. Grover," Dave said gently, "if you could show us where you keep your record folders, please?"

"Yes. Yes, of course." He stepped towards the desk. "Is it all right to…?"

"Yes. Everything has been dusted."

Grover scanned the desk and gingerly lifted a couple of magazines. "That's odd," he muttered, wiping from his fingers the forensic dust that filmed everything.

"What is?"

Caught up in his search, Grover sat down without thinking on the chair in which his friend had died so that he could get closer to the desk. He pulled open a drawer and rummaged inside. "Well, the current folder is usually kept on the desk, within easy reach. But it's not here." He got up and moved over to a filing cabinet. He took a key from his pocket, opened it, and searched inside. When he turned back to them, his expression was perplexed. "The other folders are all here, but not the current one."

"May I?" Claire joined him at the filing cabinet and looked in the drawer. There were at least a dozen ring-binder folders in the top drawer alone. She pulled the nearest one out. It had last year's date printed neatly on the front and spine.

She flipped through it, scanning the dates, signatures, and comments, all in different hands, different inks, getting a feel for the layout. "Interesting. But as you say," she said, closing the ring binder and handing it back to Grover, "not the one we are looking for." She considered for a moment. "Last night, when the killer pushed past you, did it look like he was carrying something? This missing folder for instance."

"I…I don't think so. Like I said, it all happened so fast and was such a shock but…" Grover screwed his face up in thought before shaking his head. "No. I'm fairly sure he wasn't."

"We'll have to interview Karen Haines, the cleaner, again," Dave said. "See if she remembers seeing it on him." He looked as doubtful as she felt about getting anything so useful out of that witness. "What about the folders with the befriendings in, Mr. Grover?"

"They should be in here." Grover moved over to another filing cabinet, extracted another key, and opened up the top drawer.

"Would these cabinets have been locked while Mr. Whyte was on duty?"

"Of course. Data protection is a very big thing these days, Inspector, as I'm sure you know. But Victor would have known where the key was."

"Which is…?"

Grover paused in his search through the drawer. "It's…it's over there." He pointed to a shelf by the desk and a very wilted house plant on it. "Under the pot," he admitted.

Dave went and lifted the pot. "Still here."

Grover returned to the filing cabinet drawer. "Here it is." He withdrew a ring binder and handed it over to Claire. "This is this year's."

Claire flipped through its contents, starting at the back and the most recent reports. "Victor's name is on the last but one sheet, but there doesn't seem to be anything written apart from *NS*. What does that mean?"

"No-show," said Grover. "Whoever he was supposed to meet didn't turn up. It happens from time to time. People get cold feet."

Claire flipped further back. "Okay, here's another one from Victor, presumably the last proper one he did. From six months ago." She screwed her eyes up. "Is that Baz Ronson?" She struggled with the spidery handwriting of the second signature alongside Victor's.

"Roz Joynson," Grover said. "Another of our founders, and a very good friend of Victor's. May I?" He took the folder back from Claire and read the report of the befriending she had found. "Ah yes, I remember this one. Adrian. Young lad. Deeply closeted. Came from a religious background, I think. Terrified that someone from where he lived would find out he was gay. A few of us had spoken to him over the months and he seemed to be growing in confidence all the time, so we arranged a befriending which went quite well, as you can see, but then we never heard from him again."

Claire took the folder back and looked again at the report sheet. Mercifully, it hadn't been written by the woman with the bad handwriting, so she presumed the precise and very clear italics were Victor's and it was his words she was reading. As Grover had said, the meeting seemed to have gone well. According to Victor's concise notes they had met on a Saturday afternoon in the café of a city centre supermarket. Adrian (Victor had added a note that he didn't think that was the lad's real name) had been understandably nervous but pleased to see them. They had chatted for fifteen minutes about everything from his train journey there (Adrian had been very coy about where he had travelled from) to the weather to the various gay venues there were in Worcester, with Victor and Roz suggesting that he travel over one evening to try out local night club Pharos on one of its gay nights, or possibly Gallery 48, a gay bar, and then Adrian had left them, thanking them for arranging the meeting and saying he would be in touch. And that, Grover now told them, had been the end of it.

"Ironic too," Grover said.

"Why ironic?"

"I remember Roz saying that Adrian had a strong Mancunian accent. As I'm sure you know, Manchester's got one of the most vibrant gay scenes in the country, but Adrian was so scared of friends and neighbours finding out who he really was that he had to travel all the way from there to here, Worcester of all places, just to be himself. So sad."

"Why do you think he disappeared? Could it have been something that Victor or this Roz said that they haven't recorded?" She sensed Dave's irritation with her question. *Suck it up, Sergeant,* she thought, irritated in turn by his prickliness. *I'd be asking these questions even if we were dealing with straight people.*

"No, Inspector, I do not," Grover said firmly. "There are two far more common and far more likely reasons. Firstly, and this is the one I hope didn't happen, someone at home found out that Adrian was gay, and, for whatever reason, he was driven back into the closet. Secondly, and I really hope and pray this is the one, our calls and meetings gave the lad the confidence he needed to go out and explore for himself. My fervent hope is that he is now a permanent and beautiful fixture on Canal Street."

"Fish gotta swim. Birds gotta fly," Dave said.

"Quite." Grover gave him a grateful smile, and Claire knew the connection had been made. *And he says there's no such thing as gaydar.*

Claire handed the folder to Dave. "Okay. That may well not have anything to do with Mr. Whyte's murder, but we will need to look into it, and we will need to talk to this Roz Joynson. We'd have been doing that anyway," she added, seeing Grover's objection forming. "As we will be talking to all of your operatives. We'll take this folder, too, for a closer look, if we may. And we'll send someone to pick up all the others later." She kept her tone of voice light, but there was no doubting its firmness.

"Of course."

Dave had stepped over to the office's small noticeboard and was flipping through the operator rota sheets that were pinned there. "Do you organise these, Mr. Grover?"

"Yes."

"And print them out? No disrespect, but they are very professionally done."

"No offence taken, Sergeant. No, as I think I said, we have a young computer expert. I hand him my handwritten scraps of paper, and he types them up, colour codes, prints, and laminates them."

"And do you keep the old rotas? These only seem to go back a couple of months."

"Well, the printouts are binned. Recycled I should say. But I'm sure Tom keeps the files on his computer. They're like that, aren't they, computer types?"

"Tom, you say?"

"What is it?" Claire asked, noting her sergeant's thoughtful expression.

Dave tapped the rotas on the board. "For the two months we have here, Victor was down for duty six times. Each time he was on the rota with a 'Tom', except for the last duty when he was on his own."

"Really?" Grover frowned and stepped over to the rotas himself, leaning in closely to inspect them. "That's odd. I'm sure it's wrong. It's policy to mix operators up as far as possible, when we can actually get more than one at a time on duty.

I know I didn't put Tom and Victor on together so many times." He straightened. "Tom must have made a mistake," he suggested, clearly unsure.

"Several times," Dave said.

"Hang on a minute. Give me that folder again." Claire took the befriending folder back from Dave and opened it at the penultimate page. She squinted at it. "Thought so. Look at this." She handed it back, open, to Dave, who held it so Grover, too, could see what his boss was talking about. "That last entry. The no-show. Victor's name, a date, and something else scribbled out. The name of the other person. See what it is?"

Dave squinted. The crossing out had been fairly ruthless, but the name underneath could still just be made out. "Tom."

"I thought your policy was to use one man and one woman on these befriendings?"

"Wherever possible. It may have been that there simply wasn't one of our female operators available then. Victor's usual partner on befriendings was Roz, the lady who did the previous one with him. In any case," Grover added defensively, "it was a no-show, so I suppose it doesn't really matter, does it?"

Dave handed the folder back to Claire. "Perhaps not. But I think we'd better have a word with both Roz Joynson and your young IT wiz, Tom. Probably starting with him. What did you say his surname was, please?"

"Adams."

"Tom Adams." Dave looked thoughtful. "Why does that name ring a bell?"

★

"Oh. It's you." The young man who had opened the door squinted at them, as much because he had quite obviously just got out of bed and was still adjusting to the late afternoon sunshine as in surprise at the sight of two police officers he clearly recognised on his doorstep.

"Hello, Tom," said Claire. "It's been a while."

The very first sight of the flat, with its brazen if not boastful line of empty wine bottles in the front window underneath a poster of a mashup of Margaret Thatcher and Che Guevara had made it clearer than any signpost that this was student accommodation. And it was that which had triggered the chain of associations in Dave's memory. "Of course. You remember him."

Claire had looked at him sourly. "We've already established I don't have your memory. And unless I've banged them up for something, I rarely remember people's names."

"Well, we'd wanted to lock him up, but in the end we didn't. The Jonathan Wilson case. Tom was one of the students at Wilson's sixth form college. President of Woggles. The Worcester Students…"

"Gay and Lesbian Society. Oh God, yes I remember." Claire had groaned. "He was such an irritating little prat. Now I think about it, though, I do recall him having quite a thing for you."

"Bluster and bravado. He didn't know I was gay at first, remember? He thought he was freaking out a straight copper."

"Well, he'd got your number by the end of the interview. Let's go and see if he's been pining for you since then, shall we?"

Standing on his doorstep now in a T-shirt and boxer shorts that looked like they hadn't seen the inside of a washing machine for at least four days, Tom's torch for Dave did not seem to be rekindling. "Christ. Is this what it's going to be like as an out gay male? Harassed by the police every five minutes?"

Dave tried not to roll his eyes. "I can promise you it's not. May we come in, please?"

"What do you want, then?"

"I'd really rather not discuss this on the doorstep, Tom," Claire said. Very grudgingly, the young man stepped back so there was just about enough room for Summerskill and Lyon to squeeze past him. He could, she thought, have given them more space, but that might have looked like he was making them welcome.

"Guys, it's the police," Tom shouted out as he closed the door.

"That really isn't…" Claire began, but her words were drowned out by the noise from within the flat of several people leaping from bed, muffled cursing suggestive of said people bumping into all manner of objects in their haste, a loud crashing of doors being thrown open and slammed shut, and then the sound of a toilet being flushed. Over the course of the next few minutes, it was flushed three times.

Summerskill, Lyon, and Tom Adams stood in the extremely narrow hallway, sandwiched between two muddy mountain bikes and a skateboard all propped up against the walls. "Is there somewhere we could sit and talk?" Claire asked.

Tom grunted and stalked off down the hall and into a room on the left. Claire and Dave followed into what was presumably a living room. Judging by the debris of open and largely empty pizza boxes, and opened and completely empty beer bottles, there had been an awful lot of living going on in it recently.

"Sit wherever you like," Tom said.

The officers hesitated. It was not easy to see where they could. With unconcealed annoyance, Tom swept up a pile of pizza boxes and bottles from the sofa, clearing a large enough space so that they could sit down. He dumped the rubbish behind the sofa before pulling across a stool from a nearby table, tipping the pile of magazines that had been on it onto the floor, and placing it directly in front of them as deliberately as someone planting a flag. He dropped down onto it, facing them, hands on thighs, legs wide apart.

Here we go again, Dave thought.

"Sorry to be disturbing you at this…early hour," Claire began.

"This isn't about Jonathan, is it? I mean, that was cleared up months ago, wasn't it? I read about it in the paper. It was his brother, wasn't it?"

"No, it's not about Jonathan. And it was…complicated. But that's over now. Tom, I'm guessing you've moved on from the sixth form college and are at the uni now, yes?" Tom grunted. Claire took it as a yes. "And you're also a member of the Worcester and Hereford Gay and Lesbian Switchboard, aren't you?"

"Jesus! Yes. I am? So what? It's not illegal, y'know? I mean, I know they tried to close it down once, but that was years ago. We've got out gay MPs on our side now. You can't—"

Sensing that Claire's limited store of patience was already near its end, Dave held up his hand to stop the flow of self-righteous anger. "Tom. Tom. Slow down. It's nothing like that." He allowed a few seconds for Tom's temperature to cool a little. "I'm assuming you haven't heard. About Victor Whyte."

Tom's belligerence was replaced by something else. Surprise? Wariness? "What about Victor?"

Summerskill and Lyon exchanged looks, and Dave knew his boss was delegating the next job to him. He knew she hated it, and so did he, but under the circumstances it was probably going to be better coming from him. Dave knew he'd not found a way yet to break the awful news of one person's murder to another. He had a horrible feeling he never would. "I'm sorry to have to tell you this, but Victor was killed last night."

Tom stared from one to the other of the officers. "What do you mean? Was there an accident?"

"No. It wasn't an accident. I'm afraid someone murdered him while he was doing his duty at the Switchboard."

Both officers watched the young man closely as he struggled to absorb what he had been told. "Who?"

"We don't know yet."

"You don't think that I…?"

"We're nowhere near making any accusations yet, Tom. We're at the very beginning of the investigation and have to talk to…"

"There's no way I could ever have killed Victor," Tom yelled, jumping to his feet. "I…"

"Tom. Tom." Dave held his hands out and waited again for Tom to cool and sink back onto his stool. "As I was saying, we have to talk to as many people as we can about Victor to try and build up a picture of him. We've spoken to his neighbours and now we're talking to his fellow Switchboard operators."

"And I happen to be the first one?"

"Actually no. We've already spoken to Clive Grover. Twice."

"Okay. Right." Tom's anger went down a fraction of a notch. "But me second, yeah? Why's that?"

"You were timetabled to be on duty with Victor a number of times in the past two months."

Dave bit his lip. With typical bluntness, Claire had jumped in with the business of the rotas. Not what he would have led with, but she was, he reminded himself, the boss.

"Yeah? So?"

"Nobody else was partnered up with the same person that many times. And Mr. Grover has told us he hadn't put you together that many times. He also told us that you're the guy who word processes the rotas. So, it looks as if you changed those rotas to put yourself on duty with Victor all those times. Is that right, Tom?"

Tom shifted uncomfortably on his perch. It meant less of his crotch was on display, which was clearly a relief to Claire. "Maybe."

"Maybe?"

"Yeah, all right. Yes, I did. So what?"

"Care to tell us why?"

"I…I liked him. We were friends."

"Friends? That's a bit unusual, isn't it? I mean, there was quite an age difference between you, wasn't there? Victor Whyte was seventy-two. You're, what? Eighteen? Nineteen?"

"Oh, for fuck's sake. So what? I'm not a child. I'm legally an adult. And Victor isn't…wasn't some doddering, senile old relic. He was a man, a gay man. Like me. We both worked for Switchboard, both believed in the same things. He was my friend, okay?"

"Believed in the same things?" Claire leaned forward. Tom leaned back and drew his legs together. "What *things?*"

"The right of a gay man to live an honest and open life."

"Tom." Dave dug down into his own reserves of patience to help him deal with this boy. Tom was upset, obviously and quite rightly. He was also being an outrageous prick. Summerskill and Lyon had encountered his brand of militant queerness in their last meeting with him. Neither of them was eager to put up with any more of it. "That's pretty much a given these days."

"Hah! Like you'd…" Tom stopped. Dave guessed he was recalling their last meeting. "When you interviewed me before, you know, at the college. When you said… Did you mean…?" Dave nodded. "Okay." Tom adjusted his boxers, trying to recover some dignity. "Well, maybe you needed to have met Victor and talked to him. The man was walking gay history. I mean, he lived through a time when it *was* illegal to be gay, but he still had, like, this wonderful life, you know? Met all these great gay guys. Really *lived* his life. He didn't let an unjust society get him down. He used to tell me all these stories…" Tom broke off, his head fell forward, and he covered his face with his hands.

"It's all right, Tom," said Dave. "It can take a while for something like this to really sink in."

"I'm sorry," Tom mumbled, his voice husky.

"There's no need to be. Victor obviously meant a lot to you." Dave stopped, waiting for the lad to take that as far as he wanted to.

"I really…admired him, y'know." Tom looked up at Dave with teary eyes. "He was kind and sweet, but he didn't put up with any shit. And I mean, he had had some real shit to deal with in his life. I like to think… I like to think that I'd have been like him. If I'd been around back then."

"You arranged the rota so that you and he would be on duty together," Claire said, "four times out of the five that Victor was due on. Yet on the fifth time, the night that he was murdered, you put him on the rota on his own. Why?"

Dave shot Claire a sharp look. He'd managed to bring Tom down, and now she was stirring him back up again with her blunderbuss approach.

Tom's face was stricken, as if Summerskill had hit him. "What? Are you saying that if I hadn't done that then he wouldn't have been…?" His face darkened as the further possibilities of her question hit home. "Are you saying you think I had something to do with it? You can't…" Fists clenched, face white, Tom jumped up off the stool.

"No, Tom. No," Dave said, stepping forward and placing a hand on Tom's shoulder, not quite pushing him back down but using enough pressure to prevent him rising any further and doing something rash. "These are just questions we have to ask."

Slowly Tom sank back down, his eyes fixed on Inspector Summerskill, his expression murderous.

"So why didn't you rota yourself on with Victor that night?" Claire asked, unfazed by the display of temper.

"There was a party here last night," Tom said, slowly and deliberately, obviously struggling to control himself. He jerked his head in the general direction of the mess of pizza boxes and beer bottles. "A birthday party."

"Yours?"

"No. Seb's. He's one of my flatmates. You can ask him if you like. It had been on our calendar for months. I didn't want to miss it."

"So why didn't you put someone else on with Victor?"

"Because there was no one else available," Tom said as if explaining something to an idiot. "There aren't enough volunteers these days. Are you saying it's my fault that…?"

"No, Tom, we're not," Dave said, "and yes, we know about the volunteer situation." He looked across to Claire who gave a small nod and settled back slightly on the sofa, returning the lead of the interview to him. *Would have been nice if you'd let me know before we started that we were going to be playing good cop/bad cop.* Out loud he asked, "How was Victor during your last night on Switchboard together?"

"What do you mean?"

"I mean, what was his mood? Was he happy? Sad? Did it look like anything was bothering him? Did he mention anyone who'd upset him, or that he might have upset?"

"No. No, there was nothing like that."

"Are you sure? Think carefully, Tom. It might…"

"I am thinking carefully, all right? He was good. Everything was good."

"And what about the befriendings?" Claire asked.

"What about them?"

"You've done some?"

"I think you know I have. A couple. I'm still comparatively young in the group. They prefer to use the more mature members for that."

"And the ones you did, they were with Victor, yes?"

"Yes."

"In fact, the last but one in the book was with you and Victor."

"That was a no-show."

"So we gathered. Who was it who was supposed to have shown?"

"It was weeks ago. I don't know. I can't remember. Keith. Kevin. Something like that, I think. It doesn't matter. He didn't show."

"You seem rather vague. I'd been getting the impression that Switchboard is very thorough in its operations."

"Like I said, it was weeks ago. And it had been arranged at short notice, okay? Victor had been dealing with the guy on the phone. He would have led the befriending and I would have been there as protection."

"Protection?"

"We have to protect ourselves. We arrange the meetings in public places and always make sure there are two of us there so there can be no accusations that one of us is trying to take advantage of anyone."

"Someone vulnerable," Claire muttered, more for Dave than Tom.

"I was…flattered that Victor had chosen me."

"Maybe there was no one else available," Claire said.

"Or maybe he was my friend. I mean, it went both ways, you know. It wasn't just me admiring him. He liked me too."

To Dave's annoyance, Claire leaned forward again. "Why? Why was Victor such a special friend, Tom? What was it about him in particular? I mean, there are other older men working for Switchboard. Why Victor?"

"*Special friend?* Christ! D'you think I've got a thing for old men, is that it? Jesus! I'm gay so it's got to be about sex."

"Was it?"

Bloody hell.

"No. It wasn't. All right?"

Claire stood up. Dave followed. "Thank you, Tom. You've been very helpful."

Tom stood, too, caught out by the abrupt end of the meeting. "Is that it? "

"For the moment. We'll see ourselves out. Hope your friends feel better soon."

"My friends?"

Claire made her sympathetic mum face. "Sounds like they're spending an awful lot of time on the loo. Dodgy pizza last night perhaps?"

"You sure you've finished there?" Dave asked, as soon as they were out of the door.

"I think so. Why?"

"Oh, I don't know. I thought you might want, maybe, to beat him round the head a bit, stick some burning matches under his fingernails, or drag him back to the station and throw him in a cell so that later on you could apply electric shocks to his balls."

"You're unhappy, aren't you?"

"You just came down like a ton of bricks on a young lad who's lost a friend."

"A friend who's a lot older than he is."

Dave gave Claire a quizzical look. "Yes, yes. I know that. You made that point very clearly. So what?"

Claire stopped in the street and turned to look Dave straight in the eye. She had to raise her head to do it. "Yes, I did make a bit of a thing about it. Are you saying you think that was because it was about two men?"

"No, of course not. I know you don't think that way. Obviously."

"Thank you. So, tell me, if Tom had been Thomasina…"

"*Thomasina?*"

"…or Tracey or Carol or anything, all right? If he'd been a girl, a nineteen-year-old girl, going on and on about her friendship with a seventy-two-year-old man, wouldn't you have been asking yourself what was really going on?"

Dave made himself consider her point. "Maybe."

"Maybe," Claire repeated scornfully.

"It's different for—"

Claire cut him short with a wave of her hand. "Don't go there, Dave. You can't have equality and then claim exceptions." She turned and continued on her way to their car. "I can see you don't like it, and I'm sorry, but that friendship creeps me out."

They reached their car and Claire waited for Dave, who had the key, to open it. "And I don't think Tom is telling us everything about that no-show befriending and most especially why he wasn't with Victor on that last night."

"All right. What next?"

Claire looked up at the first hints of evening in the sky. "Back to Foregate. We tidy up the day's paperwork, sort out the schedule for tomorrow's interviews, argue with Madden about budgets, and then we go home. Where I will probably be doing much the same sort of thing with my loving family." They got into the car. "You? Anything on tonight?"

"Nothing planned." In fact, Joe was coming round, and they were intending to make the most of a rare coincidence of free time.

But right then, Dave found he didn't want to tell Summerskill that.

Chapter Four

"…so, after ten minutes of mad driving through the Ronkswood estate, narrowly missing two ladies with pushchairs, one old guy on a mobility scooter, and an ice cream van, we finally get the little toerag trapped in a cul-de-sac. We jump out and Chris does the 'Would you get out of the car please, sir?' routine, but the guy doesn't open the door. I'm getting into position, thinking he's either going to make a run for it when he throws the door open or he's going to try something nasty, when suddenly Chris bursts out laughing. You'll never guess why."

Dave let his head fall to one side so that he could see Joe's on the pillow next to him. He smiled sleepily. "Because his trousers were round his ankles?"

Joe pouted. "How did you know?"

Dave kissed him on his downturned mouth. "Too early in the day for joyriding, and anyway that usually involves two or more kids. You'd said it was a midrange car so not really a target for simple theft. It was drugs, wasn't it?"

"Yeah, and he was trying to…"

"…hide them."

"Yeah. Up his…"

"I know where he was trying to hide them, Joe." Dave kissed him again. "Cretins like that barely have a brain cell between them. They all try the same tricks, thinking no one in the world will ever guess what they're up to."

"Well, that takes a lot of the surprise out of the next thirty years of my career."

Dave smiled again, and slowly ran his finger down the length of Joe's neck and over his shoulder. He was enjoying this early stage of the relationship when it was still fair game to spend time searching for all those spots that really turned the other guy on, with the right stimulation. This spot didn't seem to be doing it for Joe. It was working for Dave though.

"So how was your day?" Joe asked. "You're on that murder case, right?"

Dave sighed. As far as he had been able, when he had been with Richard he had tried not to talk about work when home. It hadn't only been because he wanted to keep work and home separate. It had been more that Richard's ideas of policing were all taken from film and television, and the differences between that and reality had always been too jarring for Dave. But Joe was different. He might be inexperienced, but he was a police officer. He'd understand in ways that Richard never could, and Dave might even be helping him, giving him insights and sharing his experience. Even so, Dave found himself not wanting to talk about this day. Its sour ending with Claire was something he didn't want to think about. "Interviews," he said shortly. "Gathering the background intel."

"How's it going?"

"Too soon to tell."

"Then why so down?"

"I'm not down. Do I seem down?"

Joe reached across and ran the back of his finger down the side of Dave's cheek. "Well, not half an hour ago. Most decidedly not. But now"—he rested the tip of one finger on the corner of Dave's mouth—"this is definitely proceeding in what we might call a southerly rather than northerly direction."

"Mmmm." Dave had been caught out. Joe had effortlessly found a spot. Dave hadn't even known about this one. He went to take the finger between his teeth, but Joe withdrew it and tapped him on the nose.

"C'mon, tell. What's getting you down?"

Dave surrendered. He'd always known that if he'd ever been someone important in a war and the enemy had sent sex spies to tease information out of him, he would have been a treacherous pushover. Joe had just proved it. "Claire," he said. "DI Summerskill."

"Boss being a bitch?"

"Er, no." Dave laughed, surprised at his instinct to reprimand a junior officer for insubordination. A bit inappropriate when said junior officer was naked in his bed with him. Joe's bluntness did make him feel uncomfortable though. He tried for a reproving expression, decided that made him feel too much like a parent, which was also uncomfortable, and gave up. "No, that's way too strong. Difficult, perhaps. She can be…high maintenance sometimes."

"You make her sound like your wife."

"Inspector and sergeant. It's an interesting relationship. And ours is… different."

"Because she's Welsh and you're English?"

Dave smiled. "Yes. Yes, that's it."

"You're a man and she's a woman."

"I'm a liberal leftie and she's…politically apathetic."

"You're gay and she's…"

"And stop right there." Dave kissed Joe. "That really doesn't mean anything to either of us."

Joe looked doubtful but he did stop.

"No, I think the only difference between us that she really doesn't like is that I'm taller than her. She hates having to look up to me. Metaphorically speaking."

Joe chuckled. "Anyway, you don't have to tell me she's hard work. The guys at the station say…"

"Whoa! Stop there. Inappropriate information. What's said at Foregate stays at Foregate."

"Yes, sir!" For a moment they sat and lay there, enjoying the silence and the intimacy.

"Do they say anything about me?" Dave asked.

Joe, eyes closed, smiled. "Sorry, but what's said in Foregate…"

"So? What do you want to do?"

"What? Now?"

"No. Well, yes. But also this Saturday."

Claire considered. "You're sure Jill is okay having the kids?"

"Yes," her husband said. "Absolutely. She may have been a bloody awful kid sister but she's actually turning out to be a pretty good aunt. For some reason she likes having Sam around. And Tony. In fact, she says she doesn't see enough of them."

Claire bit back the retort that if Jill got off her arse and tore herself away from endless lunches and shopping on her bank manager husband's credit cards then she would easily see a great deal more of her nephews. And she hadn't missed Ian's slip over Tony. Ian had never treated her eldest as anything other than his own son. Claire suspected Jill's feelings were a little less clear. *Cow.* But she was volunteering to take both kids off their hands for a whole evening so Claire supposed she could be forgiven, for the moment.

She wondered what Ian had had to do or say to get his sister to put herself out for them. How honest had he been? She hoped he hadn't told her everything. Jill was always at pains to show how perfect her marriage was. *Of course, you really have to work at it,* she'd said once, in a not too subtle dig at Claire. Claire's private opinion was that Jill "worked at it" in the same way as the girls she'd met while seconded to Vice "worked at it". But she'd held back from saying as much, which turned out to be for the best, didn't it, as now they had a free babysitter on Saturday.

Claire ran her hand through her hair and brought herself back to the question at hand. "I don't know. What about a film?"

"Anything you want to see?"

Claire didn't have a clue what was doing the rounds at that time. "Not really. Why don't we be wild and crazy and turn up, buy our popcorn, and see what we see?"

"Right. You do remember the last time we did that? I never knew a subtitled film about mountain canoeing could last so long." He laughed. It had a forced ring to it.

Claire laughed, too, and was depressed at how fake that also sounded. She did remember that film, but the memory seemed unreal somehow, like something that had happened to two other people. "Maybe just a meal, then?"

"A candlelit meal for two?"

Was he being sarcastic? *Let it go.* "I was thinking more Pizza Lodge. It's a week till payday. We could take our own candles."

"Could do."

Is that a yes or a no?

"And what about tonight?"

What about tonight? What did we used to do before Sam came along? And how did we even manage whatever it was when Tony would have been around anyway? Claire struggled to remember. She'd be forever grateful to her mam for the support she'd given before Ian had come along, when Claire had been a mum on her own, working hard to raise a child and make her way in the police service. Had she looked after Tony all that time Claire and Ian were getting together—and doing whatever? She couldn't remember. "Anything on telly?"

Ian reached for a paper, and for the next couple of minutes they tried to find something that appealed to both of them. They settled for a film that the write-up suggested might have enough action for him and sufficient story for her. Within about ten minutes, it was clear they had both been misled. "Cup of tea?" Ian said.

"Yeah. I'll pause the film if you like."

"No, let it run." And he was up and into the kitchen. By the time he came back, the plot had lumbered to a place he couldn't possibly understand without Claire explaining it to him, and she had paid so little attention there was no way she could do that. He'd been gone quite a while. *Texting someone?* Claire shoved the thought to the back of her mind.

They sat for another ten minutes, clasping their mugs, sipping their tea, and staring at the screen. An advert break came and went without either of them particularly registering it.

Of course, there had been the sex in the past. That was definitely something they used to do when her mam looked after Tony. And that, of course, had led to Sam. She loved Sam with all her heart. They both did. But she couldn't help wondering if his birth had marked the beginning of the end. Was that when they had begun to drift apart? She caught up in motherhood and work; he caught up in work. And the other woman at work.

Claire's stomach knotted, the unwanted tea sitting in it like acid. She wasn't going to think about Ms. Cassie Grant. She'd discovered the affair, more through heavy hints dropped by her eldest son than through any detective skills of her own. Ian had admitted it, said it meant nothing and that it was over. And she had believed him.

So, here they were, trying to move on.

Should she suggest sex? She gripped her mug. No.

"Y'know," Ian said, "I hate to say this, but I really do have a ton of marking I could do with getting out of the way as soon as possible. Would you mind if…?"

"No. That's fine. I've got a pile of reviews I need to wrap up too. Dave'll give me his disapproving routine again if I haven't got them done by the end of the week."

"Right. Dave. Of course." Ian got to his feet. "You know, I thought you were the one who was supposed to be in charge."

"What do you mean? Of course, I'm the one who—"

"I can use the kitchen if you want to use the table in here. Or would you rather be out there?"

What she would rather have done was deal with that crack about Dave. But now wasn't the time, was it? Her sister-in-law's words about "working at it" came back to her. God, she really disliked that stuck-up bitch. "No. If you're happy with the kitchen, that's fine. Thanks."

"Right. Okay. See you in a bit then."

"Yeah."

He left, and Claire tried not to admit to herself what a relief it was.

"So come on," Joe insisted, when the two of them finally got round to food that evening, "what was so bad about your day?" Reluctantly, but still too blissed-out to refuse Joe anything, Dave outlined his spat with Claire.

Joe's brows furrowed. "That's it?"

"Yes."

"She gave an irritating college kid a rough time?"

"Yes. And yes, he is irritating. But it was what she picked up on. The age thing. It felt a bit too close to giving in to gay stereotypes."

"I dunno. It is a bit creepy."

"What? Don't you start."

"But it is." Joe laughed. "I wouldn't fancy you if you were seventy and all wrinkly."

"But I'm going to be, one day. I hope. You going to drop me then? You'll be the same, too, you know."

Joe wagged a finger in denial. "Nah. I'll always be younger than you, remember? Besides"—he patted his own cheek—"black don't crack, y'know?"

"Moving on," said Dave, unwilling to talk any longer about the difference in their ages, "we don't even know that there was anything between Tom and Victor more than the simple friendship Tom says."

"Right," Joe scoffed, reaching for the last piece of pizza on the table.

"Oh, come on. You're as bad as Claire. Inspector—"

"I know who she is, Dave. And, for what it's worth, I think she might be right. But I also think it doesn't matter. It's a bit…icky, but to each his own, and it's not illegal so who are we to worry?" He stood from the table. "Puddin'?"

Crossed Lines | - 49 - | Steve Burford

"It's in the fridge."

Joe leaned across the table to kiss him before gathering their plates and taking them to the kitchen. Pizza crumbs could be a bit uncomfortable when you were dining naked, Dave thought as he watched Joe, but the views were so much nicer.

As he waited for Joe to come back, he thought about what had been said. For the most part, he and Joe were in agreement. Why, then, did he feel so rattled? Why did he feel so defensive about whatever relationship Victor and Tom might or might not have had, especially when he really did think it had been nothing more than a friendship with a little bit of hero worship thrown in on Tom's part? Was he letting his reaction against gay stereotyping blind him to a potentially important aspect of this latest case? Or was he being defensive because of his own relationship with Joe? That would be ridiculous. The age difference between him and Joe was nothing like that between Victor and Tom.

How much older than him was Sean Cullen?

"Ta-da!" proclaimed Joe, re-entering the room, arms held out, a heaped bowl of ice cream in each hand.

"My, my," Dave murmured. "Is that a Flake, or are you just pleased to see me?"

Chapter Five

The following morning at the station got off to a cool start. Conscious of their disagreement the day before, Claire and Dave were more formal and polite with each other than usual. "Trouble in paradise," Jenny Trent whispered to Sergeant Cortez, one of the other officers who shared their office. Cortez looked bemused. His own relationship with his immediate boss, DI Rudge, was considerably simpler.

First job of the day for Summerskill and Lyon was a visit to Roz Joynson, the Switchboard operator who had gone on that last befriending with Victor. She wasn't at the home address they had been given, a modest maisonette. "Try the library, love," a woman next door said as she was hanging out her washing.

"Bookworm, eh?" said Dave.

"Nah. She works there."

"Isn't she in her seventies as well?" Claire asked as they got back into their car.

"The way things are going in this country, we'll all be working that long."

"Maybe I should take up Cullen's Fitness First after all. Make sure I've still got what it takes to chase bad boys in my dotage."

Worcester Library, formerly a dour nineteenth-century building, assumed by local children to have once been a jail, had in recent years, and after a huge injection of cash, been relocated in a brand-new, purpose-built complex down by the race-track, and rechristened, for reasons no one was sure of, The Hive. It was, quite literally, a glittering addition to Worcester's architecture, as its main building had been sheathed in a golden alloy. "Bit like visiting a biscuit tin," Dave said as they made their way in.

"Tony loves it," Claire said. "Much bigger selection of books."

"He'll go far, that lad."

An inquiry at the desk, and they were directed, not to some checkout point as they had half expected, but to a room in the basement signposted "Archives". There, they found a small woman dressed in purple and black, hunched over a table illuminated by an incredibly bright Anglepoise lamp, laying out what appeared to be sweet wrappers. "Hullo," she said, looking up at them over a huge pair of glasses like the bottoms of two wine bottles. She took both the identity cards they held out to her and examined then under the lamp. "Come to arrest me?" she asked with a smile as she handed the cards back.

"I don't think so," Claire said.

"Good. I've got a ton of work to do and that would really get in the way." The woman removed the glasses, revealing two heavily kohled eyes. "Fancy a cup of tea? I'm Roz by the way, but I'm guessing you know that."

"Thanks, Roz. I'm Claire and this is Dave."

In short order, Roz found them two cups of truly vile tea from a nearby machine, and they pulled up chairs around the table on which lay the papers she had been examining. "Sweet wrappers," she confirmed. "Want to feel old? You will when they start giving you things you used to buy as a kid and tell you to archive them as history." She leaned on the table, holding her plastic cup in both hands, a profusion of silver and jade rings and bracelets on her fingers and wrists. She blew on her tea, wrinkling her nose at the smell that arose from it. "You've come to ask me about Victor, haven't you? I couldn't believe it when Clive told me. Horrid. Absolutely horrid. Victor was such a lovely man."

"How long had you known him?" Dave asked.

"Oh, we went back centuries, darlin'. We met when Worcester's gay scene was one room in one pub, and we could only use that when the landlord wasn't using it to store barrels. I'm a Worcester girl born and bred, but Victor had come down here from somewhere up north. Young, dumb and full of…enthusiasm." She sighed sadly. "It wasn't easy being here and queer back then, but somehow, everything still seemed so hopeful. Now look at us. Me an aging hippy and Victor…" She stopped and looked at the cup clasped in her wrinkled hands. "Sorry, sweethearts. Bit maudlin there. I thought coming into work might stave that off. Daft old bird."

"You worked on Switchboard together?" Claire prompted.

"Darlin', we *started* it. The Worcester and Hereford Gay Switchboard." Roz chuckled. "No Lesbian in those days. We were all quite happy, men and women, to be G for gay. And no B, T, Q, or bloody Plus either. Made the letterheads a lot neater. Just the three of us: me, Victor, and a guy called Gerald Reeves. We saw a gap in the market, as it were, and went for it. The big cities already had their switchboards, but they didn't know what it was like out in the sticks. We definitely did. Started out in a backroom in Gerald's house. Bit of fundraising, and after a year we were able to start renting an office. We moved into the one in the Halo Centre about ten years ago when we actually got a grant from the local government." She gave a barked laugh. "We couldn't believe it. Money from the council to support poofs and dykes. Time was they wanted us all thrown into prison for corrupting the local young farmers. Poor old Gerald would never have believed it."

"He's…not with us any more?" Dave asked.

"We lost him twenty years ago. AIDS related."

"I'm sorry," Claire said.

"He was knocked over by a bus with a big 'Don't Die of Ignorance' poster on its side." Roz cackled. "Sorry, couldn't resist that. It was true about the bus, mind you, though not about the poster. Do you remember those? No, of course you don't. You're much too young. Lord, what is it they say about when the police start looking young?"

"Did Victor…?" Dave began.

Roz reached across and patted him on the hand. "I digress. I know. Don't worry, I'm not going gaga yet. It's…helping a bit. Remembering the good times. Is that okay?"

"Of course it is," said Dave.

Roz patted his hand again and then reached into a voluminous sleeve for a handkerchief which she used to dab carefully at her kohl-lined eyes. "Victor was marvellous at it," she said. "So kind and patient with the callers. And a wonderful voice. I used to tease him that he should be one of those deep-voiced, breathy men who do the trailers for films. They only work for American films, though, don't they? British films these days are all about pensioners finding love in India, aren't they? You don't really want a basso profundo summing up one of those."

"Would you say there were any callers that Victor had…problems with? Where he might have heard something odd, or said something that might have offended someone?"

Roz was incredulous. "Enough to make someone want to kill him? I really can't think of anything like that. That wasn't Victor at all. Everyone liked him. Some callers asked for him especially. In fact…" She stopped. "Oh dear."

"What is it?" asked Claire.

"A sudden vision of Clive Grover wagging his finger at me. He is a lovely boy, really, but he is very strict about confidentiality, and I think I might have been about to breach it, a tiny bit."

Claire tried not to smile at the description of fifty-something, stuffy Clive as "a lovely boy". "Don't worry. We've already had that discussion with Mr. Grover. He understands that there is information we have to share."

"That's a relief. Well, ordinarily, I wouldn't have mentioned it, because in a way it's the exact opposite of what you were asking, but there was one caller. Dale. He was a bit of a joke among the operators. Not in a nasty way, I hasten to say. But he only ever wanted to talk to Victor. I was on duty a couple of times when he called, but we didn't get much beyond saying hello. He'd always ask for Victor, and then if we told him that Victor wasn't there, Dale would politely say he'd try again another day and ring off."

"Couldn't the operators have simply told him when Victor was going to be on duty? It would have saved your time and his?"

"Oh, Clive would not have been happy with that. Strict Switchboard policy not to give out rota details over the phone."

"Though if anyone wanted to, they could walk into the Halo Centre and read the rota pinned to the noticeboard."

"Spotted that loophole, did you? It seems never to have occurred to Clive, and I've not had the heart to point it out to him. Mind you, it didn't seem to occur to Dale either."

"Perhaps," said Claire to Dave, "because he lives too far away to easily drop in and check the board."

"Or because, for whatever reason, he didn't want to be seen by people who might recognise him and ask what he was doing there. It also suggests that he wouldn't have known Victor was on duty the night he was killed."

Claire turned back to Roz who had been fascinated by their exchange. "Can you tell us anything else about this Dale?"

"I'm afraid not. Like I said, I only spoke to him briefly a couple of times. Bit of a Black Country twang to his vowels perhaps, but I'm no Professor Higgins. Youngish, I'd say, twenties or thirties, but the phone can be deceptive, can't it? I'm told I sound like a young Marlene Dietrich."

"Yeah, I can get that," said Dave.

"Aren't you the sweetest thing!"

Claire rose. "Well, thank you very much for your help, Ms. Joynson."

"Roz, please. And you're very welcome."

"It's been a pleasure meeting you, Roz." Dave also rose and reached out to shake her hand. "I hope we meet again sometime. I'd enjoy hearing more about local history."

Roz clasped his large hand in her small one and looked up at him earnestly. "D'you know, sweetheart, I have the feeling we will meet again." She placed her other hand on his too. "And I hope you catch the person who did this. Victor was special. I hope you catch the bastard who killed him and cut his bollocks off."

"We'll do our best" was all Dave could think of to say.

"Oh, before we go," Claire said. "Tom Adams. You know him, of course?"

"Of course. Sweet boy."

"Hm. He and Victor were on duty a lot together."

"We all end up on duty with each other at some point."

"But Victor had been on duty with Tom at least four times in the last two months."

Roz pursed her lips but didn't look too concerned to hear that. "Oh?"

"Were they friends, do you know?"

"Yes. I think so. We're all friends, really."

"But were Tom and Victor especially friendly?" Claire was aware that Dave's eyes were on her, not on Roz, and she had a good idea what their expression would be. *Tough.*

Roz tilted her head to one side as she regarded Claire. "They got on well. Victor was a very kind, generous man. Tom is a nice lad. A bit full on, but he's young. Better get all that *sturm und drang* out of the way now rather than never, yes?"

"Victor didn't have a boyfriend, did he?"

"Oh, darlin'. I think we should all stop talking about boyfriends and girlfriends after a certain age, don't you? Victor certainly never used that word, even back in the day. But, no, there hasn't been anyone special in his life for a few years now."

"Had there been?"

Roz frowned briefly, as if puzzled at this new line of questioning. "Of course. Not long after I first met him, Victor took up with Roy. They were together for ten years. Then there was Philip, and then when that came to an end, all quite amicably

I might add, there was Lesley. Not that he jumped straight from one to the other, you understand. There were periods when he was on his own, *alone and palely loitering* I suppose you might say."

"And when did he finish with…Lesley, was it?"

"About two years ago. Although saying that Victor finished with him sounds a bit harsh. It had run its course, that's all. I'm sure you appreciate how that can happen, Inspector." She smiled archly at Dave. "You may not yet, Sergeant. You're far too young to have experienced a love long enough to have paled and died."

Claire's expression was stony, either because she was narked at the suggestion she was so much older and battered by the world than Dave, or because she did not want to dwell on long-term love turned cold. "That's quite a lot of…partners."

"Really? Three, over fifty or so years. There are gay men I know who would describe that as a positively monk-like existence." She looked again to Dave who this time avoided her eye. She looked back to Claire. "Perhaps you've been lucky, darlin', and found *the one.*"

"Were these all local men?" Claire asked. "Would you be able to provide full names and addresses so we could maybe find them and speak to them?"

"Well, yes, I suppose so. For Philip and Lesley certainly. I think they're both on my Christmas card list, but…"

"Were any of these men much younger than Mr. Whyte?"

"Does it matter, sweetheart?"

"It might."

"D'you know, I'm not sure I could tell."

Despite her words, she gave off the very strong impression that she could.

Back at the station, Summerskill and Lyon were greeted by two distinctly different pieces of news.

"They've found your records," Jenny said as they walked into their office, pointing to a ring binder in a plastic evidence pouch on Claire's desk.

"The Switchboard records for this year?" Claire held up the pouch and peered inside. "Where was it?"

"Still in the Halo Centre but outside the Switchboard office. Stuffed behind a pile of noticeboards left in one corner by the exit. Whoever tried to hide it hadn't done a very good job. It was found last night by one of the cleaners."

"Karen Haines?" Dave asked.

Jenny shrugged. "No idea."

"Wish I could have evidence dropped into my lap like that, m'girl," a dour DI Rudge said from his side of the office.

"Wouldn't do you any good, Jim," Claire said. "You'd still have to work out what it meant, and you know you're shit at that without me on your team. No offence," she added for the benefit of Sergeant Cortez sitting at the desk next to his boss.

"None taken." This was almost certainly true. Praise and blame alike seemed to slide off Cortez like water off an indifferent duck. Claire had once suggested to Dave in an unguarded moment that this might be because the impossibly handsome man was so wrapped up in his own appearance he hadn't got time for anyone else's opinions about him. That, or his sublime indifference was a defence mechanism that helped him survive working with the infamously abrasive DI Rudge.

Claire handed the pouch to Dave. "Get that to forensics. See if they can lift some prints."

"That might have to wait," Jenny said. "Superintendent Madden wants to see you."

"What now? Okay. Dave, you can still—"

"No," said Jenny, "not you, Inspector. Sergeant Lyon."

Dave appeared to be as surprised as Claire. "What about?" he asked.

"How should I know?"

"Okay then," said Claire. "Jenny, you take the folder to forensics. Remind Pete he still owes me one for the drink I bought him Christmas before last. He's a liar if he says he bought me one back. And you"—she looked to Dave—"had better head upstairs. Pretty quick."

Dave was gone for ten minutes, during which time Claire busied herself rearranging the piles of overdue paperwork on her desk and tried her best not to look as if she was wondering what the hell Madden wanted her sergeant for.

"Your man been up to things you don't know about, girlie?" Rudge asked.

"Has yours?" Claire snapped. "What am I saying? Terry doesn't get up to anything unless you put a rocket up his arse."

"That what you do for Lyon?" Cortez drawled. "Figures."

"That comment…" Claire began, but Rudge grunted a laugh, and shoved a folder over to Cortez to look at, and Cortez swivelled on his chair to discuss it with his boss, turning his back on her.

Claire sat and fumed, both at Cortez's banter and at her own failure to challenge it.

When Dave came back, Rudge and Cortez paid him no attention, though Claire knew they were as curious as she was to find out what their boss had wanted him for and were listening closely. "Well?" She tried to read Dave's expression. It could have been surprise or confusion. Maybe both. He didn't look happy.

"There's going to be a press call for local telly news about the Whyte case."

"Not that bloody Moody woman again," Claire said, recalling their involvement with the local media during their last case.

"Probably." Dave looked as if he was bracing himself. "And Madden wants me to front it."

Without looking, Claire knew that Cortez and Rudge had both stopped what they were doing and were now openly listening to her and Dave.

"Why?"

"The usual. Public interest. Plea for information. Y'know."

"No, I mean, why you?"

"Madden said it would be good experience for me."

"Right. Yes, I suppose it would be. Any thoughts on how you're going to explain that a sergeant is fronting the case, not the inspector who is actually in charge of it?"

Dave's expression became a lot clearer to read. He was definitely unhappy. "He said you don't enjoy appearing in front of a camera."

Damn Madden. Claire fumed inwardly. *Manipulative bastard.* He was right, of course. She loathed press calls, so insisting on leading this one, even though it should have been her, would have looked like blatant attention-seeking. Also, much as she wanted to bite Dave's head off, she didn't want to do it in front of Rudge and Cortez as she was still angry with them for Cortez's earlier off-colour remark. And this wasn't Dave's fault, the small, most rational part of her mind reminded her. He hadn't asked to be pushed into the limelight. Had he?

Dave lowered his voice. "Can I have a word?" It was obvious he wanted to speak to her out of earshot of the others.

"No, that's fine, Sergeant." Claire hated herself immediately for rebuffing him, but also knew she couldn't trust her temper alone with him right then. "Do you know when this call is happening?"

"In about an hour, I think, but—"

"Then you'd better go and get ready for it, hadn't you? Wouldn't do to be on local television with a shiny nose." She glanced down at her desk. "Oh, and you'd better take this. Looks like Jenny forgot it." She tossed Dave the bagged Switchboard folder, then sat down at her desk, gave her mouse a couple of savage swipes to wake up her computer, and made it clear that she was far too busy to talk to anyone.

Dave stood for a moment, holding the bag. "Yes, ma'am," he said, and left the room.

There was a frigid silence in the room before Rudge spoke. "Not feeling so politically correct now, are you, girlie?"

Outside the office, Dave was as unhappy as Claire. He'd thought at first there'd been some mistake when Madden had told him of his decision, and then an uncomfortable suspicion had raised its head. "Are you putting me forward for this because I'm gay, sir, and the case involves a gay man?"

Madden had regarded him with the utterly unreadable face that was his trademark and, some said, the secret of his success. "I've given you my reason, Sergeant. One of my many duties is the overseeing of the professional development of the officers stationed here at Foregate Street. *All of the officers.* And I believe that this will be good for yours. Unless you're planning on making some public statement about your private life during the call—which, incidentally, I do not recommend— I can't see that your orientation makes the slightest difference. Can you?"

Dave faced up to his superior officer, the man largely responsible for his appointment to his current post as part of an equal opportunities/minorities quota initiative. "With respect, sir, it looks like tokenism."

Madden gave a small smile, as warm as a crack in a block of ice. "Only if you make it so, Sergeant. I don't know about you, but I have never been a great believer in gaydar, so I'm fairly certain the majority of the viewing public will not appreciate that you are gay. So, you will do this press call and accept it as the CPD opportunity it is meant to be. And, if you are worried that Detective Inspector Summerskill will see some slight in this"—he smiled again, another glacial fissure—"you can refer her to me. Dismissed."

Dave shook his head over how easily Madden had worked him, even using his own scepticism about gaydar against him. And as for CPD… Dave snorted. The only thing Continued Personal Development was good for was ticking boxes in the annual review, and they both knew it. When it came to career progression in this job, like any other bloody job, the only thing that got you to the top…

Dave stopped dead in his tracks, as yet another horrible suspicion reared up in his head. Only one other person in recent months had expressed any interest in his career path. Was it a coincidence that person was a close friend of Madden's? "Shit! Sean!"

For a moment, Dave almost forgot the plastic wallet he was carrying, nearly overwhelmed by an urge to go to Sean Cullen then and there, to find out if what he suspected was the truth, that the MP had pulled strings to get him this opportunity. He squashed the impulse. Any further delay with the folder she'd given him would definitely not improve Claire's mood. He resumed his walk to forensics, picking up the pace to deliver the damn wallet as quickly as possible so that then he could go and deal with Sean.

Before he had gone more than half a dozen steps, he literally ran into Joe who had come hurtling round a corner.

"Hey, hey, hey, movie star." And before Dave could stop him, Joe had thrown his arms around him and planted a big kiss on his lips.

"For Christ's sake." Both men whirled round, Joe still with his arms round Dave.

"Inspector Rudge." Joe dropped his arms and straightened to attention, though he was still grinning broadly.

Rudge glowered at the two of them. "I came out to have a word, Sergeant," he said, "about the proper way to work with an inspector. But I see I've interrupted a little celebration." His face wrinkled with distaste. "You might like to keep it in your own home. We'll talk later. When you're less…busy." He turned and stalked away from them down the corridor.

"Shit!"

"Embarrassing," said Joe.

"Embarrassing! It's a bloody sight more serious than that, Joe."

"What do you mean? You're going to be on telly. It'll be a laugh. I thought you'd be happy. I'm happy for you and I was showing it. Rudge is an old crusty. So what?"

"Joe, it's not good news."

"Why not? Gets you exposure. Gotta be good for the career."

"Why is everyone so bloody concerned about where my career is going all of a sudden? What I'm more concerned about is my career right now. And what with Summerskill bent out of shape because of this press call and now Rudge catching you all over me in the corridor, that is not looking too good."

"Aw, c'mon. I was hardly all over you. And as for Summerskill, you ask me, it won't do her any harm to be taken down a peg or two. Do her good to be reminded she's got an up-and-coming officer thrusting up from below." As he said that, Joe laughed and went to hold Dave again.

Alarmed, Dave stepped back. "Joe!" He looked round to make sure they weren't going to be caught out a second time. "Not in the station. And that's not how I work, okay?"

Joe stepped back, too, though with obvious reluctance, and dropped his arms to his side. "Okay. Though I think you're making too big a thing of it. As always. Good thing someone up there is looking out for you."

Dave regarded the enthusiastic young recruit in front of him. *If you only knew.*

"David. This is an unexpected pleasure."

Dave stood on the doorstep of Sean Cullen's apartment, torn between wanting to rip into the MP right there and then, and not wanting to be seen by any passers-by. "Can I come in?"

"Such enthusiasm. Of course. Always." Stepping back, Cullen welcomed Dave in with an extravagant bow. "You know where the bedroom is."

"That's not why I've come, Sean."

"Isn't it? How disappointing. Oh well. In that case, let me see if I can tempt you to something in the kitchen instead. I was about to have a coffee."

Cullen led the way to his luxuriously appointed kitchen, which was larger than Dave's kitchen, living room, and bedroom combined. At Sean's invitation, Dave took one of the gleaming bar stools set around the breakfast bar, though he would much rather have remained standing, and waited, quietly simmering, while Sean went through the elaborate process that made his gleaming monster of a coffee machine produce two tiny cups of perfect espresso.

"So," Cullen began, pulling up a stool next to him and resting one hand on Dave's thigh, "if it isn't an urge to work off some excess energy with a spot of mutually beneficial fucking, to what do I owe the pleasure of this visit?"

"I think you know very well."

"Melodramatic, but I have to admit, I think I do." Sean made no move to take his hand away. "And you're welcome. If you'd like some tips on how to deal with the media, I am a recent graduate of my party's latest 'How to Handle Social and Anti-Social Media' course."

"Why?"

"To help you look your best on the screen. I mean, it actually begins with the way you stand, if you can believe…"

"I mean, why did you get Madden to make me the television face of the investigation?"

Cullen laughed and shook his head. "Your chief superintendent and I are close friends, have been for a number of years, actually, long before he became a policeman and I became an MP. But I still very much doubt I could get him to do anything if he didn't want to do it already. I suggested it, yes. I confess. That's all. I thought it would be good for your career, for the Worcester police, and, frankly, for the gay community. And so did he, though his order of priorities may differ from mine. You have friends in high places, David. I told you when we first met, that can only be a good thing." He squeezed Dave's leg before finally taking his hand away. "Brioche?"

"And what are those *friends* going to want in return?"

Cullen affected an incredulous expression. "Do you really think you have anything that Superintendent Madden is going to want? And as for what I might want…" He pretended to consider. "Well, a kiss wouldn't go amiss. Nothing chaste, mind you. Tongues and all."

"You know you've screwed around with my relationship with my inspector? Summerskill thinks I've gone behind her back to make myself look good."

"Then tell her you haven't. If your relationship is that good, she'll believe you. It is, after all, the truth."

"It's not that simple, is it?"

Cullen pantomimed confusion. "Isn't it? Isn't it really? You do have a habit of making things much more complicated than they need to be, David. You do know that, don't you?" He shifted his bar stool a little closer to Dave's. "Now, about that kiss."

"You know I'm…going out with someone now?"

"'Going out with'. How very Mills and Boon. Yes, of course I know about you and Constable Jones." He shrugged. "So?"

The two men sat on their bar stools. Cullen reached across and took Dave's coffee cup from him.

★

"You don't have a room set aside for media interviews?"

"No."

Sarah Moody, reporter with local television news programme *Midlands Now*, raised an exquisitely pencilled eyebrow and looked around Interview Room Three. "And this is really the best you think you have?"

"Yes," said Dave.

Moody turned to her cameraman. "I think we'll take it outside, Reg. On those steps leading up to the station. Pan across from that big sign, take in that statue thing on the corner and then in on me and—" She turned back to Dave. "I'm sorry, what did you say your name was again?"

"Sergeant David Lyon."

"In on Sergeant Lyon. Now is that David or Dave? For the captions. And is it Lyon with an *i*"—Moody made what he presumed was meant to be a roar and clawed the air—"or Lyon with a *y* as in the tea rooms?"

"It's David. And Lyon with a *y*. As in the city."

"Nice. I'll try and remember. All right, let's get out and get this done. We need to get a move on if we're going to make this evening's show." Moody cast one last disparaging look around Interview Room Three which really was, had she known it, the best the station had to offer for the purpose, before sweeping out with her cameraman. Dave followed them, cursing Madden and Cullen, and glaring balefully at anyone foolish enough to catch his eye on the way.

★

"Mr. Philip Day?"

"Aye?"

Claire held up her ID card. "Detective Claire Summerskill. I wonder if I might have a word?"

"S'pose. Ye'd best come in." The thickset man who had opened the door stood back, and Claire stepped into the modest terraced house. It hadn't occurred to her that it might have been a good idea to take backup along with her on an interview with anyone who had been a partner of Victor Whyte, and that over twenty years ago. Now, looking up at the burly Scot with the large arms and not very welcoming expression, she wondered if she might have let her preconceptions overrule her good sense.

Day led the way into the living room, a room almost completely filled by a huge sofa and two armchairs, both in floral print. There was a strange, musky smell in the air that she knew she recognised from somewhere but couldn't immediately place. Day gestured to one of the armchairs. "You'll no mind the hairs?" he said, in a tone that was more statement than question, and his comment triggered her recognition of the smell, even before two bolts of yapping brown fur shot through the door and began jumping up her legs.

"Candy! Ruby! Down!" Another man came running into the room. He was as heavily built as Day and about the same age, but although flustered, seemed friendly enough. "Sorry about this," he said as he pulled the two small dogs to him by their collars. "They get a bit excited when we have visitors, so I normally try to keep them in the kitchen." He stood up with both dogs cradled in his arms. They licked his face enthusiastically. He looked from Claire to Philip Day and back again, clearly expecting some kind of introduction. "Hi. I'm Greg," he said when none was forthcoming. He tried to hold out his hand but had to abandon that when the struggling dogs looked as if they might escape his embrace. "You here to see Philip?"

"Yes."

"I'll take these two out of your way, then. Would you like some tea?"

"Thank you. That would be lovely."

Greg gave Claire a cheerful smile and hurried from the living room. As he passed his partner, he gave him a questioning look. Day shrugged.

As Day closed the door and came to sit on the armchair across the room from her, Claire snuck a quick look around the room. It was chintzier than she would have expected from two such burly men, but then the two small, yappy-type dogs didn't match the profile either.

"Terriers?" she asked, in the hope that her interest might soften Day up a little.

"Aye," he said, sitting down.

Claire took in the framed photos on the mantelpiece and shelf, most of them of dogs either like the two she'd just seen or the nasty little snappers themselves. Several of the frames had rosettes stuck in the corners. The largest photo in the very centre of the mantelpiece had a gold rosette attached and was a closeup of

Philip Day and Greg, holding a terrier and beaming joyously into the camera. *So, you can actually smile, then?* "Do you show them?"

"Aye."

A Scot from the accent, the little she had heard of it, and from the attitude behind it, she guessed more Glasgow than Edinburgh. She abandoned any more attempts at ice-breaking small talk. "I wonder if I could ask you—?"

"Is this about Victor?"

"Yes, it is. I'm assuming you've heard about what has happened to him?"

Day gestured to the television in the corner. "Saw it on the news last night." He narrowed his eyes as if checking something. "You're no the police officer in charge."

"Actually, I am," Claire said stiffly. "The man on the television is my sergeant."

Day looked uninterested either way. "So how come ye're here, then? Ye're not after thinking I did it, are you?"

"No, Mr. Day, I'm not. I'm just trying to get a clearer picture of the sort of man Victor Whyte was."

Day looked sceptical. "He was a good man. A very good man. But it was a long time ago we were together."

"Over twenty years, I believe."

"Aye." Day's eyes narrowed again suspiciously. "How did you get my name and address?"

"Roz Joynson."

For a moment, Day's expression softened and there was even the hint of a smile, like a ray of watery sunshine on a craggy highland mountain. "Oh aye, Roz. She's a sweetheart that one." Then the moment passed, and the friendly face was gone. "So, what more do you want to know?"

"You were together for quite a long time, I think?"

"Seven years."

"And you stayed in touch after you split up?"

"Aye. Christmas cards. The odd meeting in the pub, that kind of thing. Not so much recently. Like you said, it was over twenty years ago."

"In all that time, was there anyone who Victor…fell out with?"

"You mean enough to want to kill him?" Day's tone was almost contemptuous. "No."

"And you," Claire went on, choosing her words carefully, "parted on good terms."

"Aye," said Day slowly.

"As good as terms can be, I suppose, when you're breaking up with someone?"

Day eyed her. "You'll be wanting to know why we split up?" Claire said nothing and waited. "He didnae like dogs."

Claire glanced again at all the pictures around the room, and at the hair on her trousers that it was going to take ages to brush off. "I can see how that might be a dealbreaker." Another person might have been put off, intimidated even, by Day's unwavering stoniness, but Claire was unmoved and regarded him now, trying for an accurate estimate of his age. She suspected that genetics and environment both would have given Day a weathered look probably from his early twenties, but now he had to be at least in his mid to late fifties. Which meant, he would have been… "Do you mind my asking, Mr. Day, how old were you when you met Victor?"

For the first time, she saw something other than suspicious hostility in the man's eyes. Not unreasonably, it was surprise at such an apparently irrelevant question. She waited, hoping he wouldn't be awkward about answering. The looked-for answer was pretty much the main reason she had come here in the first place.

"Twenty-five," Day said. "Or thereabouts. Why?"

Twenty-five. And Victor would have been, what, forty-one?

"Just filling in the picture, Mr. Day."

The Scot looked as if he was about to say something, but at that point Greg re-entered, elbowing the door open, and bearing a large tray laden with tea things. "Light refreshments, anyone?"

Oh God. Even the cups have pictures of dogs on them. "Actually," she said, rising from her chair, "I think I have to go."

"All right, Sergeant," Moody said wearily, "we're going to go for a third take. Don't worry if anything goes wrong. Let us deal with it. We can sort it out in editing. Okay?"

"Okay." Standing on the steps of Foregate Street station, Dave was not comforted by thoughts of what Moody and her colleagues could do to his interview in their editing suite. He had seen what they had done to Claire on their last case. He was determined not to let himself be caught out in any unguarded moments. Unfortunately, this was resulting in a facial expression of perpetual astonishment, and a camera performance that could only be described, even kindly, as wooden.

"Relax," Moody said with a grim tone and face that did nothing to encourage same. She turned to her cameraman, muttered something that Dave couldn't quite make out, and began her introduction to camera again. "I'm standing on the steps of Worcester Foregate police station talking to Sergeant Dave Lyons who is leading the investigation into the recent murder of seventy-two-year-old member of the gay community, Victor Whyte."

"I'm not," said Dave. "Sorry. I mean, I'm not leading the investigation. That's Detective Inspector Summerskill. And I'm Dave Lyon. No *s*. As I said."

"Take four, Reg," Moody said.

"We took less time covering the Olympics," Reg muttered.

"And do you have to describe him that way?"

Moody stopped in the act of rearranging her fringe which the cold wind was not treating well. "Who? What way?"

"Victor. Member of the gay community."

Dave guessed Moody was trying to frown at him but suspected Botox made that tricky. "He was gay, wasn't he? He was killed in a gay venue, wasn't he?"

"Yes. Well, I mean, I'm not sure I'd describe the Switchboard office as a venue. That makes it sound like a nightclub. And yes, he was gay. But he was a lot of other things too."

"Such as?"

Dave racked his memory for what they knew about Victor. It was so much easier when your victim was straight. Then they became *loving father of two* or *beloved grandfather of five*. Something more human than *member of the gay community*. "He was…a chemist."

"At seventy-two?"

"No. He'd retired."

"Is there anyone who is likely to be embarrassed by us saying he was gay? Would he have objected?"

"No, and I doubt it."

"Are *you* bothered by his being gay?"

"Of course not. It just seems…reductive I suppose."

Moody smiled. Cosmetic chemistry and her true feelings robbed it of any warmth. "Sergeant, we're filming a one-minute news report here, not a ninety-minute biopic. Reg, take four. I'm standing on the steps of Worcester Foregate Street police station, and here…"

"Hi, Dave. Ooops, sorry." Coming up the steps, Chris McNeil pulled a guilty face and held his hands up in apology. *Didn't see,* he mouthed, pointing to the camera.

Dave dropped the hand he had automatically raised in greeting. "Take five?" he suggested to Moody.

"Wow. I mean, I don't want to be rude or anything, but is this normal? I haven't seen Victor in nearly two years. And we'd stopped being an item at least three years before that. I mean, I was really shocked and very sad to hear about what had happened, but I never thought I'd have the police coming to talk to me about it."

Lesley Walker was younger than Philip Day, mid to late forties Claire guessed, and much slighter than Day, with a good head of salt-and-pepper hair and a beard to match. His home was a real contrast too. While Day, Greg, and their substitute children had been crammed into a tiny terrace, Walker had welcomed her into a quite large, detached residence. She looked around the room she had been shown into. No dogs, thank God, but something about the wallpaper, furnishings, and glass ornaments suggested a much older householder than the one she was seeing. "Do you live on your own, Mr. Walker?" she asked. Perhaps there was an older partner in the background somewhere. Someone as old as Victor perhaps?

"I do now, sadly. Mum passed away four years ago. I was back living here by then, and I think Dad was glad to have someone else around the place. That generation, y'know? Not used to looking after themselves, and he couldn't boil an egg or sew on a button to save his life. He died over a year ago, leaving me here on my own." He held his arms out. "A lonely goldfish in a large bowl. Tea?"

"No, thank you." Claire launched into her routine about building up a picture of Victor Whyte, and Walker listened politely. Even to her, it was beginning to sound stale. Walker happily outlined his relationship with Victor, and as he talked about what a good, kind, and generous man Victor had been, Claire couldn't help feeling glad that Dave wasn't with her to see her pursuing this particular line of investigation. It was beginning to make her feel a bit grubby herself. She almost had to force herself to ask the question that was the main reason for her being there. "So, how old was Victor when he started going out with you?"

And there it was again, that look of surprise at this apparently irrelevant question. "I suppose he'd passed the big five-oh by then."

Claire had calculated that Victor would have been fifty-four. "And yourself? If you don't mind me asking."

"I was coming up to the big three-oh."

"Twenty-nine. Quite an age difference." *Even bigger than that between Victor and Philip Day, although Walker had been older than Day when he'd first met Victor. Still not as big as the difference between Victor and Tom Adams.*

Lesley Walker laughed uncertainly. "I suppose it was. It never really seemed to matter to us. Victor was—I hate to use the cliché, but it was true—young at heart. Very *vital.*" Too late, Claire realised she may have been letting some of what she was thinking show on her face, as Walker went on, "I may have a Peter Pan youthfulness, Inspector, but I can assure you I was well over the age of consent when I first met Victor. Well over. If you're wondering whether he took advantage of me, I can categorically tell you he did not."

"That's not what I meant to suggest at all."

"If anything," Lesley pressed on, "it was the other way round. I mean, I came on to him." He smiled fondly at the memory. "Cheltenham racecourse."

"You were betting on horses?"

"Good God, no. The clubhouse. They used to have a gay night there once every month. Victor was working for Switchboard, and they always had an outreach stand there, y'know, for any guys who were just coming out and were a bit confused."

"Vulnerable?" Claire hadn't been able to help herself.

"Yeah. Good word."

"And were you vulnerable?"

"Me? Good Lord, no. I'd been on the scene since…well, for years, trust me. I was there with a guy I was kind of seeing at the time, but Victor, well, he blew that guy out of the water. Not in an aggressive, competitive way. I mean, he was just so much more…sexy." Walker smiled dreamily. "Some men get better and better as they get older, don't you think?"

Claire thought of Ian. "Some do."

"Not that I was a slapper," Walker went on. "I mean Victor and I were together for nearly twelve years."

"How did it end?"

"There was another guy," he said happily. "A younger guy."

"For Victor?"

"No, for me." Walker turned wistful. "My bad, as they say. Derek was a laugh, but I was a fool to drop Victor for him. Some people can't be happy with what they've got, can they?"

Claire didn't answer.

"Well, that's got to be the hottest video I've watched in bed—ever."

Dave let himself flop back on his pillow, mortified. "You're biased."

Joe reached for the remote. "Let's watch that bit again where they zoom in really close on your face. I reckon they knew you'd have the women and gay guys melting with that shot."

Dave snatched the remote from him and dropped it down his side of the bed. "You mean that moment when you can see the look of fear in my eyes that we're going to have to go for a tenth take? No thank you. I'll be reliving that often enough in my dreams tonight."

Joe grinned and cuddled up. "Seriously. You did well. You came across as calm, confident, and in control."

"Which is the whole problem. I'm not. In control that is. Summerskill is. And you should know by now that everything I was saying was police-speak for 'We haven't got a clue who killed Victor Whyte, not even a hint as to why anyone would want to.' Anyone who knows anything about how police work is going to think that was why I was put out there, to take the flak."

"Maybe. Or maybe the gay community will see it as a positive sign that a gay man is leading an investigation into the murder of a gay man."

"Yeah, right. A gay *sergeant*. Like a gay victim doesn't rate a full inspector."

"You are determined to be a glass-half-empty sort of person, aren't you?"

"In any case," Dave went on, wanting to move past an increasingly common accusation, "how is the community going to know that I'm gay? I wasn't wearing a pink triangle and my rainbow T-shirt was in the wash."

"They know."

"What?" Dave propped himself up on his elbow to look at Joe. "You saying I came across as gay on the television?"

"Would that bother you? Okay, you didn't mention Cher, Kylie, or Madonna, and you kept your wrist resolutely firm, so you came across as really, really hetero. But it's all over social media that you're gay."

"What!" Dave shot up in the bed.

"I mean local social media," Joe backtracked. "It's cool. It's all positive. Well, the feeds I follow are."

"How the hell…?" Dave sank back on his pillow and stared up at the ceiling while he worked through this latest development. He knew how the hell. Because he knew someone who had recently been on a course about how to handle social media.

Chapter Six

"Saw you on the telly last night," Claire said to Dave as she walked into their office the next morning. "It was good."

"Nine takes," Dave said. "Moody said it was a record."

"Amazing how much weight the camera puts on you, though, isn't it?"

"Years too. If you remember?"

They both relaxed slightly. An awkward moment had been successfully navigated.

The Switchboard folder of call sheets they'd sent to forensics was waiting for them on Claire's desk with a report attached. "Okay. As you'd expect. Evidence that an attempt was made to wipe it clean, though this was clumsily done so there are multiple prints. They've run it through the database, and nothing's come up. Great." She slapped the report back on the desk. "You know the drill. Everyone on Switchboard needs to be printed and ticked off."

"Halo Centre cleaners too?"

"Why not? It's only time and money. Cancel the visits to the other Switchboard members. Call them in to get their dabs done and we'll talk to them here. Get Grover, Joynson, and Adams in too. Jen"—she picked up the report again and addressed WPC Trent who had entered the office—"get this photocopied for Sergeant Lyon, please."

"That'll teach me to play messenger. Visitor for Sergeant Lyon," Trent said.

"Fans?" Claire suggested. "Tony tells me you're quite the local gay poster boy on social media."

Dave winced and glanced across at Rudge and Cortez. "I don't…"

"Emily Tufton," said Trent, dropping the contact sheet his visitor had been obliged to fill out onto Dave's desk. "She says she's a friend of Tom Adams and wants to talk to somebody about the Switchboard case. I've put her in Interview Three."

"Shit. He's not here, too, is he?" asked Claire.

"No, just the girl."

"Okay. Dave, you deal with that, and I'll get on with setting up the prints work. Jen, for you." And she tossed the Switchboard folder and attached report to Trent, who caught it with ill grace and left the office. Dave followed. Claire sat down at her desk and began to sort out the telephone numbers and addresses they were going to need for the fingerprinting session.

Across the room, at his own desk, DI Rudge put down the papers he was working on. "Terry," he said to his sergeant, "you picked up that Purcell file I asked you for?"

"Purcell? But you told me to take that down to—"

"Yeah, well now I want you to bring it back up."

"But I thought you said—"

"Back. Up." Rudge waited.

Light dawned. "Oh right. Yeah. Purcell. I'll go and get it." Cortez stood up. "How long do you think it's going to take me?"

"No more than ten minutes I should think."

"Time for a quick canteen stop, then," Cortez said, heading for the door. "To be on the safe side." He left.

"That was subtle," said Claire, without looking up.

"It's my middle name."

"Really? I thought that was Fogey, as in—"

"I get what it's in. Not one of your sharper darts, girlie."

"I'm in one of my blunter moods." With a sigh, Claire put down her paper-work. "Okay. What is it? What have I done wrong this time?"

Rudge's naturally hard face softened. He might almost have been smiling in a sad kind of way. "You're not doing anything wrong. Not at the moment, anyhow. It's what you've got to do."

"And what have I got to do?"

"You've got to get rid of Sergeant Lyon."

★

Emily Tufton wasn't what Dave had expected, and for that he was grateful. He assumed she was the same age as Tom, and a student at the university like him, but her neat skirt, blouse, and jacket were a world away from his student activist denim with badge accessories. She looked, he thought, like a waitress from a mid-range restaurant. When he entered the room, she immediately stood up.

"Please," he said, gesturing for her to sit back down and offering his hand for her to shake. "I'm Sergeant Dave Lyon."

"Emily Tufton. Sorry, I'm a bit nervous. I've never been in a police station before, and this room…" She looked around at the pale-green, bare walls, the worn wooden table with fixed chairs on either side. "It's making me feel a bit like I've been arrested," she said with a short, breathless laugh.

"Trust me, this is much cosier than the ones we use for people who *have* been arrested." He felt a little sorry for her. "Would you like a coffee? Tea?"

"No thank you."

"Don't blame you. It's all horrible. Well, what can I do for you today? Am I right that you're a friend of Tom Adams?" He sat back and waited. He had a feeling he might have to coax this one, but again he was pleasantly surprised.

Emily sat up, took a deep breath, looked him straight in the eye, and said, "Tom thinks he knows who killed Victor Whyte."

"And why would I want to do that?" Claire asked.

"You're not daft, m'girl. You know why."

"Well, I must be dafter than I look, because I cannot think of a single reason why I would want to say goodbye to Dave. So, stop beating around the bush and tell me."

Rudge leaned back in his chair. "All right. Firstly, he's ambitious."

"So am I. So were you, once. It's not a crime."

"No, but when you put your career over your cases it's bad for the team, for working efficiency. When a junior officer sets out to get one over his immediate superior in order to get a foot up the ladder, it undermines us all."

"You're talking about that television call, aren't you?"

"Yes, I am talking about that television call."

"Jim, I don't give a damn about that. You know I hate the bloody things. I was grateful Dave did it."

"And you're grateful for the way it makes him look as if he's in charge?"

"He's not in charge. You know it. I know it. Anybody who matters knows it."

"That's not the story coming across on social media."

"*You* are quoting social media? The man who'd still rather use an abacus than a computer if he had the choice? Is this your grandkids telling you what all their friends are saying on their smartphones?"

"Who put him on that call?"

"Madden, of course."

"Of course. And you think Madden woke up that morning and thought, 'Who can I do a favour for today? I know. Sergeant Lyon. Let's put him on television and make him a star. That'll please him.' Someone put the idea in his head, Claire. By which I mean, someone went up to Madden and asked if he could do it."

"Dave wouldn't do that."

"You reckon?"

"Yes, I do. Now, if that's all…"

"You think you know him?"

"I think I'm getting to know him, yes. I think I know him well enough by now to know that he wouldn't—"

"What do you think about his new boyfriend, then?"

Claire felt a sudden and familiar ache in her temple that signalled one bitch of a headache was on its way—literally and metaphorically. "Joe? What about him?"

Dave was frankly sceptical of Emily's claim. If she had turned out to be the kind of friend he would have expected of Tom, someone who wore her heart and her political allegiances on her sleeve and lapels, then he would probably have remained so. But this young woman was so earnest he put his scepticism to one side and determined to hear her out. "And how does Tom know this?"

Emily gave him a watery smile. "I don't really know."

Dave felt all his scepticism creeping back.

"He's been really upset these last couple of days," Emily said in a rushed response to Dave's expression.

"Because of the death of Victor Whyte?"

"Yes. They were very close."

"And has he told you who he thinks the killer was?"

Emily shook her head. "I don't think he meant to tell me anything at all but, well, I made him. I knew that something was getting to him. Honestly, I was starting to get worried. He hasn't seemed to know what to do with himself. And then when he told me that he'd seen the killer, I…"

"Wait. Hold on there a minute." Dave felt the interview suddenly shift into something much more serious. "He saw him? When? When Victor was being murdered?"

"No. Today."

"Where?"

"Outside the Halo Centre."

Dave cast his mind to the Switchboard rotas. "What was he doing there? Switchboard's closed for the foreseeable, and he's not due to be on duty again for weeks."

"I think he wanted to go somewhere where he could remember Victor." Emily sighed. "Tom may come across as a bit hardnosed, but he's got a really soft side to him. No, really. He didn't know where else he could go. So, he went there today, and then when I called on him in his flat a couple of hours ago, he was curled up in a ball on his bed. He said he's seen this man outside the Halo Centre and now he was afraid he'd done something wrong, and he might have seen the murderer."

"I'm sorry, Emily, but I have to ask, why did he send you to tell us this? Why not come himself?"

"I think," Emily said, obviously choosing her words with care, "that he finds it difficult to engage with the police."

"That's very diplomatic of you."

"Look, I know Tom isn't always the easiest person to deal with. But he is a good person at heart. In his defence, he's had a hard time of it these past couple of years. His parents were very down with the whole gay thing. He lost a few friends when he came out. He even thinks some of his teachers might have been homophobic. No, really," she said, seeing Dave's reaction. "I was at school with him, and I think he might have been right. Anyway, it's all made him very mistrustful of authority figures."

And we probably didn't help rebuild that trust. Summerskill definitely didn't.

"Whether he's right or wrong now, or if he's just being Tom, the simple fact is, he's in a bad way. Even before this business outside the Centre, he's not been in to uni for the last two days, and he's hardly talking to his flatmates. Maybe I should have gone to someone at uni, the student liaison officer or something, but I thought…"

"You've done the right thing, Emily. You're a good friend." She flashed him a grateful smile. A disturbing thought struck Dave. She'd come to the station and asked for him, not for Claire. Why? *Please let it not be because of that bloody television interview.*

"I can see why Tom likes you."

"I'm sorry?" Caught up in his own gloomy thoughts, Dave thought he might have misheard.

"Well, has a grudging respect at least." Emily lowered her voice to a conspiratorial whisper. "Though I'm afraid he's not too keen on your partner. Between you and me, I think he has a problem with strong women."

Who doesn't? And there's the reason Emily asked for me. "Well, he obviously doesn't have a problem with you, Emily, so I'm afraid I may have to disagree with you there." She fairly glowed with pleasure at the compliment. "C'mon. I think we need to have another word with Tom, to find out what's got him so spooked."

"Could you come on your own?" Emily said quickly.

Dave considered. The simple answer was no. It was quite inappropriate for him to see this disturbed young man on his own, especially after Emily had spoken of his grudging respect. But she'd also made clear what Tom's feelings for Claire were, and for that matter, Dave knew what Summerskill's were for him. In his head, Dave ran through the names of station officers who he knew should be available there and then chose from them the ones least likely to rattle Tom's cage. Two came to mind. As a woman, Jenny Trent would probably have been ideal. A shame Dave couldn't stand her. That left only one other person. He hesitated, but really there was no other choice.

"Come on," he said, standing and opening the door. "I have an officer guaranteed not to upset Tom. His name is Constable Jones, but I'm sure he won't mind you calling him Joe."

★

"Look, Jim, if this is going where I think it's going, then maybe we should stop right here."

"Claire, I've never kowtowed to the right-on brigade and I'm not going to now. I didn't think you did either."

"It's politically correct, not right-on, you old fossil, but that's not the point."

"Then shut your yap and maybe I'll get to the point." Jim spoke calmly, as if his words contained nothing that might be considered offensive at all. For years, Claire had worked with him as his sergeant. He had been her friend and her mentor, though he would have laughed out loud if she'd ever have described him openly as either. He'd have killed her if she'd ever called him a father figure. But there it was, and for a moment Claire felt like the sergeant she had been when she'd first been posted to work for him. She shut up and she listened, even though she knew she was not going to like what she was going to hear.

"I'm not going to say I don't like gay people. I don't like what gay people *do*, and I've been doing this job long enough to remember when we used to bang them up for doing it sooner than recruit them. But times change. What they do is their business now, and I was ready to overlook it with Lyon—"

"Big of you."

Rudge raised a warning finger. "—because he looked like he had the makings of a good sergeant. And I even thought he'd be good for you."

"What's that supposed to mean?"

"But he's overstepped the mark."

"How? I've already said, I don't give a damn about—"

"I'm not talking about the bloody television programme now. I'm talking about Constable Joe Jones. Your sergeant is carrying on with another officer. A junior officer."

Claire laughed out loud though her face and neck were flushed with anger. "Carrying on! My God, is this the fifties? Do you want to take him down into the cells and leave him there overnight with the roughest bigots you can drag in off the streets? That's what they used to do to gays, wasn't it? Was that what you used to do?"

"I'd say it if it was a woman he was…he was having a relationship with."

"Like hell you would. Jen and Terry have been flirting since day one and you've turned a blind eye to it. Even though Terry's supposed to have a long-term girlfriend."

"That's just larking around."

"You reckon? I don't think Debs would say that if she ever found out."

Rudge rose from his chair, and even now Claire had to fight the urge to shrink back into her own. He was a short man, maybe only an inch taller than her, but his squat frame had a presence when he was angry, and he was angry now. He jabbed the air with his finger as he spoke. "It's different, Claire, and you know it is. And I'm thinking of young Joe Jones as much as anything."

"What? Are you saying Dave's corrupted him? Turned him to the dark side? It's not like vampirism, Jim. Joe is an adult."

"He's younger than Lyon."

"Not that much younger."

"And a junior officer. I've seen it before. I think Lyon is a user."

"What the hell is that supposed to mean?"

"He uses people."

"And this is based on what? The first relationship we have seen that is still only weeks old?"

"And what about the boyfriend before Jones? From what I hear, Lyon used him to get somewhere to live when he moved here from Redditch."

Amazed, as much that Jim knew anything about Dave's personal circumstances as that he could put such a spin on them, Claire didn't know what to say. "How did you…?" she began. *Jenny.* She tried again. "It wasn't like that."

"And what about the other one? The photo on the desk guy?"

Now, she didn't know whether to laugh or cry. *That damn photo. Stupid idea, Dave!* "That was a picture off the internet. Dave put it on his desk to make it clear right from the start that he was gay. He was being honest."

"I know it was a fake picture. D'you think I'm stupid, girl? But honest? Hardly."

Claire raised her hands as if in surrender. "All right. I hear what you're saying, Jim, and you know what? It's all a pile of crap. It's a pile of festering, homophobic crap, and if you're worried about the morale of this station, then so am I, and for the sake of that morale, I am calling Dave back in here right now and we are getting this out in the open." Claire stabbed at the intercom on her desk. "Jenny. Has Sergeant Lyon finished in Interview Room Three yet?"

"He finished three minutes ago. Last I saw, he was heading out with the young lady he'd been speaking with."

"Damn. Did he say where he was going?"

"No." There was a pause. "He took PC Jones with him. Should I give them a call? Tell them you want to see them?"

Across the office, Rudge sat back down, leaned back, and looked at her without saying a word.

★

Although when he opened the door to them this time, Tom was not, mercifully, in his boxers, the boy looked every bit as dishevelled as the last time Dave had seen him. His face, though, was more drawn, and there were dark patches under his eyes. Dave braced himself for the usual political attack, but it didn't come. "Hello, Em," Tom said dully.

"Hi, Tom."

Tom looked at Dave, his handsome, uniformed companion, and then back at Emily. "What's going on?"

With Emily's help, Tom was persuaded to allow them in, and they were shown into the living room Summerskill and Lyon had interviewed him in previously. Dave hoped that the pizza boxes scattered around were different from the ones that had been there the last time. Muttering apologies, Emily cleared spaces for them all to sit, Joe giving her a hand with the boxes. When they were all seated—if not comfortably, at least not on cardboard—she took her friend's hand in hers and began. "Tom, you're scared, and you need help. I've gone and got it. I went to Foregate Street and spoke to Sergeant Lyon. You were right. He's cool"—she shot Dave a grateful look—"and he's said he wants to help you."

"Why don't you tell us what's been bothering you, Tom?" Dave said.

"Bothering!"

Prickly as ever. "Disturbing, then. Irritating. Annoying." He paused. "Frightening. Emily said you think you might know something about Victor's killer." Tom snorted. "She said you knew who he was."

"Of course, I don't know who he was," Tom snapped, his head down, his eyes fixed on the floor.

"But, Tom," Emily said softly, "you said…"

"I was worked up, okay? I'm…I'm upset about Victor. He was killed, right? Horribly. It's got to me. I don't know what to think any more. I wish you'd all leave me alone so I can think."

Dave looked at Tom, who sat head bowed, hands clasped. There was no doubt he was in pain. "I know you don't want to hear this right now," he said, wary of setting the lad off again, "but I do understand what you're feeling. It's hard, and you're bound to feel this way." He glanced at Emily. "But you've got friends who are worried about you, and they're going to stay worried until you tell us what is upsetting you so much." It was true. It was also emotional blackmail, and Dave felt guilty using it, in large part because Joe was seeing him do it.

Tom sat, head still down, and Dave wasn't sure if he was thinking about what he'd said or whether he'd switched off completely and was ignoring them all, but then he raised his head, a determined expression on his face. "I don't know who killed Victor," he said, "not for sure. But there is someone who might be involved."

"Who?"

"The guy from the befriending."

Dave thought back to their conversations with Clive Grover, and their review of the Switchboard records. "Adrian? The guy from Manchester?"

"No." At a reproachful look from Emily, Tom moderated his instinctively hostile reaction. "The guy from the last befriending Victor and I did together."

"The no-show?"

"Yes."

"So, he did show?"

"Duh. Sorry," Tom said after another look from Emily.

"Why was it recorded as a no-show, then?"

"Because that was what Victor wanted."

"All right. Tell me then what really happened at the befriending. Who did you and Victor meet?"

"I didn't meet him," Tom said quickly.

Emily reached across and took his hand. "Tell them what happened, Tom."

"All right." Tom took a second to prepare himself before speaking. "Victor called me up, out of the blue, asking me if I'd go with him to this befriending. He said he couldn't get anyone else as they were all too busy or couldn't be bothered, whatever. I said yes. I didn't have anything else to do and...I was happy to do something for him. So, we turned up at the café..."

"Which café?" Dave asked automatically.

"Bumbles in town. Usual deal, public place so no one could accuse us of any hanky-panky. Bit less crowded than the usual supermarket caff we use, but it was cool."

"Thanks. Go on."

"Well, at first, it really was a no-show. We must have sat there for a good twenty, thirty minutes waiting. People are coming and going, and that's when we begin to realise that the guy at the table across from us isn't. He's been there the whole time, on his own, and now we can see that he's looking at us every time he thinks we aren't looking at him. That's when Victor knows it's the man we've come to meet."

"Victor hadn't seen him before?"

"It was a befriending. You've never met the guy you're meeting before. That's the point."

Don't snap. Keep calm. Let him talk. "Understood. What happened next?"

"That was when Victor asked me to leave."

"What? Why? I thought the whole point was that there were always two of you there. Wasn't that why Victor had asked you to go along in the first place?"

"Yes. I know that. Victor said he knew the guy wouldn't come over while I was there."

"So, you left?"

"No, not straight away. I told him that I should stay, that it could be trouble if I didn't, but he asked me again to leave, and said that he'd tell me later what had happened. And he asked me not to tell anyone."

"And how was he? I mean, what was his mood? Did he seem sad, worried, eager? Scared?"

"No, none of those things. He was the usual Victor. Quiet and sweet but firm. He was smiling. He…" Tom looked down at Emily's hand still holding his. "He patted my hand. So, in the end, I said yes. I left."

"But you didn't go away, did you?"

Tom sniffed heavily and shook his head. "I did at first. I walked up and down the high street for a bit, trying to tell myself I'd done the right thing. Must have done that for about twenty minutes or so. And then I went back to the café. I thought by then the guy might have gone but that Victor might still be there, and we could talk a bit. Befriendings can be quite short. But he was still there, sitting at Victor's table now, and they were talking."

"How did they seem?" Dave asked. "Were they arguing? Did the other man look angry? Sad?"

"I couldn't see his face; he had his back to me, and I was trying hard not to be seen looking through the window. But I saw Victor's face. He was smiling. He looked really happy." Tom sniffed again, straightened up, and looked at both police officers. "And then I went home."

"Victor said he'd tell you what happened. Did he?"

"No. No, we never got to talk about it."

Dave ran through the chronology of events in his head as best he could without actually taking out his notepad. "But you could have done, couldn't you? If you'd been on duty with him that last time?"

"How many times? I've told you. I couldn't do that duty. I had…other things going on."

"Your flatmate's birthday party, yes, you said." Dave caught Emily's quick look at Tom, the slight frown. He had a feeling that the birthday alibi wouldn't hold up to an investigation. The pizza boxes and beer bottles had looked like corroboration at the time. Now they were looking like part of this flat's typical décor.

"What did you think was going on?"

"How should I know? I—"

"Tom." Dave leaned forward, his tone not unfriendly but firm. "What do you think was going on?"

"I think…I think Victor was in love. I think he'd finally found someone new."

"But this must have been, what, ten or more days before he died. And no one we've spoken to so far has said anything about Victor having a new partner. Why was he keeping it so quiet?"

"Because he'd done it wrong, hadn't he? You know what they're like on Switchboard. You've met Clive. They'd have thrown him off for being unprofessional or something."

"Is that why you didn't say anything about this when we spoke the last time?"

"Yes. No. I don't know. You turned up on the doorstep telling me that the guy I…that my friend had been killed. I didn't even think of that befriending at first. Why should I? Like you said, it had been days before. It had looked like a good thing for Victor. And I'd promised him I wouldn't say anything about it. But then I saw the guy again, and it got me to thinking."

"Emily said you saw him outside the Halo Centre."

"Yeah."

"What was he doing?"

"I dunno. Walking. He'd gone before it clicked who he was."

"Was he trying to go in?"

"I've told you I don't know. I don't think so. I was too caught up in my own thoughts to pay much attention to what anyone else was doing."

"Can you describe him?"

"Tallish, I suppose. Darkish hair, bit grey round the sides. Blue donkey jacket type coat, that's about it."

"Clean-shaven?"

"Yeah."

"How old?"

"You'll be asking for his fucking inside leg measurement in a minute."

"Roughly, Tom."

"Old. Older than you even."

"As old as Victor?"

"No. Maybe fifties. Could have been late forties. I dunno. I'm rubbish at guessing ages."

"Okay. Thanks for that. I'm going to ask you to come down to the station to have a go with one of our artists, see if we can get some kind of picture together."

"I've told you, I can hardly remember what he looked like."

"But you recognised him, even if it wasn't at first."

"Yes. I suppose I did, but—"

"Tom," said Emily.

Tom subsided. "Okay. I'll come."

"Do you think that was the killer?" Joe asked as they drove back to Foregate Street.

"I don't know. It doesn't seem to fit together. Victor had this meeting with the guy days previously, and it sounded like it made him happy. What could have happened in ten days to turn the man into someone so full of hatred that he'd strangle Victor? The main reason I'm doubtful, though, is why would he come back to the Halo Centre in the day? He could hardly have been expecting Victor to be there if the last time he'd seen him it had been with a telephone cord around his neck."

"Don't killers always return to the scene of the crime?"

"Only in bad telly programmes. If it was that easy, we could skip over all that tricky investigating business and just sit by the bodies with the cuffs waiting for murderers to come back. Don't forget, we only have Tom's side of that befriending. There might have been more, or a lot less to it than he was suggesting. It was partial."

"You mean because he was in love with Victor?"

"Or infatuated."

"And hurt that he was being sidelined?"

"Or plain jealous."

They pulled into the station carpark.

"Do you really think Tom was in love with Victor?" Dave asked, as they got out.

"Yeah. I think he was. You could see it in his eyes."

"You are such a romantic."

"One of us has to be."

"Hm. Do you think Victor loved him back?"

Joe shrugged. "We'll probably never know, will we?"

Dave felt the chill in the office the instant he walked back in.

"Where have you been?" Claire said.

"I think I might have a lead." He outlined his visit to Tom. "I've asked him to come here in the next hour, and I've called Paul in to try and get together a picture of the man."

"You took Constable Jones."

"Yes," said Dave, noting that this was a statement not a question, and wary of this unexpected turn of direction.

"Was that wise?"

"Was it unwise?"

"C'mon, Dave, don't play daft."

"I'm not being daft. Why shouldn't I have taken Constable Jones?"

"Tell me first why you did."

"It was a quick decision. Adams sounded desperate. I wanted to get to him quickly. Constable Jones was available."

"Was he the only officer available?"

Dave hesitated. "No. WPC Trent was also available. I chose Constable Jones."

"Passing over the more experienced Trent because…?"

Dave steeled himself, but he was damned if he was going to dodge the issue. "Because I think she has an issue with gay people."

Now it was Claire's turn to hesitate. "That's a serious allegation."

"I'm not making an allegation. I'm giving you a reason." Dave waited. He knew Jenny and Claire had been close friends. He knew their friendship had become strained for some reason. Now he wondered if any friendship he might have with his boss had also been laid to rest.

"Why didn't you come to me?"

"Tom had expressed…a disinclination to talk with you."

Claire nodded. Dave knew that would have bothered her less than any accusations against her friend. "All right," she said finally. "I'll want detailed write-ups from both of you on my desk by the end of the day."

"Of course." It was only standard procedure. Though they both knew that, under any other circumstances, Claire would have been happy with a short note from either of them, and that only when they could manage it.

"Moving on." Claire threw him a photocopy of the Switchboard call sheets they had hoped would yield something. "These give us almost nothing. Victor dealt with about half a dozen different callers over the past few months, ranging from obvious joke calls to requests for information about cruising grounds, lesbian bars, and, on one occasion, a request for a gay bed and breakfast." She looked up at her sergeant. "What the hell is a gay bed and breakfast?"

"You get the bed, but you can tell they really don't want you to stay for the breakfast the next morning."

"Right." Claire returned to her notes. "The only caller of any interest is the guy Roz Joynson told us about.

"Dale?"

"Correct." Claire passed him the folder back. "Frequent caller. Only ever wants to talk to Victor. And yet, when Victor comes to record the calls…" She tapped a section she had highlighted.

"In low spirits. Will call again later."

"And this one." She indicated a second.

"Not in a good way but will call back. And then he doesn't."

"Or he does, but Victor doesn't record the calls."

"You'll note of course who is on duty with him when the majority of these calls are taken?"

"Tom."

"Correct again."

"Because Tom had been fiddling the rotas to make sure of it. You think these calls lasted longer and more was said? That Tom went along with Victor fudging the records the way he went along with the unorthodox befriending?"

"I think you have some more questions you can ask that young man when you see him."

Dave thought about what he'd just been told. "D'you think this Dale could be the same guy who Tom saw at the befriending and then outside the Halo Centre?"

"Could be, and if it is then it looks like he doesn't know Victor is dead, which means…"

"He's a false trail."

"Exactly. And it occurs to me"—Claire took the photocopies back from Dave to check her highlighting—"we could soon find out. Dale doesn't always call on the same days, but Thursday after nine is far and away the most common time." She looked up. "Doing anything tonight?"

"I—"

"Good. I'll meet you at the Halo at seven thirty. Don't be late."

"*Me* be late?"

"Now, you say you've got Adams in with Paul? Let's go and have another word with him."

"Wouldn't it be better if—?"

"Relax. I'll try not to be Scary Summerskill. Besides, he's got to learn how to deal with forthright women at some point in his life."

"Haven't we all?" Dave murmured as he followed his boss out of the office.

★

"I can't make tonight."

Even over the phone, Joe's disappointment was clear. "Why's that, then?"

"Summerskill wants me to go with her to a Switchboard session at the Halo Centre. There's a chance that guy Adams told us about might ring tonight."

"Couldn't she do that one on her own?"

Dave snorted. "First privilege of rank. You get to spread the misery around."

"So, you reckon it's going to be misery?"

"Figure of speech. It should be okay." He hoped.

"Well, you be careful."

"Sorry? I'll be sitting by a phone not taking part in a shootout." He was re-lieved to hear Joe's laughter. Another advantage of a copper as a boyfriend. Richard would have been royally pissed off by something like this.

"I'm not worried about bad guys. I'm thinking about the good guys. Specifi-cally, Summerskill."

"You have lost me completely."

Joe chuckled. "It was one of the things they warned us about in training. All very coded, but there, y'know?"

"What, like *don't fall for the sexy new recruit at your station?*"

"Nah. That came under perks of the job. I was referring to the long-hours-working-closely-together-breeds-intimacy scenario."

"Ah. I must have missed that lecture."

"You? Miss a lecture? I doubt it. Seriously, though, the number of coppers who leave their partners for other coppers is huge, and the most commonly cited cause of said coppers getting together is being thrown together in high-pressure situations like stakeouts. So, you watch out."

"Thank you for the refresher, Constable. A couple of points for you to con-sider. Firstly, there isn't much that is high-pressure about watching someone answer phones. And secondly—" Dave lowered his voice and turned his body slightly so there was absolutely no chance of anyone overhearing what he was saying. "—I was kind of hoping you'd noticed, maybe when we were in bed together, that I'm thoroughly gay. You can rest assured I will be immune to any advances DI Summerskill might make."

"She may be tempted. She is only human."

"Don't bet on it. I'll call you later, after Switchboard."

"Later, then. Bye for now. Love you."

"Bye for now."

"Whistle stop," Claire said, kissing her youngest, Sam, and ruffling her eldest, Tony's, hair despite his best efforts to avoid her. "Any of that stew left?" She dropped down into her seat at the kitchen table and lifted the lid of the casserole dish.

Ian, meal already finished, pushed his plate to one side. "Why's that?"

"Working on the Whyte case." Claire ladled a sizeable portion of the stew onto her plate. "I'll be at the Halo Centre till ten. Should be back by half past."

"Can I get down, Mummy?" asked Sam.

"Don't you want to sit for a bit and tell your old mam what you did at school today?"

"No," said Sam with crushing honesty.

"Right. And I don't suppose you do either?" she asked Tony.

"Nothing to tell."

"In that case, you can take your brother upstairs and keep an eye on him till it's time for bed. Go." She raised her voice to drown out the complaints from both of them. "How was your day?" she asked Ian, as the two boys left the kitchen and headed upstairs.

"Same old, same old." Ian got up and started clearing the table.

"Leave that. You can do it when I've left."

"It's okay." He began to load the dishwasher. "By the way," he said, with his back to her. "This weekend."

This Saturday. The night out. The first night out they'd had together since she could remember. Claire carried on eating her stew and waited.

"I'm afraid we can't do it."

Claire stared down at her plate, pushing the food around. "Why not?"

"Sister called. She's double-booked. She's very sorry."

"We can get someone else."

"It's a bit short notice, isn't it?"

"We can try. There's…"

"No, Claire." Ian stood up from the dishwasher to face her, though she continued to sit with her back to him. "I don't think so. I'd…rather not."

Claire put her fork down, pushed the plate to one side, and turned on her chair to face her husband. "So that's that, is it? Saturday cancelled because you'd rather not?"

"Why not? You've cancelled tonight at the drop of a hat."

"That's work!"

"Well maybe I'd like to work on Saturday too. You're not the only one with a job that eats into private time, remember."

"Oh right. Got another of your 'meetings', have you? On Saturday night?"

"Why shouldn't I spend as much time with my colleagues as you spend with yours?"

"Except it isn't colleagues plural, is it, Ian? It's colleague singular. And feminine." She stood, neck flushed red with anger. Ian looked pale but said nothing. "Right. I'm off. Don't wait up. I'll be late." She left the kitchen without looking back at her husband.

Chapter Seven

"I know what you're thinking, sweetheart," Roz Joynson said to Dave.

"I'm hoping you don't." Dave looked away from the picture of the lad with the perfect bum.

Roz narrowed her eyes as if focusing her powers of perception. "You're wondering why that attractive young man would rush to define himself in such a narrow way when he still has his whole life in front of him with time enough to choose from the vast range of potential experiences open to human sexuality."

"Well…"

"Or you're thinking, what a great arse. Depressing, really, isn't it?"

"I'm sorry?"

"The urge to define, to limit. Not the arse. That is, frankly, magnificent. It's not only the men either. Women do it too. I wasted so many years trying to decide if I was a diesel dyke, scissor sister, or lipstick lesbian I very nearly ran out of time to actually *be* any of them. In the end I decided I was mainly a librarian, and everything else was gravy."

Dave regarded their evening's companion on Switchboard duty. He had indeed tried earlier to categorise Roz, though the labels he'd considered hadn't had so much to do with her sexuality as her flagrant bohemianism. Aging hippy, her own description, had been a front-runner but now, after the unsettling accuracy of her mind reading, he wondered if New Age witch might be nearer the mark. Looking at her silver bracelets, purple (and grey) streaked hair, and heavy eyeliner, librarian wouldn't have been a first choice.

The two of them stood, like art lovers in a gallery, contemplating the poster again and its model's best feature. "You could bounce pennies off that," Roz said.

"Would you want to?"

"Only if I could have dinner with Naomi Campbell afterwards."

"Sorry I'm late. Have I missed anything?" Claire stood in the Switchboard office doorway, taking in the sight of Roz and Dave admiring the safer sex poster. "I'm guessing not." She put down the carrier bags she was carrying and joined them in front of the picture. "That has got to be Photoshopped, hasn't it? I mean, I've never known a guy with as great a behind as that." She looked at Dave and then at Roz. Both seemed thoughtful as if reviewing arses they had known.

With some reluctance, they eventually all turned their minds away from the perfect glutes and back to the office and the work they had ahead of them. Roz, that night's operative on duty, had been contacted by Clive Grover and had generously agreed to be accompanied by the two officers. She had thoughtfully brought in a chair from the main hall outside the office, but that still meant one of them had to use the chair in which Victor Whyte had been killed. With obvious awkwardness, Claire took it.

The chairs, along with two desks facing each other and pushed together and two filing cabinets, pretty much filled the entire room. On the desks were two small piles of manuals, reference books, and magazines, a computer that made even the dated hardware of Foregate police station look futuristic, and a card index file which Dave had studied as one might study an artefact in a museum. The walls were covered with a number of dogeared posters, many featuring young men as built and undressed as the hottie on the rug even as they proclaimed important messages about safer sex, domestic violence, and the importance of equality for all. There were rainbows everywhere. There was also, of course, a landline telephone.

Roz filled them in on what the night's duty would involve.

"The first thing we do is check the logbook folder to see who has called since the last time we were on duty, and if anyone has made any notes or advice for operators about callers who might ring back."

"Ah yes." Claire reached into one of the shopping bags she had brought with her and pulled out the folder that she and Dave had gone through earlier.

"Thanks," said Roz. "I'll have a look in a bit. That may well be the busiest time of the evening. After that, we sit here and make idle chat and wait for…the phone to ring." Dave noted the slight hesitation, and Roz's glance down at the solitary phone on the desk. There should have been two. One had been removed, for obvious reasons. "We can put the calls onto speaker so that you'll be able to hear. After each call, we make notes in the folder and then—" She paused to add a little spurious suspense. "—we wait for the next call." She folded her arms and sat back. "A monkey could do it really. As long as it was gay."

"Right. Well, thanks for that, Roz. I suppose we need to make ourselves comfy, then, and see what the night brings." Claire reached into her second bag and pulled out several packs of biscuits and bags of crisps. "What have you brought?" she asked Dave.

"Some report sheets to fill out."

"I meant foodwise."

"Er, nothing. I had something to eat before I came."

"So did I. What's your point? Have you never been on a stakeout? You do know what happens on stakeouts, right?"

Dave thought back to what Tom had said. "I'm not sure…"

"We eat a lot of crap." She pulled out one last bag of crisps.

"Ooh, maybe I should have considered the police as a career option," Roz said, reaching for one of the packs of biscuits. "Fancy a coffee? Tea?" She rose. "There's a small kitchen on the other side of the hall. I'll sterilise the mugs so you should be okay. Unless the milk's gone off again. Back in a tick." And with a cheery wave she was gone.

Summerskill and Lyon sat in the office, looking around at the tiny room they'd be sharing for the next two and a half hours, trying not to let their eyes be drawn back to the lad on the rug. "You know, this didn't really need both of us," Dave ventured finally.

"I do."

Dave looked at his boss. There was something distracted about her, something a little fake about her good humour. Was she still angry with him? "I could have done it on my own. I'd have been happy to."

"You could have brought Joe." Claire held up her hands in apology. "Sorry. I did not mean anything by that. I'm just… I've got something on my mind. Look, I think things got a little…strained between us today. And over the last couple of days to be honest. I thought a bit of a stakeout might give us a little breathing space, a chance to get us back on the same page. And I needed to get out of the house."

"This is hardly a stakeout."

"Would you rather we were in a freezing car?"

"Fair point. Although that would only be marginally less cramped than this office. And we wouldn't have someone who looks like she could have been a groupie for the Stones in the sixties with us."

"I think I like Roz."

"Actually, I think I do too. Though I'm uneasy with anyone who wears that much kohl. I had a girlfriend once who plastered her eyes like that."

"You had a *girlfriend?*"

Roz re-entered bearing three mugs. "Here you go. This is a charity centre, so this is all free trade, caffeine free, and gender neutral so it doesn't really matter which is tea or coffee as they all taste the same." She put a mug each in front of Dave and Claire. "If you want sugar, we keep our own in the pot over there." She smiled sadly. "Victor always used to bring a little jar of honey. He literally was very sweet." She raised her mug in the direction of Victor's chair as if toasting her absent colleague.

"Did you know him well?" Claire asked.

"As well as two people with absolutely no sexual interest in each other can. We're two of the oldest members on Switchboard. *Were,* I suppose I should say now, by which I mean we were two of the longest-serving members. As I think I told you, we were part of the team that set the Board up." She sipped from her mug. "Actually, who am I kidding? We *were* the two oldest members, full stop. By a long chalk. Never sure which of us was the oldest though. I always lie and Victor didn't care." She looked down into the mug she was cradling. "No point lying any more. I'm definitely the oldest now."

"And when was Switchboard set up?" Dave asked, to divert Roz's mind from melancholy thoughts.

"Nineteen seventy and frozen to death," Roz said with an exaggerated shudder. "When dinosaurs still ruled the earth, and both of you would have been little more than glints in the eyes of your heterosexual fathers and sighs in the breath of your heterosexual mothers. Did I tell you by the way"—she waved her mug airily—"that I'm also a poet as well as a librarian?"

"Different times," said Dave, diplomatically avoiding the question.

"Sweetheart, you have no idea. Gay people were like a different species back then. You might have been okay if you lived in London or one of the other big cities, but piddling little Worcester? Or even worse, one of the tiny villages scattered around the counties! If you were a man, you grew up thinking all gay males were like the mincing queens they trotted out on teatime sitcoms. And if you were a gay woman, you thought you were some kind of unique freak as you didn't even get that. Okay," she conceded, "I exaggerate slightly for effect, but only slightly. No positive role models. A constant barrage of hatred from the media. No internet.

No one to turn to for help or advice. It wasn't easy. That's why we set up Switchboard." Roz drained her mug and set it down on a desk with a thump as if it had been an empty pint glass in a bar. "We started picking up new members straight away. Pretty soon we had a solid core of nearly thirty. Over the years people came and went and often came back, but it stayed more or less at that number. Until recently of course. We even moved up from one telephone to two." Her gaze moved to the spot next to Claire's elbow. "Back to one again now."

"What was it that happened recently?" Claire asked. "You're saying your numbers fell?"

"Progress, darling." Roz gave an expansive wave of her hand. "A lot of it, I have to say, for the better. It's still no walk in the park coming out as gay in this brave new world, but it's a damn sight easier than it used to be. People talk about it now. Everyone knows someone who's gay or knows someone who knows someone who's gay. Mainly, of course, there's the internet. All the advice you could ever want or need at the click of a mouse, and all in the privacy of your own bedroom. People don't need Aunty Roz and her friends on the end of a crackly line any more telling them that it's not the end of the world because they fancy someone with the same tackle as them. They don't even need us to tell them where the local cruising grounds and cottages are." She tapped the side of her nose and winked. "Not that we ever did that of course. Not really part of the charter, y'know?" She leaned back slightly, as if to take in the sight of Dave better. "We don't even have to warn them about pretty policemen trying to entrap them round the loos. You ever do any of that, sweetheart?"

"Not in the way you mean," Dave said.

"You can even order a shag online now, can't you?" Roz continued. "Like a pizza. On your phone even. Can you imagine?" She cackled again. "I had to trek halfway across the county for the promise of a kiss when I was young. I wouldn't have had the energy left to lift a book let alone catalogue one if I'd been able to summon up a pretty lass every time I was feeling a bit frisky. You ever done that, darlin?" she asked Dave.

"I…" Dave began, very conscious of Claire's leaning in, the better to hear his answer. Fortunately for him, the phone rang.

"Duty calls." Roz reached over the desk to pick up the phone's receiver. "We'll come back to that in a minute. Hello. You're through to Worcester and Hereford Gay and Lesbian Switchboard. My name's Roz. How can I help you?" She flipped the switch that put the caller on speakerphone, and the two police officers sat back to listen.

★

As she watched Roz in action, Claire was reminded of a poem she'd been made to read when she'd been a kid back in Pontypridd Comprehensive. The poem had been about a woman vowing to wear purple when she grew old. The teacher had explained it meant she was planning to do and say whatever she damn well wanted to when she was old. Young Claire had thought that was a great life plan. She hadn't understood at the time why the woman had to wait until then. Looking at Roz now with her artistically streaked hair, billowy black blouse, and dangling silver jewellery, she noted now how her manner had changed when she spoke: still warm and cheerful but with a serious, more professional tone. This, Claire thought, was a woman she could respect.

"Hello?" Roz said again. "Worcester and Hereford Gay and Lesbian Switchboard here. I'm not sure if you can hear me, but at the moment, I'm afraid I can't hear you." There was no response. "I do know that it can be a bit difficult at first to talk to someone you don't know, but I can promise you that we're here to listen and to help you in any way we can." From the speaker, behind the normal background hiss of a landline, there was a muffled sound that might have been someone breathing or might have been the receiver brushing against skin. "I'm afraid I'm the only operative here at the moment, but if you're a man and you'd rather talk to another man, we do have a male operative on duty next week." Roz paused again, giving the caller a chance to say something, but again all that came from the speaker was an indeterminate sound. "I'm sorry, but I'm afraid I'm still having trouble hearing you. If you're not able to speak, perhaps you could give the phone a tap so that I know you can hear me." Both Summerskill and Lyon found themselves leaning into the speaker, willing the reluctant caller to say something.

There was sudden barrage of raps from the speaker, making Claire jump backwards. It was followed by what sounded to her suspiciously like laughter in the distance. "Okay." Roz sounded unfazed. "Now, how about I do a bit of a run through of the sorts of things that people tend to ask when they call us here, and if there's anything you want me to talk about in more detail you can give the phone a tap again and I'll know what to focus on. How's that?"

There was a pause, and then an eruption of noise. "Queers!" yelled a voice.

"Well," said Roz, "that is what some people call gay people. It's actually what some gay people call themselves these days, but it's really not the friendliest way of talking to someone you don't know."

There was another pause; then, "Queers! Queers! Queers!" the excited voice shouted again, and this time there was no doubt about the raucous laughter in the background.

"Now, how about we…?" Roz began. There was a click, and then the dialling tone. "And that," she said, replacing the receiver, "is the kind of call that makes up about half of what we get these days."

"Bigots," Claire muttered. After nearly a year of working with him, she'd come to understand some of the crap Dave had to deal with simply because he was gay. A lot of it was what he had called microaggressions, and some of that, initially at least, had even come from her. Now she wondered how often he had to deal with such naked hatred and hostility. She wanted to ask him but knew he wouldn't want to tell her. Her fists itched to punch the face of the obnoxious shit who had just called in.

"Kids," said Roz. "Probably."

"Well, whoever it was, respect to you for staying so calm and polite," said Dave.

"If it had been me, I'd have given them a right mouthful," said Claire.

"It's what kids do, isn't it, darlin'? They meet up at night in their little gangs, looking for something that's going to give them a bit of a thrill, a bit of a laugh, and one of them says, 'Why don't we give those poofs at the Centre a prank call?' What you've got to remember is that lad—and sorry, but it is usually lads—had us on his mind to begin with. He might even have our number already. And at least one of his mates was keen to give it a try. You've got to ask yourself why that was. Maybe, a call like that one is a kind of test run, done with the security of mates around. And maybe, if he hears someone reasonable and normal on the other end, the lad who suggested the call or who egged it on will feel a bit braver about ringing us again later, on his own, and possibly even start talking about what's really on his tiny mind." She shrugged. "Who knows? Better to be positive, in an increasingly negative world." She looked up at Dave from under her purple-and-grey fringe. "Did you ever call a helpline when you were a nipper, Sergeant?"

"Why, Roz, whatever makes you think I'm gay?" Dave said with a smile.

"It's the way he walks, isn't it?" Claire teased. "Or is it the way he talks? Go on, tell him he has a gay voice. I've heard that's a thing." Dave laughed, and it struck Claire that she'd never seen or heard her sergeant so relaxed when talking about his sexuality. It should have been this easy at work. But it wasn't.

"Darlin'," said Roz, "if only it was that easy. Relax, handsome; you could pass for straight, if you wanted to lower your standards that far. It wasn't the walk, and it wasn't the talk. It was the way you checked out these posters the boys have put up in here. Straight men don't know where to look with all these pecs and butts on display." She smiled, with a touch of regret, at Claire. "And the way you checked them out made it quite clear that you were straight. Shame."

"You should be the detective, Roz. So come on"—Claire turned her chair to look straight at Dave, not ready to let him off the hook that easily—"did you ring a switchboard when you were young and confused?" A thought struck. "Did you ring this one? You were local, weren't you?"

"Wrong in almost every respect. I was never confused—"

"Never young too," Claire said in an aside to Roz.

"—and I'm not from around here. Born and bred in Birmingham."

"No accent, darlin'," Roz murmured, "thank God. How did you do it, then? How did you find your fairy wings and fly the straight nest?"

Dave shifted awkwardly in his chair. "I…" To Claire's fascination, she could tell that he didn't want to meet her eye. He cleared his throat. "Research."

Roz waited for more. "I'm sorry?" she said, when no more was forthcoming.

"Research," Dave said more firmly though still avoiding his amused boss's eye. "I bought as many of the gay papers as I could, drew up a list of gay shops, pubs, and clubs, put them on a map, and began to check them out."

"That's…different," Roz said.

"Was there a spreadsheet involved? I bet there was," Claire said. "He's very methodical you know." She relented slightly in her mockery. "It's what makes him quite a good cop actually. You should see his notebook."

"Very brave though," Roz said quietly.

"I'm sorry?"

"Going out into the big gay world on your own when you were…? How old?"

"Seventeen."

Claire finally caught his eye. There was something… She let it go. For now.

"Must have been quite scary," Roz said.

Dave hesitated. "It was…challenging."

"Get your wings singed?"

Dave looked down. "A couple of times."

Roz reached over and patted his hand. "Only makes 'em stronger. Like I said. Brave boy. Now," she said to Claire, "*that's* why I think he must be a good policeman."

"You said that kids' call was like half of the calls you get these days," said Dave, keen to change the subject. "What's the other half like?"

Roz chuckled. The deflection tactic was obvious, but she went with it. "From one extreme to the other I'm afraid, sweetheart. The old, run-of-the-mill, 'Am I a monster?' or, 'Where can I find a boy stroke girlfriend?' questions can all be answered online now. We still get a few of them, of course, especially from the less computer literate."

She's looking at me, Claire thought. *Bloody hell! She is good!*

"But the rest nowadays tend to be from people whose problems are less easily dealt with or who are in such a bad place they're desperate for some kind of human contact. Kids and adults who aren't uncertain about their sexuality so much as their actual gender identity. Sex workers who can't get out of the trade. Same-sex abuse victims. You wouldn't believe some of the things I've heard. Breaks your heart, some of them." She sighed. "No, I'm afraid the good old days of 'Can you give me the address of the best local S&M leather dungeon?' are long gone. That was a simpler, more innocent time." She shook her head and then brightened again. "Any more of those cheese and onion crisps left, sweetheart?"

Dave passed a packet across, and for a few minutes the conversation drifted into how the smaller size of crisp packets and chocolate bars was another sign of how the world was falling headlong into hell.

There was a knock at the door. Karen Haines, wearing the overalls they'd seen her in on the night of Victor's murder, stuck her head into the office. "Bin," she said tonelessly. They assumed it was meant to be a question.

"Already taken to the recycling, darlin'," said Roz.

Her expression suggesting that in some way Roz had snubbed her, Karen withdrew, closing the door behind her.

"Not the greenest plant in the garden, our Karen," Roz said. "I think she's rumbled me as the bitch who spirits away the office scrap paper before she can dump it in the nearest landfill."

"You know she was here on the night of the murder?" said Claire. "Along with Clive Grover. She was on the scene before him, in fact."

"Yes, I read about it in the paper. The reporter said Karen was 'shocked'. I was impressed he could perceive that much of a reaction. 'Taciturn' doesn't come close to describing what she's like normally. I shouldn't run her down though. She is actually a bloody good cleaner. Raised the bar quite a bit since she started here." Roz gave another throaty chuckle. "I think some of the others get a bit freaked out by what we do." She waved a heavily ringed hand at the walls. "Or by our posters. This carpet sometimes doesn't see a Hoover for weeks, and I don't think the shelves know what a feather duster looks like. But Karen trundles round and does the business without fear or favour. Without a smile, too, but that's by the by."

"You don't suppose," Claire ventured, "that she might have a vested interest?

"What, because she's built like a navvy and has a resting bitch face, you think she might be a lesbian?" Roz roared. "There are exceptions that prove the rule, darlin'. She's got a man. Leastways, I've heard she's been seen with a man." Roz's expression abruptly became conspiratorial. "Now, completely unconnected with that and apropos of absolutely nothing, there is a small issue I fear I am going to have to raise with you at some point this evening." She lowered her voice. "I have to make a small confession."

"Go on," said Claire. Dave sat up a little.

"I am," said Roz, "what you might call an addict. Now, that didn't used to matter so much in days of yore when everyone was, or when there were more of us here to go around, and we could rota on at least two people every night. But when there's only one of you at a time, it is a bit more awkward." She nodded towards the wall, and Claire was worried she was making some oblique reference to the safer sex advocated by so many of the posters. But then she saw the "No Smoking" sign and understood. "I'm sorry, but I can't last an entire night without popping out at least twice for a fag, and right now I'm gasping. I'd spark up in here, but I couldn't do that to you." She assumed a hopeful expression. "Could I?" Claire made an ambiguous noise. Dave's face was more explicit. "Fair enough. Look, I'll only be five minutes. I have to go round the back of the building to a charming little spot full of weeds and tin cans. It totally enhances the experience."

"But what if the phone rings?" asked Dave. "I know it's still early for the caller we're expecting, but there could be someone else."

Roz pulled on an extravagantly furred coat. "Sweetheart, these days we're more likely to get a cold call about double glazing than a genuine plea for help. That fake effort we had makes this one of the busiest nights I've had for weeks. But if it does go, you can nip outside and give me a shout. Or better still," she said, reaching into her huge handbag, rummaging around, and pulling out a packet of cigarettes and a lighter, "why not answer it yourself? A tad unethical, but you're used to handling the public, aren't you?" She turned a dazzling smile on him. "And I'm sure you've got tons of personal experience you can draw on. You'll be able to keep any soul in distress chatting away till I get back." She laughed. "It was you talking about Karen that set me gasping, truth be told. She's caught me lighting up in here loads of times, but never says a word, bless her. Just sniffs and gives the room a good blast with some nasty floral spray. Anyway, back in a jiffy. TTFN." With a cheery wave, Roz left the room.

★

"Are you going to bust her when she comes back or shall I?"

"You caught it too?" Claire said. "The whiff of weed on her coat? Bet you a pound she comes back in sucking a mint."

"Nah, I think it'll be a spray of some kind. Toilet water." Dave clicked his fingers. "Patchouli."

"Good guess, Sergeant. Okay. You're on."

The two officers sat and waited. The office was a lot quieter without Roz. Strangely, though, it felt smaller.

"I have got some of the latest personnel evaluations that need to be written up." Dave eyed the ancient computer on the desk. "In fact, if that thing actually works, I could possibly make a start on…"

"You remember what I said? Stakeout. No one writes reports on a stakeout."

"Well, no, not usually I suppose. But then, as also pointed out, we're not sitting in some freezing car in the middle of the night keeping an eye out for some malefactor up to no good."

"*Malefactor?*"

"The poetess is rubbing off on me."

"Whatever. Have a crisp."

"I ate before we came, so no. Thank you."

Claire helped herself. Dave saw it again, that distracted look he'd noticed earlier. "When we first got together," she said through a mouthful of smoky bacon, "Ian would always make me up a snack box when I was on a stakeout. All sorts of healthy shit to see me through the night." She wrinkled her nose. "I used to chuck half of it away. More than half, actually. You know I can't be doing with crap like that. He used to put these daft messages in them, too, you know, all lovey-dovey.

Some of them quite racy. Course, that was the other reason I had to chuck most of it away. In case there was something too spicy in the chickpea wrap, or too hot in the hummus." She gave her head a small shake. "Joe ever slipped something into your lunch box? And even as I'm saying that, I realise it's an unfortunate choice of words."

"No. He has not. He hasn't got near my lunch box, which is a completely irony-free statement. It's still a bit early days yet for either of us to be making packed lunches for the other."

"Early days is when the daft stuff happens." Claire leaned forward over the desk, resting her chin in her hands. "Come on. Tell me how it's going. I need to hear some good stuff. And I want to know every disgusting detail."

"You know I could just lend you some gay porn. I've even got some that's got a bit of a story to it, if you like. Can't see the point myself, but I'm told that's what the ladies…"

"Are you and Joe the real thing or not?"

Dave gave up trying to avoid the question. He'd seen her at work in the interview rooms and knew how dogged she was in pursuit of the answers she wanted. "We are in a relationship."

"*Iesu Grist.* Could you be more millennial? Say what you mean, man!"

"It's…good."

Claire waited and then threw herself back into her chair when she realised there was nothing more on offer. "*Good?* This from a man who can spin out a traffic accident report into over two thousand words?"

"Detail is important."

"Exactly. Two guys bump into each other. Bang. It's all over. That's a car accident. Now I want to know if the same thing's happening between you and PC Joe."

"Like I said…"

"All right. Starter for ten. How does it compare to other relationships you've had? I mean, you have had other relationships, right?" Claire stopped, as if unexpectedly struck by the feeling that she might have gone a step too far. "Sorry, that was a bit…"

"No, it's fine. It's okay."

"No. No, it's not. I'm only messing around. And I can tell you meant what you said. But…I go too far. Sometimes."

Caught off guard by this unexpected apology and wary of some new and hitherto unseen tactic, Dave was mildly surprised. "No. Really. It's fine. It's…"

"Don't say banter," she warned.

"Conversation?"

She smiled. "I prefer gossip."

"Not scuttlebutt?" he said. "Is that a Welsh word by the way?"

"I guess I forgot for a moment there that you're…"

"Not one of the girls?"

"That's not what I was going to say."

"And not one of the boys either?"

The unexpected bitterness of Dave's comment took them both by surprise.

"Now that's…" Claire had been about to say "unfair". But was it? How many months had Dave been with them at Foregate Street? There was always an awkward period of adjustment when a new guy joined an established team. That was only to be expected. But somehow, with Dave, that awkwardness was persisting. "Look, it's not a boys or girls thing. And it's definitely not a gay/straight thing either; you know that."

"Ah." Dave nodded. "It's me being spiky again, isn't it?"

Claire threw her hands up. "That bloody memory of yours!" She knew he was referring to what she'd called him some weeks previously during an admittedly heavy-handed effort to team build. "I'm your boss. That's all it boils down to. It makes a difference. You'll find out yourself when you get promoted."

"Yeah, come the day. Look, that wasn't meant to be a dig. I know, all right, that I can be…standoffish. You're not the only one who's pointed that out to me recently." He pressed on, before she could probe that titbit. "The thing is, I guess I'm not that used to talking to people. About personal things. Maybe that's what happens when you grow up hiding something pretty fundamental about yourself from your nearest and dearest. At least at first. I suppose it becomes a bit of a habit."

"I'm sorry." It was possibly the last thing Claire actually wanted to say to him, but she really didn't know what else to say.

"Oh no!" Dave shook his head vehemently. "No, no. That wasn't some plea for sympathy. Being a gay kid was challenging. Okay. So what? Whose life isn't?

It's not an excuse or a plea for pity. I'm just saying it made me who I am. And actually, I'm quite happy with who I am."

"Okay. I get that." Claire nodded, and then, to break the tension a little but mainly because she couldn't help herself, she sang quietly, "*I am what I am, and what I am needs no…*"

"And you can stop that."

"Fair enough. Look, thanks for telling me that. I appreciate it. I am your boss…"

"Technically."

"Literally. And sometimes I forget that. If you must know, I still find it a bit…tricky at times. Dealing with people, I mean. Now that I'm so important."

"I am genuinely surprised."

"What? That I think I'm important?"

"God, no. That you find it difficult dealing with people."

"I said 'tricky'."

"It's always looked to me like you've found being in charge pretty natural."

"Hah. Well, part of that is because I'm from a long line of Pontypridd women." Claire exaggerated her Welsh accent. "We don't take no shit, see?" She laughed. "I suppose the rest comes from being a mam. You learn a few tricks dealing with kids."

Dave smiled. "That how you see me? A kid? Like Rudge sees you?"

Claire threw her head back. "God, you are impossible, Lyon. Here's me, trying to do a bit of team building."

"Is that what this is? I thought you were fishing for scuttlebutt about me and Joe."

"I should be so lucky! So far, all I've got is 'good'. That's less than I get from Tony when I ask him how his day at school went."

"All right." Dave sat back in his chair. "If you must know, it's going quite well."

"Steady on there, tiger."

"There were things we had to sort out, right at the start—quite a few things, actually, and still a fair few more to be honest, but…" He wobbled his hand in the air to suggest reasonable progress.

"Bloody hell, man. Have all your relationships been this hard work? They're supposed to be fun, y'know. Adventures. Especially for—"

"Gay guys?"

"—young men," she lied. "You're making it sound like a performance review."

"Yeah well, we might both be young men," Dave said, not blind to her lie for an instant, "but one of us is a sergeant and one of us is a constable."

"So? You're a low-life sergeant and I'm a high and mighty inspector. It doesn't really matter in the broad scheme of things."

"I'll remind you of that next time you get me to fetch you a coffee. And you've just said how hard you find it being an inspector."

"I said 'tricky'. Look, I don't know why you found it so hard—"

"Challenging."

"—getting together with Joe. Everyone knew it could be a good thing between the pair of you the minute he walked into the station."

"Exactly, and that was one of the problems. People didn't think it was a *good* thing. They thought it was an *inevitable* thing. Half the station, largely though not exclusively the female half, had this rosy, fluffy idea that two gay policemen would have to fall for each other, as if there were no other gay men in the world for either of them."

"If there are, you didn't seem to be having any luck finding them."

"And the other half," Dave said, ignoring the interruption, "obviously thought we wouldn't be able to keep our hands off each other, because that's what gay men are like."

"So, you determined to prove both sides wrong?"

"Yes."

"Even though they were both right."

"They were not. We didn't rip our clothes off and jump into bed at the first opportunity."

Claire leaned forward again. "So, when did you jump into bed?"

"No comment."

"*Ych a fe.* Were you this slow off the mark with Richard?"

Dave sobered slightly. "Richard wasn't really a boyfriend."

"No?" Claire thought back to the guy Dave had brought along to her home for her "getting to know you" dinner shortly after he'd joined the station. And to what Rudge had said to her earlier. "I'm pretty sure that's how you introduced him. And you were living together."

"Only until I got my own place."

"Oh. Okay. How…practical." In the back of her mind, she heard Rudge's words again: *He's a user.* "Okay. Richard's not in the picture anymore. He's around, though, isn't he? He teaches at one of the local primaries, doesn't he?"

"Grove Park. And we're friends. It's not going to be a problem."

"Right. So, the field's clear for you and Joe, then? No other skeletons, in or out of the closet?" It had been a light-hearted question. She'd assumed she'd known the answer. She was surprised when Dave hesitated.

"I'm back. Miss me?"

Claire struggled not to show the irritation she felt at Roz's return.

"Didn't know you'd gone," Dave said. "We've been so busy answering calls. Phone's been ringing off the hook."

"And I'm the reincarnation of Mata Hari," Roz said, hanging her heavy fur on the hook behind the door. She was sucking a mint. "Seriously, though, anyone call while I was out punishing my lungs?"

"Not even someone trying to change your electricity supplier."

Roz glanced at the call sheet folder. "I must record that earlier call. I'll confess, I often leave it till right at the end of the evening, and then I end up missing my bus."

"We can give you a lift."

"Thank you, sweetheart." Roz pulled the folder towards her. "Clive is a real stickler for keeping this up to date." She chuckled as if at a private joke. "Oh yes, he can be very strict." Sensing something under the words, Dave and Claire looked at Roz quizzically. "Have you met Trevor, his partner?"

"Briefly. He made us tea when we went round to Clive's place."

Roz snorted. "I'll bet he did."

"Are we missing something?"

"He's Clive's slave."

"What!"

"Not in a Vietnamese nail bar/Polish car wash kind of way. Clive and Trevor have a Master/slave kind of thing going on. They're both heavily into the S&M leather scene. You wouldn't believe the piercings Clive has got under those fusty outfits he wears during the day. Apparently, it's a nightmare trying to get through airport security with him. He used to visit me quite regularly for lunch at the library until they installed those scanners to stop gits stealing the books. His metal bits would set the alarms off."

Claire thought again of the portly, stuffy Clive Grover, trying to picture him in this new light. She quickly stopped. It was not a pretty picture.

"Trevor makes nice cakes," Dave said.

"How about you, Roz?" Claire asked, as much to get her mind off the image of a geared-up Clive as out of any real desire to know. "Do you have a partner?" Too late, she wondered if this innocent question was going to lead to more lurid revelations. She thought again of that poem. She'd applauded the idea of older women wearing purple. She wasn't sure she was ready to celebrate them wearing PVC or rubber.

"Lord, no, dear. The Lady of Shalott, me, sitting in my ivory tower in splendid isolation. Here I am, ready to offer my life's stored wisdom to any young lovely with wit enough to grab me, but all too often I'm passed over in favour of superficial glamour: a wrinkle-free face and tits that don't need scaffolding. I think the cats are also a problem."

"Ah." Dave nodded. "Too many?"

"Not any. Can't stand 'em, and that tends to put the Sapphics off. No idea why but they love the furry little shit-spreaders."

"Victor seems to have done okay for partners?" Claire said. "Although you say he didn't have anyone as such at the end? Seems a shame he was on his own when everybody says he was so lovely." She felt slightly guilty turning a pleasant enough chat into a fishing expedition, but she knew Dave would understand. Perhaps Victor had said something to Roz about the man from the befriending, the man whom Tom had said had made Victor look so happy.

"Claire, Claire, Claire," Roz said like a reproving mother. "Don't tell me a modern, high-achieving woman like you still thinks we all need another person to make us complete? If I want that kind of satisfaction, I've got things…"

"Yes, but Victor," Claire said, eager to prevent Roz telling them exactly how she filled any void in her life.

"Victor was a serial monogamist, bless him. Three relationships in all the years I knew him, and each one of them lasted a good stretch. There'd been something before he moved down to Worcester but he was only young then so it can't have been more than a fling I suppose. A flexing of those wings, you know." She winked again at Dave.

"But nothing at the end?"

"Not that I know to, darlin'."

Okay, so Roz didn't seem to know anything about Tom's mystery man, but what, Claire wondered, might she know about Tom himself? The lad made no secret of his affection for Victor, but how reciprocal had Victor's feelings been? "He'd never been close to anyone on the Switchboard team?" She knew again that Dave would know where she was going with this. She hoped it didn't set back the rapprochement they'd been enjoying tonight.

Roz roared. "Good God, no. You have met us all, haven't you, darlin'? Who on Earth would Victor want to get off with out of us poor remnants?"

"Tom?"

"Tom?" Claire noted that Roz wasn't outraged by her suggestion. She had feared she would spring to a heated defence of her old friend, and that would be the end to the evening's friendly chat. But she appeared to be considering her question without any bad feeling.

"I'm fairly sure not, sweetheart," she said.

"Not even…"

"Fucking?" Roz asked with perfect equanimity. "No, I don't think so."

"It wouldn't have been illegal."

Roz guffawed. "I do know that, darlin'. But it's not a question of legality, or even morality come to that. It's a question of *taste,* sweetheart. Tom was hardly Victor's type."

"Didn't he like younger men?"

"Oh, Claire. Who doesn't prefer a bit of younger meat now and again? It's nice not to have to overlook the bits that sag, don't you agree, Sergeant?"

"So, he did," Claire insisted, "like younger men?"

"If you're asking whether that was his thing, then I would say no."

"His last two partners were younger than him." Across the desk, Dave reacted with surprise. That appeared to be news to him.

"Sweetheart, one partner is always going to be younger than the other. And yes, I know I'm being disingenuous there. I know what you're getting at, so I'll answer you in as straight a way as I can manage. Question: do I think that Victor had a thing for young boys? Answer: no. Question: do I think that Tom had a thing for Victor? Answer: yes. I don't think there was any, how shall we put it, consummation, but if there had been I would have said good luck to him."

"For landing a lad young enough to be his grandson?"

"For landing a catch like Victor. I was talking about Tom. What is Tom likely to end up with in the next ten years? Some spotty inadequate who doesn't know his arse from his elbow and who hasn't got a clue how the world wags. Victor could have opened that boy's eyes to all manner of things, and I'm not just talking about sex." She grinned broadly. "Although the great secret they don't tell you until it's almost too late is that sex keeps getting better the older you get. Good news, eh, Sergeant?" She nudged Dave hard enough to make him wince. "It's not who you do, it's what you do, and the more you do it the better you get. Don't let them make you think you always have to be chasing twinks."

"I'll bear that in mind," said Dave.

Roz folded her arms and looked at Claire rather in the manner of someone issuing a challenge. "Some people say that gays and lesbians are only interested in younger partners. They kind of forget that for that to work, logically, there must be an equal number of gays and lesbians who are only interested in older partners."

"You don't think, then, that Tom might have strangled Victor in some kind of lover's tiff?" Dave asked the question, but he was looking at Claire as he did. She knew he was pouring cold water on her line of investigation with his deliberately outrageous question.

Roz howled with laughter. "Tom is a lovely boy, but he's a total snowflake. Victor would have flattened him if he'd tried anything like that. Not that I think for one second he would have. Tom's a good lad. His heart is in the right place, at least it is when he isn't wearing it on his sleeve. He needs to grow up a bit, that's all. Get a boyfriend."

"Always good advice," Dave said.

"Do you have a boyf, Sergeant?" Roz asked. "Is there a Lyon cub handcuffed in a cell somewhere waiting for you?"

"You have a most lurid imagination, Roz," Dave said.

Roz chuckled. "I spend my working days in a library and a deal of my spare time in this room on my own. My imagination has to have some outlet."

"His name is Joe. He's a police officer too. And"—Dave glanced at Claire—"it's early days."

Roz clapped her hands. "Good for you." She turned her attention to Claire. "And what about the inspector? Who massages your feet at the end of a day pounding the beat?"

"I'm married," Claire said.

Roz nodded. "And how's that working out for you?"

"It's good. Thank you. Five years of marriage, one husband, and two sons. All good. Nothing to write home about."

Dave watched his boss thoughtfully. He thought he'd enjoy her turn squirming under Roz's bludgeoning questions, but Claire's responses were short, brittle. He thought quickly about how he could change the subject.

"Two kids under five and holding down a full-time job like police inspector. I'm impressed."

"Actually, the oldest is thirteen, going on fourteen."

Roz leaned forward. "Do tell."

The Switchboard phone rang. It was a toss-up who was more relieved: Claire or Dave.

Roz picked up the receiver. "Worcester and Hereford Gay and Lesbian Switchboard. Roz here. How can I help you? Oh hello, darlin'." She covered the receiver with one hand. "It's Clive." She returned to the phone. "Yes, yes, they're here. Yes, including the dishy one. And Inspector Summerskill." She winked at them. "Want me to put this one on speaker?"

"No, no. You carry on."

While Roz chatted to Clive Grover, Dave pulled up his chair closer to Claire. "Saved by the bell?"

"Hoist by my own petard, if we're swapping clichés."

It was only another minute before Roz put the phone back down. "The boss, checking up that all was well. Couldn't hear any chains in the background, so he and Trevor must be having a quiet night in. Now, where were we?"

"Y'know, I'd love another cup of coffee, Roz," said Dave.

"Someone's not getting any sleep tonight." Roz got to her feet and collected their mugs. "And not for a good reason. Okey-dokey. Back in a jiffy." She left the office.

"D'you think she noticed?" Claire said eventually.

"I think she may have felt the temperature drop a degree or two."

Claire nodded. "I thought tonight might have taken my mind off it. I didn't expect to be cross-examined."

"I thought…" Dave began slowly.

"That Ian and I were working things out? Trying again? Yes. Yes, we were. Are."

"But…?"

"I…don't think it's working," Claire said, finally admitting something to herself as much as to her sergeant.

"I'm sorry."

"Don't be," she snapped. She ran her hand through her hair. "I'm sorry. I mean, thanks. I know you mean well. I appreciate it. But it's home stuff, isn't it? It should be left at home. And yes," she said, not blind to the reproving look in Dave's eyes, "the word you are looking for is hypocrite."

"Oh, I do love a bit of hypocrisy," Roz declared as she sailed back in with mugs in hand. "Two faces are always so much better value for money than one, I always say." She set the mugs down on the desk and settled herself back into her chair. "Now then, where were we?" She blew into her mug and looked at Claire over the rim of it. "The state of your marriage, I think, sweetheart."

Both Summerskill and Lyon opened their mouths to speak.

The phone rang again.

Roz dealt with the call with brisk efficiency. "A hang-up. Probably a wrong number. I have been asked to deliver a pizza before now. Could have been our kids from earlier again. Could have been someone trying to pluck up the courage to talk to us but bottling out. Who knows? Now, where…?"

"Have you ever had a partner, Roz?" Claire asked. Dave hid his smile behind his mug. As a stalling manoeuvre, his boss's tactic was pretty obvious. He guessed from Roz's smile she thought so, too, but she was game enough to go along with it. For the moment at least.

"One," she replied. "The love of my life. We were together for fifteen wonderful years." She took a sip of her tea and smiled wistfully.

"She's…? I mean, you're not together anymore?"

"No, darlin'." Roz looked up and smiled brightly. "I cheated on her."

"Oh."

"Yes, entirely my fault. Bright young thing called Alison. Started at the library. Teeth, hair, glasses, and an interest in medieval lyrics. Just the way I like them. I couldn't resist. Tess found out and that was that. So stupid. Even turned out that Alison's interest in *Gawain and the Green Knight* was as fake as her teeth and hair. It was all about getting into my knickers. Tess went off and was last heard of in some commune in the Forest of Dean, and Alison is now heading up her own library in Bradford. So perhaps there is some justice in the world after all." She shook herself and turned cheerfully to Summerskill and Lyon. "Anyone else cheated on their partner recently?"

"No," said Claire.

"C'mon, Roz," said Dave.

Roz looked from one to the other of them. "Interesting," she said.

"What do you mean?" asked Claire.

Roz spread her hands. "Everyone cheats, darlings. It's human nature."

Claire gestured at Dave. "Well, he's only been with his…with Joe a couple of weeks. Give him a chance."

"So, you," Roz said, pointing at Claire, "are deflecting. And you"—pointing at Dave—"aren't answering." She leaned back in her chair. "As I said, interesting."

Claire snorted and waited for her sergeant to come back at Roz. He didn't. She frowned at him, inviting him to reply. He looked away.

"I think," Roz said slowly, "that I feel the need for another cigarette. All this openness and honesty. You know what to do." She hurriedly gathered her things and left again.

"Well?" said Claire, after waiting long enough to be sure Roz was out of hearing range.

"What?"

"Roz was right. You weren't answering her question."

"I wasn't aware I was under oath."

"And you're doing it again. Have you cheated on Joe?"

"For God's sake! Like you've said, we've only been seeing each other for a couple of weeks."

"And still not answering!"

"You can't cheat on someone if you haven't made a commitment."

Claire looked at her sergeant in frank surprise. "You have!"

"I don't think it's part of your job description to rake me over the coals about my private life."

"I've told you about how things are with me and Ian."

"That was your choice." Dave stopped. He rubbed his hand over his face. "I'm sorry. That wasn't fair. I appreciate your telling me that. I really do."

"And you're both officers under me. So, if this is going to affect your work…"

"What happened to work and private life being separate?"

"That rather went out the window when you started going out with a colleague, didn't it?" Again, Rudge's words from earlier came back to her. "And now, I'm sorry. You're right. But I wasn't talking to you as your boss. I was talking as your friend." She paused. "That okay?"

Dave nodded. "Yeah, it is. Thank you."

For a moment, they sat in silence, each thinking about what they'd said, each trying on for size this latest stage of their relationship. "Look, it's not cheating," Dave said finally, "not really. Not in any way that means anything. It's been sex, all right? That's all. A couple of times. I think I've got feelings for Joe, feelings that I hope will grow. I don't feel that way about…the other guy. There is definitely no future there."

"That's bullshit, Dave," Claire said calmly. "It's never *just* about sex. And don't tell me it's different when it's between men because I don't believe that. Or maybe, I don't believe it about you. I think you're better than that."

Dave looked at the floor. "Maybe I'm not. Maybe you're a rotten judge of character."

"Up yours, Sergeant." Claire thought for a moment. "Who the hell is it, anyway? You're not telling me it's someone in the station, are you? It's got to be. You haven't had time to look anywhere else." She sat up, unable to hide her pleasure in the thrill of the chase." It's not Simmonds, is it? I've always wondered about Simmonds. But I can't believe anyone would pass over a good-looking lad like Joe for pasty-faced Max."

"It's not always about looks, you know? But no, it is not Max. God, no!"

"Then who? It's not like you have a social life. When you're not at work you're studying for promotion so who on earth have you had time to…?" Claire stopped, her face a picture of horrified suspicion. "Someone you've met through work but who isn't a copper." In her mind, a series of previously disparate pieces fell into an unexpected and wholly distasteful picture. "Someone who comes and goes as he bloody well pleases, gets his friend in high places to push you up the ladder, who doesn't give a damn about anyone else, and who gets to call you David. It's Cullen, isn't it?" Dave's stone face was the clearest confirmation she could have asked for. "What the…" She ran both hands through her hair. "I mean what the actual fuck!"

"Look, it's…"

"What are you even thinking? The guy is slimy, a sleazy, slimy… I mean what is it? Is it the sex? Is it the power? I mean, he's an MP but for Worcester for God's sake. Or is it his connections that get you going? He and Chief Superintendent Madden are secret handshake buddies, so he can get the boss to look after you at work. Maybe they'll even induct you into the lodge. You can all roll up your trouser legs together. Or take them off altogether. No stopping you then." She stopped, unable to hide her disappointment, as another memory came to her. *He's a user.* That's what Jim had said to her about Dave. She hadn't wanted to believe it. But now?

"You're making a whole mountain range out of a molehill. It isn't like that at all."

"You're sleeping with Sean Cullen behind your new boyfriend's back, and yes, I am going to call him that, even if you won't, but it isn't like that? I've heard better defences from bellends I've caught with their arms full of knocked-off car parts. So, come on, what is it like?" She waited, bracing herself for a typical Dave comeback, for a fierce denial. She didn't care what it was. She was going to shout at him anyway. She'd had enough. Enough of men lying and cheating and thinking they could do what they wanted with whoever they wanted and damn the consequences, and if they thought that they could…

"I don't know what it's like," Dave said.

That was not the response she had expected.

She looked at him, slumped in the chair like the air had been let out of him. He looked strangely alone, and it occurred to her for the first time that essentially he was. He had family, a father and brother, but he never seemed to see them. He had no friends in the station, and, as she had pointed out, that was pretty much his life. If he did find himself caught up in a bad personal place, who was he going to talk to? Come to that, who had she got these days? Once it would have been Jenny, but that door seemed to have been closed. Maybe they only had each other.

Perhaps she should stop shouting.

She thought over what she knew of Cullen. He was very handsome and very successful. But she didn't believe Dave was that shallow. And Cullen was also very clearly cynical and manipulative, so maybe… "Has he got anything on you?"

"Of course he hasn't," Dave snapped.

Claire abandoned psychology. "Then how the hell have you ended up in his bed?"

"Look. It started before I met Joe, all right?"

"Presumably during the Best murder case. That was when he first raised his head."

"Not during. I'm not that stupid. Afterwards." She noticed he didn't say how soon afterwards.

"So, some time after we closed an investigation in which he was implicated and came out of smelling like shit, not that long after either presumably given how recent that was, you started shagging."

"He called me. We met. He was obviously out to get me in his bed. Fair enough. He's good-looking. I was flattered. Things with Richard had fizzled out before they'd even started, and there wasn't anyone else. I'd been looking around. It had all been depressingly awful. And Cullen is…exciting. He's charismatic. An arrogant, annoying, self-absorbed, conceited cock. But charismatic. I thought, why not? So, I did."

"Maybe I should have had a romp with his partner in crime, Sue Green. I think she was sending out the right signals."

"We proved Sue Green was implicated in something dodgy. Cullen was cleared."

"Legally. Morally, he was a sleazeball."

"Do you honestly think I'd have gone with him if he'd done something illegal? He hadn't, so I did. And it was good. Great, actually. Physically, I mean." Claire held up her hands. "Oh, so now you don't want details? Anyway, there was nothing emotional about it. Nothing at all."

"Really?"

"Really."

"Funny."

Dave frowned. "What is?"

"That's exactly what Ian said about his first fling with that bitch Cassie Grant. Course, the first fling led to the second fling and so on and so on. I don't know when a fling becomes a thing, and the *only physical* tips over into the emotional. Perhaps it happens later for gay men." She looked Dave straight in the eyes. "But it will happen."

Dave looked away. "There is no way I could ever end up as Sean Cullen's partner."

"No? But you didn't go with him just the once, did you?"

"No."

"And you've been with him since you've got together with Joe?"

The answer to this was longer coming. "Yes."

"Does that mean poor old Joe is some kind of second best?"

"No!"

"Then what is it with Cullen?" She didn't want to ask him, but Claire knew she had to. "Did you get Cullen to ask Madden for the television interview?"

"No," Dave said immediately. "In fact, as soon as I got that bloody thing, I went round to his place to ask him what the hell he was thinking."

"And you told him you'd got a new boyfriend and didn't want to see him again?"

"No," Dave conceded slowly.

"That was one of the times you shagged him, wasn't it?"

Dave nodded.

"Jesus, Dave. I thought you were better than that."

"Yes, well maybe I did, too, which is why I feel so bad about it now."

"What about Joe?"

"What about him?"

"Are you with him or not with him? Are you going to mess him about?"

"No!"

"Then what are you going to do?"

"I…don't know."

"You can't seriously be thinking of carrying on with Cullen? Please don't even try to tell me he's misunderstood and that if I got to know him, I'd come to love him too."

Dave gave a small and mirthless smile. "I won't. The more I get to know him, the more of a callous, arrogant bastard I see he is. But…"

"But what?"

"Look, Sean's exciting. I've never known anyone like him. He plays by his own rules."

"He can afford to. He's a rich git."

"I love my job, I really do. But being with Sean reminds me there's more to life than work. Maybe having a partner who's also a policeman isn't such a good idea."

"Try having one who's a teacher. Sounds to me like poor old Joe can't hope to hold a candle to Cullen. So, cut him loose. It's not fair to cheat on him."

Dave shook his head unhappily. "I think Joe already feels more for me than Sean ever will."

"It's about what you feel, though, isn't it, not about what Joe feels. And definitely not about what Cullen feels."

"I have no idea what Sean feels. I don't know if he feels anything at all. He's never mentioned any previous partners, so, as far as I know, I'm the latest in a long string of casual flings. I haven't known either of them that long, but I already know far more about Joe than I do about Sean. Sean could throw me over tomorrow. Joe… I think Joe could be around for a lot longer than that. And that would be…nice." He looked up at his superior officer. "So?"

"You asking for my advice?"

"No."

"Thought not. So, all I'll say is, sort it, Sergeant. Quickly. For everyone's sake."

"Yes, ma'am. And you?"

"I will if you will."

"Air cleared, darlings?" Roz inquired as she breezed back into the office, so on cue she might almost have been listening at the door.

"A few things cleared up," said Claire.

"Which reminds me," Roz said. "I have got to get my records up to date." She reached for the call sheet folder. "Don't want Clive playing the Nazi commandant with me. No matter how much he might enjoy it. Here you go." She reached into a magazine rack by the side of her desk and, after a brief inspection, pulled out a couple of magazines which she handed to Claire and Dave. "*Dyke* for you," she said to Claire. "Don't worry, no full frontals or pullouts. It's all pretty serious stuff for the right-on politicals. Never touch it myself. And for you," she said to Dave, "*Velcro*. Not a political slogan in sight. I think the boys keep it here to raise their spirits when the nights are really dull." With a cheerful wink she turned to her work of recording the night's calls so far.

"Swap?" Claire offered Dave her magazine.

"No chance."

"Thought not." Claire flipped through *Dyke*. "Where are the knitting patterns or recipes?"

"There is quite a spicy piece about what you can do in a kitchen with all the tools to hand," Roz said as she found her place in the folder. "That's strange."

"I'll say." Claire stared aghast at the article Roz had mentioned. "That can't be safe."

"No. This." Roz tapped the folder. Dave and Claire put down their magazines and turned to see what she was talking about. "I wouldn't have noticed only the sheets were in a bit of a mess. Like they'd been taken out and not put back in properly."

"That'll have been Jen," Claire said. "One of our officers. I asked her to photocopy the sheets. Sorry about that."

"No, that's no problem. It's this." She turned the folder round on the desk so the officers could see and pointed to a page.

"It looks like an ordinary day's entry to me," Claire said. "One wrong number, a guy called Mickey who was almost certainly a prank call, and someone wanting a Salami Special. Is that some kind of gay code?"

"No, it's a pizza, darlin'. And yes, I remember those calls because I was on duty that night. Look." Roz indicated the small box marked "Operator(s)" at the top of the page and her initials within it.

"Okay," said Dave, "then what…?"

"But this isn't my handwriting. These are the entries I made, as near as I can remember, but not the ones I wrote. They've been rewritten."

"Do you know who by? Can you recognise the handwriting?"

"Oh yes." Roz turned the sheet over for the next day's records: the same handwriting but a different set of initials in the "Operator(s)" box. "It's Victor's."

There could be little doubt. The neat precision of Victor Whyte's handwriting bore scant resemblance to Roz's chaotic scrawl. The police officers studied the records of the night when Victor had been on duty. There were two calls recorded. *"Martin at quarter past eight,"* Claire read. *"In usual good spirits—think he likes to say hello,* and an anonymous request for the nearest GUM clinic." She looked at the date. It was from a good three months previously.

"You don't suppose," Dave ventured, "that Victor took your day and copied it out because, well, your handwriting is a little tricky to decipher."

"I don't know what you mean, darlin'."

Claire pushed the folder back to Roz. "Can you see if there are any other entries like that in Victor's writing but not from him?"

Roz quickly looked through the folder. She found two others, both from within a fortnight of the first entry she had found. The entries, both Victor's copies and his genuine comments, seemed to contain nothing out of the ordinary.

"None later than these?" Claire asked.

"None that I can see, sweetheart, no."

"They don't seem to have anything in common."

"Except," said Dave, "all the entries were made the day before or after a day Victor was on duty."

"I don't think the other operators' entries are the forgeries," Claire said. "They're copies of what was there originally. I think Victor's own entries for the days he was on duty are the forgeries, or at least, they're alterations of what was there originally."

"But what on earth could that have been?" said Roz. "Those entries were made near the start of the year. We've had at least two review meetings since then when all the operators sit down and we go through the call sheets discussing the various callers and sharing our thoughts. Clive is very strict about them."

"I'm sure he is," said Dave.

"But there was never anything odd mentioned. Certainly nothing that would warrant going back and being erased from history."

"Unless," Claire mused, "Victor had written something in those three records which seemed quite innocuous at the time, but which later events made more significant in some way."

"He could have pulled the sheets out," said Dave.

"That would have left noticeable gaps."

Roz gave a sad smile. "And it would have meant losing records. Victor wouldn't do that to us. He respected our work too much. No, this would have been typical of him."

"Do you think this has something to do with the folder's disappearance after Victor's death?"

"I'm guessing yes," said Claire. "At the least, someone was trying to prevent us from seeing the folder, perhaps from seeing the changes. At the most, they were trying to smuggle the thing out of the building, perhaps to destroy it, but could only get it as far as that hiding place in the hall where it was found before they could come back for it."

Focused as they were on their thoughts, the sudden ring of the phone made them all jump. Roz checked the office clock. "Nine o'clock. This should be Dale." She cleared her throat and picked up the phone. "Hello. Worcester and Hereford Gay and Lesbian Switchboard. My name's Roz. How can I help you?" There was a pause. "Hello, Dale." Roz flipped the switch that made the phone call public.

"Hello, Roz." A soft voice, not effeminate but light and quiet. Perhaps Dale was having to keep his voice down for fear of being heard. "Is Victor there?"

"No, Dale, I'm afraid he isn't at the moment."

"Oh. Might he be coming in later?"

Roz bit her lip. "No, Dale, sweetheart," she said. "I'm afraid he won't."

"Then I'll…"

"No, Dale, please wait. I've got somebody else here to talk to you."

"Somebody else?" Dale's voice became suspicious. Claire knew they could lose him if they didn't play it right. "No. No, I don't want to talk to anyone else. Only Victor. If he's not there, then…"

"Sweetheart, Victor's gone," Roz said.

The silence at the end was broken only by the faint hiss from the speaker. Claire willed the man to hold on. "What do you mean, gone?"

Roz held the phone out to Claire and Dave. *I can't,* she mouthed.

Automatically, Claire went to take the receiver, but then she indicated that it be passed to Dave. They hadn't discussed this, but right now it was obvious that it was a man Dale needed to talk to.

"Hello, Dale," said Dave. "Please don't be alarmed, but my name is Dave, Detective Sergeant Dave Lyon from Worcester Police. I'm afraid we have some sad news about Victor."

"Is he…is he in some kind of trouble?"

"No, Dale. I'm afraid he isn't. Victor is dead. He was killed in this office last week by person or persons unknown." Silence. Dave pressed on. "We'd like to talk to you about Victor, but please understand that is not because we suspect you of being directly involved in his death."

"Then why…?"

"At the moment, we're looking into the calls Victor received while he was working as an operator here. Do you know that he spoke to you more than to anybody else over these past few months?"

There was a sound that might have been a sob at the other end of the phone. "He was a good man." The three listeners had to strain to hear the words.

"Yes. Yes, we know. And we want very much to find out who killed him. That's why we're speaking to everyone who had contact with him recently. Will you let us talk to you, please, Dale? We can come to you if you let us know…"

"No!"

"That's okay. Don't worry." *And don't put the phone down!* "We understand how difficult things can be for people who call this switchboard."

"No. No, you don't." They could hear now the tears in Dale's voice.

"Dale. I do, mate." Dave glanced at Claire who nodded. "I'm gay myself, so I know…"

"You don't understand at all," said the voice at the other end of the line. "I'm not gay."

Chapter Eight

"Morning, all."

"You're late."

"That's how you know it's me, not some imposter." Claire hung her coat up and looked around the office. There was something in the air, above and beyond the latest cologne Terry Cortez was trying out. "What's up? And where's Dave?" No use assuming that he was even later than her. He was never late, except when she made him pick her up first.

"Madden's office," Jenny said.

Claire ignored Jim's harrumph. "What for?"

Jenny shrugged. "Hard to keep up with the life of a media superstar."

"Yes, but don't worry. I will try to keep it real with the little people," said Dave, walking in and catching the end of Jenny's comment. He nodded his good morning to Claire. "Meeting with Dale at two?"

"Yes. And what did Madden want?"

Dave looked around the room at Claire, Trent, Rudge and Cortez. No one was even pretending not to be listening this time. "I've been asked to give an interview about the case."

"Another television interview?" Claire said. "And you thought Moody didn't like you."

"Actually, no," said Dave reluctantly "This is an interview for a magazine, *Campaign*."

"And what the hell is *Campaign* when it's at home?" Rudge growled.

"One of the biggest mainstream gay magazines in the UK at the moment, of course." Claire recalled Clive Grover's list of the magazines the Gay and Lesbian

Switchboard advertised in. "What?" she said, catching Dave's expression of faint disbelief. "It's only people's names I can't remember. Magazines I'm good on."

"So, Sergeant Lyon is going to become a pinup boy as well, eh?" Jenny poked Sergeant Cortez in the side. "Eat your heart out, Tel. I know you've always fancied yourself as a bit of a model."

"That's…" Rudge had a face like a threatening storm cloud.

"Not the kind of magazine it is," Dave interrupted quickly. "The clue is kind of in the name."

"It's camp?" Claire said.

"Yeah, that is an in-joke I think we could all have done without. No, it's a campaigning magazine, a bit more serious than its rival." He hesitated, apparently unsure whether he was making matters better or worse. "A bit more political." He looked across to Claire.

Claire knew the others in the room were waiting for her to kick off at this latest example of her subordinate officer's grandstanding. She was pretty sure at least one of them wanted her to. And maybe before her night on the switchboard with Dave, she would have done. Now though… "Good for you," she said, and she meant it. "Be good for the gay community and the police." Her intentions were good, but even she cringed a little inwardly at how earnestly they came out. *My God. I'll be going on bloody gay pride marches next. Or turning into a chief superintendent.* She was slightly surprised to see that Dave still looked unhappy. It occurred to her that he hadn't yet told them everything.

"They want to do a human-interest story on me," Dave went on.

"Barking up the wrong tree on both counts there," said Jenny in what was almost an aside to Cortez. Cortez smirked.

"And to get the full picture, they want to interview you as well."

Cortez's smirk vanished.

"What?" rumbled Rudge dangerously. "We've all got to flash our scanties?"

"I've said, it's not that kind of magazine."

"Wishful thinking, Jim," said Claire.

"And they want to interview all of us?" Jenny Trent sounded disbelieving.

For the first time since this looming car crash had begun, Dave looked almost happy. He nearly smiled. "Not quite everyone, Constable. I doubt you'll be required."

"And I'm damn sure I won't be either," declared Rudge.

Claire saw Dave's unhappiness return. "Chief Superintendent Madden would like the *Campaign* reporter to interview as many senior officers as possible. He is very keen—" As he spoke, Dave turned slowly so it could be seen he was speaking to everyone present—he just happened to finish facing in DI Rudge's direction. "—that Foregate Street station be shown as the inclusive place he wants it to look."

There was a chilly silence.

"Right, well, that's fair enough, isn't it?" said Claire, giving a challenging look to all around her. "We give interviews to local papers all the time. Be nice to achieve a larger circulation for a change. It's got quite a good circulation, has it?" she asked Dave.

"Millions I guess," he said gloomily.

"Right." Claire tried to get her head round a figure that was much larger than she had been imagining. "They won't want to put us on the cover, will they?"

"Trust me, ma'am, I don't think you'd appeal to their key demographic."

Uncertain whether she was relieved or put out by that, Claire assumed an air of deliberate positivity. "Right, well, it's going to happen whatever, so let's get it done and dusted with and move on. Worse things happen at sea, and least said, soonest mended."

"Red sky at night?" Dave murmured.

Claire shot him an *I'm trying to help here* look. She spun her chair back to her desk and reached for a file. "When are these interviews happening, anyway?"

"Today."

"What?" Claire spun her chair round again to face her sergeant.

"In fact, their reporter is waiting for me now, apparently, in Interview Room Three. So, if anyone wants me in the next half hour or so, that's where I'll be. The reporter's name is Vince Simonson by the way, and I'm told he's looking forward to meeting us." He flashed one last hint of a smile at Jenny. "Well, most of us anyway." He turned and left the office.

"Hang on a minute," Claire called out, as she got up and followed him.

"Look, I'm sorry about this," Dave began as soon as the office door was closed.

Claire waved his apology to one side. "It's fine. I know you haven't set this up."

"I tried to talk Madden out of it, and when he wouldn't budge, I tried to get him to postpone but he wouldn't. This Simonson guy has been trying for days to set this up, apparently. Somehow, the messages he's been leaving haven't been getting through."

"Odd." Claire knew what Dave was thinking. She thought the same.

"Anyway, if he does me first and then you, we shouldn't have any problem meeting up with Dale at the arranged time."

"Okay. One thing before you go. Do you think Cullen is behind this?"

Dave's expression was grim. "I don't know. But I aim to find out."

Was it internalised homophobia, Dave wondered, that had led him to fear Vince Simonson would be outrageously camp, exactly the kind of queen to raise DI Rudge's hackles and sour relations between him and his superior officer even more? Or was it because the reporter worked for a magazine with a dreadful pun for a title? Either way, Dave pushed the question to the back of his mind for future examination and focused on the ordeal ahead.

First appearances suggested it might not be such an ordeal after all.

Vince Simonson was in his thirties, rather conservatively dressed in jacket and tie, although the simple cut of his clothes suggested both taste and cost, and when he rose to shake Dave's hand, his grip was firm and his smile warm. He was also quite good-looking. Good teeth. Dave's spirits rose a little. "Sorry about the room," he said.

"Oh, I've been in worse. Rooms in general," Simonson added quickly, "not police interview rooms."

Dave relaxed a little bit more. "Sorry about the tea too."

"Again, worse." Vince took out his phone and laid it on the table between them. "Do you mind if I record our interview?"

Right. Not just a friendly chat. Remember that. Dave sat up a little straighter in his chair. "Go ahead." He indicated the digital recorder securely fixed to the wall on one side of the table. "Conversations in here generally are." *Though usually, I'm the one asking the questions.*

"Okay then. Well, I suppose we'd better start at the beginning, hadn't we? When did you first know that you wanted to be a policeman?" Simonson smiled. "Please tell me it wasn't because of the uniform."

"Well, that didn't hurt."

Simonson looked surprised, and mentally Dave kicked himself. Here he'd been worrying that the reporter would be camp and the first answer he gave suggested his career was all about the look.

Shit shit shit shit shit.

★

The interview took an hour.

It felt much longer.

To Dave's relief, Simonson didn't follow up that flip comment about uniform, but took him through a series of clear, sensible questions that fleshed out his background, reasons for becoming a policeman, and career to date. Dave had expected more of a focus on the Whyte case and less on him, but the questions were fair, and as they talked, he began to relax again and to forget that the man interviewing him was a "gay reporter". After all, it had been unfair of him, hadn't it, to think that Simonson's sexuality was going to make a difference, any more than Joe Public should expect him to be any different because he was a "gay policeman". He realised he must still have been showing some vestiges of his nerves when the reporter said, "You seem a bit tense, if you don't mind my saying."

"Sorry." Dave deliberately tried to look more relaxed. It had precisely the opposite effect.

"Not a criticism. An observation." Simonson pulled a self-deprecating expression. "I have a reporter's eye for body language."

"Feeling the weight of responsibility, I suppose." Simonson raised an eyebrow. "I'm speaking on behalf of a lot of other people here."

"Gay people?"

"Police people. Specifically, the people here, at Foregate. I think I can speak for them more than I can for gay people in general."

"Interesting."

Is it? Shit!

"Let's talk about Foregate Street," Simonson went on. "How did you come to end up here, Dave?"

Dave hesitated. *End up?* Why not *stationed?* "I'm sorry?"

"What I mean is, you start off in Birmingham, the country's second city. You train there, then you move to…" He consulted his notes. "Redditch, and then you end up here." He looked up and gave that apparently genuine smile again. "I mean, it's not exactly a fast track to the top, is it? Would you say that Worcester is going to be a challenge to a man of your calibre?"

Should he say, Dave wondered, that as a percentage of its population, Worcester's crime rate was depressingly challenging, due in no small part to the city's drawing into itself large numbers of disaffected youth from the rural areas surrounding it on every side? He decided not to. He didn't know what *Campaign's* circulation figures were in Worcester, but there was no point in pissing off any locals who might chance to read this article. "You go where the opportunities take you, Vince," he said.

"Isn't that true?" The reporter gave Dave a look of wry sympathy that he no longer completely believed. He pressed on. "You were at Redditch, what, five years? Don't officers on the way up move on faster than that normally? Especially officers with as good a record as yours?"

"There are no hard and fast rules." Dave pointedly looked up at the clock on the wall. "I don't mean to hurry you, but if we could get on to the Whyte murder investigation, I'd really appreciate it, especially if you're going to be interviewing DI Summerskill next. We're both due to be somewhere else by two."

"Of course. But before we do, can I ask, do you think you've been held back in your career as a police officer because you're gay?"

Dave blinked. This was not the line of questioning he'd been expecting. He was damn certain it wasn't the sort of questioning Madden had anticipated when he'd talked about positive publicity. "Are you implying there's some kind of institutionalised homophobia in the service?"

"Are you?"

"Please, Mr. Stevenson, this isn't some sort of television psychiatry session."

"Please, Vince. And no, it isn't. I'd hoped it was an honest discussion between two gay men about the state of the police force in this country today, specifically about its attitude to queer people."

Dave gave a meaningful look at Stevenson's notebook. "Is it? I thought it was an interview with a police officer about an ongoing investigation. And it's police *service*, not force."

"Some might say you are ducking the issue, Dave."

"Some might say you're missing the point, Mr. Simonson."

Simonson grinned. Dave thought there was something of the shark about it. "Don't you feel you have a duty to speak out for other gay men and women?"

"What makes you say I don't?"

"You refuse to consider that your relatively slow progress in *the service* might be down to your sexuality?"

"Perhaps because you would have to convince me first that it was."

"You don't strike me as a naïve man, Dave."

"Good."

"So, don't you think that by passively accepting prejudice you're actually colluding with it? If I pretended to be straight in the *Campaign* office…"

"I suspect no one could get away with that there."

"Touché."

"And I don't pretend to be anything."

"I'm glad to hear it."

"My sexuality is my own business, and that's true of every other officer."

"Good for you. But"—Simonson smiled again—"you have let yourself be set up as the poster child for this current investigation, haven't you? Is that the service using you to reassure all us queers that we're getting a fair deal, or is it actually you using your sexuality, the sexuality that is *your own business*, to give your career the bit of a boost it seems to need?"

Dave rose from his chair. "I think we have come to the end of this interview."

Simonson remained seated, looking up at Dave calmly from his fixed chair. "But you still haven't answered my question, Sergeant. Do you think that your progression up the ranks has been slower by comparison with other men of similar abilities and achievements simply because you are gay?"

Dave leaned forward, planted his fists on the desk, and looked Simonson squarely in the eyes. "No."

It was the reporter who broke eye contact, ostensibly to look back down at his notes. "And the case that you're working on now, the murder of Victor Whyte, a gay man. Do you think you were put on this specifically because you are a gay man too?"

"Again, no."

"Are you the leading officer in this case?"

"Definitely not. DI Summerskill is in charge."

"A woman."

"You should have been a detective, Mr. Simonson."

"So, there's only two of you?"

"We are the detectives on the case, so we are at the front, if you like, but we're supported by…"

"Isn't that quite a small frontline force? Wouldn't there have been more detectives on the case if the murder victim had been, I don't know, *Victoria* Whyte, a young charity worker?"

Dave almost laughed, reminded of his own use of gender reversal in his recent argument with Claire. "And if it had been Victoria, would you be here interviewing me now?"

"A fair point, well made. Let's talk a little bit about the case, then."

"I think that would be a very good idea."

"I understand, then, that Victor Whyte was…"

"One moment, please, before we get on to that. Can I ask you a question?"

Simonson put his notebook down. "Of course."

"Do you know Sean Cullen?" Dave studied his face closely for any sign of reaction. Definitely a flicker of something. Surprise? Guilt?

"That's the local MP, isn't it? I wouldn't say that I know him, though I have met him. He's been in the *Campaign* offices a couple of times, and we've run articles that have featured him, about politics and about sport. He's what we call a 'Good Gay', a successful role model in several different fields. Why?"

"I was thinking what a great subject for an interview he'd make."

I certainly intend to be asking him a few questions later.

"I understand that you are the lead officer in the case of the murder of Victor Whyte. Is that correct?"

"Yes, it is," said Claire.

Vince Simonson smiled. "I'm sure you'll understand that, given the readership of our magazine, our main interest is in Sergeant Lyon, but we in no way intend that to be a slight to yourself."

"Thank you."

"So, what is it like working with a gay man?"

Claire blinked. "I'm sorry. What do you mean?"

"What makes working with Dave different from working with a straight man?"

Caught unawares by the unexpected direction of the question, Claire floundered for a moment, genuinely unsure where to begin. Until she realised she didn't have to begin. "I'm sorry, but I thought we were here to talk about the Victor Whyte case?"

"Oh definitely, but as I'm sure you appreciate, *Campaign* is a magazine, not a newspaper. We look for the human angle in our stories."

"Victor Whyte was human."

Simonson laughed good-humouredly. "And gay."

"Well, yes."

"Does that bother you?"

Increasingly Claire had the almost dreamlike sensation of this interview not following any logic she could see. "Why the…why should that bother me?"

Simonson looked up to the ceiling as if considering. "Oh, I don't know. Do you think perhaps some people might see it as more appropriate for a woman to investigate the murder of a gay man? That she might bring more…sympathy to the case than her straight colleagues?"

Claire folded her arms and looked stonily at the reporter. "I'm just as sympathetic as the next man. And I mean that literally."

"I see." Simons made a note on his pad, and like Dave before her, Claire found that she did not like this feeling of being on the other side of the interview process in this room. "Which brings us back to my original question. What is it like working with a gay man?"

This time, Claire was ready for him. "I don't know. Because I don't think of it as working with a gay man. I think of it as working with Sergeant Lyon."

"So, what is like working with Sergeant Lyon?"

Wrong-footed again, Claire took refuge behind police speak. "Sergeant Lyon is an experienced and highly capable officer." It was all she could do to keep the habitual witness-stand singsong out of her voice. "He has a proven track record when it comes to…"

"What is he like as a person?"

"I hardly think…"

"Sensitive? Thoughtful? Empathetic?" Simonson leaned forward. "Obstinate? Opinionated? A touch arrogant?"

"Is this human interest or character assassination?"

"Oh, come on, Claire. Just between us, Dave has got a bit of a stick up his arse, right?"

Claire stood up. "I think this interview is at an end, Mr. Simonson."

"Do you think Foregate Street station is a good place for a gay man to work?"

Halfway to the door, Claire stopped and turned back. "Yes."

"Seriously?"

Claire took a couple of steps back towards the reporter. "I think Foregate Street station is a good place for any man, or woman, gay, straight, bi, or any other flavour people come in, so long as they do the bloody job. And Dave Lyon definitely does the bloody job."

"Thank you, Inspector," said Simonson, scribbling away in his notepad. "That really will make for a great end quote." He looked up and smiled. "Would you mind sending in Inspector Rudge, please?"

★

"Inspector Rudge. Thank you so much for agreeing to…"

"I didn't agree." Rudge sat down heavily. "I was ordered. You've got five minutes before I knock this on the head and get back to some real work."

Simonson cleared his throat and reshuffled his notes. "Okay. About Sergeant Lyon."

"No comment."

"I'm sorry?"

"No comment. I am not currently Sergeant Lyon's commanding officer. That would be Detective Inspector Summerskill. You need to ask her." Rudge gave a smile that was like a fissure in a cliff face. "I'm sure she'll give you a straight answer. If you'll pardon the expression."

Simonson eyed Rudge rather in the way a young boxer might eye a much heavier, older opponent. "What is your opinion of gay men in the police force, Inspector?"

"No comment."

"Inspector Rudge, we're not going to get very far if…"

"Look, son." Rudge's tone had assumed a gruff familiarity that had misled and undone many a young offender in the past. "I'm getting on a bit, been round the block, old dog, new tricks, all that kind of thing. I'm not going to be around much longer—"

"I can assure you you look in perfect…"

"—in the service, I mean, so what I have to say about anything has as much impact as a wet fart in an open field. So…no comment."

Simonson coloured. "Very well. You say you've been around a while. A policeman all your adult life?" Rudge nodded. "So, you'll have been part of the police persecution of gay people that used to take place twenty, thirty years ago." Rudge sat eying him, waiting. Simonson swallowed. "Yes?"

Rudge leaned in a little and lowered his voice, so that Simonson had to lean forward, too, to hear him. "Before 1967, it was illegal for men to bugger each other. After 1967, it was illegal until they were twenty-one. After 1994, it was illegal until they were eighteen. Since 2000, it's been illegal until they are sixteen. As a policeman it has been my duty to arrest people for illegal practices, and this I have done, and will do until the day I retire, according to whatever the law at the time demands. That's my job." He leaned forward even further, bringing his face as close to Simonson's as he could with a desk between them. "What's yours?"

"Thought you might need this."

Vince Simonson left off rubbing the back of his neck and opened his eyes to this unexpected voice. "Thanks. It's not a double whisky, is it?"

"Only coffee, I'm afraid." Jenny Trent closed the interview room door behind her, put a mug in front of the shattered looking reporter, and sat herself down in front of him. "But it's better than the stuff they gave you from the machine. And it might help your recovery."

Simonson drank gratefully from the mug and gave an approving thumbs-up. "Is he always that brutal?"

"DI Rudge?" Jenny considered. "Yes. Although he has his favourites. And his not so favourites."

His reporter's instincts teased, Simonson cupped his mug and swirled its contents. "And which are you?"

"Oh, Rudge is an old softy when it comes to the girls, real old school. I'm all right."

"Old school? Yes, that would be one way to describe it, I guess." He looked up from his coffee. "That must make work a bit tricky these days."

"He's okay. As long as people don't rock the boat." Jenny sat, facing the reporter across the table, and waited.

Vince Simonson put down his mug and reached for his notepad. "Tell me, what's it like working with Sergeant Lyon?"

★

"Excuse me, Officer, but do you have the time?"

"Er, yeah, sure." Joe Jones checked his wristwatch. "Half eleven." He nodded towards the station clock on the wall that was very large and very visible. "As it says."

"Sorry," said Vince Simonson. "That's something I've always wanted to do."

"I'm sorry?"

"Ask a policeman the time. Symbol of the good old days, isn't it? When bobbies had their beat, clipped the ears of naughty kids, and everyone felt free to ask a copper the time of day."

"Ah, right. Well, I guess times have changed, sir. If you'll excuse me."

Joe went to walk past the man, but Simonson stepped to one side and without actually blocking his path made it difficult for Joe to move on. "I was wondering if I could have a word."

"If there's something you want to report, sir, then the desk sergeant is over…"

"I meant a word with you, Constable Jones."

Joe looked more closely at the other man. "I'm sorry. Do I know you?"

"Vince Simonson." He held out his hand. "I'm here doing a piece for *Campaign*. I don't think I have to tell you what *Campaign* is, do I?"

Joe clicked his fingers in recognition. "Oh yeah, that's right. I heard we had a reporter coming in."

"In fact, I've not long been speaking with your boyfriend, Dave Lyon. He was very helpful. Is there a problem, Joe? I may call you Joe, may I? Only I noticed you looked around then when I mentioned your boyfriend. It's not a secret, is it?"

"It's not a secret, no, but…" Joe struggled for words. "It's kind of personal, y'know? I mean, it's not something we go blabbing about around work, and well, we're still early days. Maybe *boyfriend* is a bit too soon." He stopped, uncomfortably aware that he was gabbling away about his private life to a man he'd only just met.

"A friend with benefits, perhaps?" Simonson grinned.

Some of Joe's natural cheeriness faded. "Well, nice meeting you, Mr. Simonson, but I really do need to be getting on. You know how it is. Kids' ears to clip and all that."

"Sorry." Simonson didn't move. "I didn't mean to embarrass you. I had no idea that it was so difficult for gay men in the police force to be open and honest about who they are in their place of work."

"It's not like that. It's…" Joe stopped. "How did you know who I was? Dave, Sergeant Lyon didn't tell you, did he?"

Simonson waved his finger. "Joe. Reporters are like police. We don't grass on our informers. And my sources tell me you really don't have any need to be so coy about your relationship with the handsome Sergeant Lyon. Apparently, it's quite the talk of the station."

"Well, we really shouldn't put too much faith in gossip now, should we, sir?"

"So, tell me, what's it like being a gay policeman at Foregate Street station?"

"Much the same as being a gay policeman in any other station I imagine."

"I can see why you and Dave would get on. You both have a tendency to dodge questions."

"Only if the questions don't mean anything. This is the twenty-first century, Mr. Simonson. No one cares any more if you're gay or not. There wasn't a box or anything I had to tick on the application form."

"I'll bet there was one about heritage, though, wasn't there? But that's a conversation for another day." Simonson moved on quickly as Joe's eyes narrowed. "You don't think then that there's any resentment towards you?"

"Resentment? Resentment over what?"

"That you've attached yourself to an older, senior officer. Did you feel you had to do that? Strength in numbers, that kind of thing? A necessary defence mechanism: the only two gay officers in the station, looking after each other in the face of, what was it, 'institutionalised homophobia'. And I'm quoting Dave there. I'm assuming by the way that you two are the only gays in the building? Present company excepted, of course."

"I don't know, and I don't care," said Joe. "But what you said, the way you've made it sound, it's…bull."

Simonson stepped closer to the constable and lowered his voice. "Then tell me what it *is* like, Joe, so I can tell the real story in *Campaign*."

Joe, the taller of the two men, bent his head slightly and lowered his voice, too, as if joining in with the confidentiality. "The real story, Mr. Simonson? Or the story you want to tell?"

Simonson stepped back. "Again, I can see why you and Dave are an item. You're both very suspicious people."

"I like to think we're both very honest people. And we can be that here in Foregate with no problems. And it's because I'm an honest person that I can tell you this." Joe lowered his voice again as if sharing a secret. "I've read *Campaign*. Not very often but enough to know that I think it's a pile of shite."

Chapter Nine

"How was it for you?"

"Not what I was expecting," Dave said. "You?"

"I think," Claire said carefully, "that Mr. Simonson had an agenda. And it wasn't to make you look good."

"Sometimes I think the police may be going further to make up for past bad relations than the gay community is. Sorry."

"You're apologising on behalf of the gay community?"

"God, no. I'm sorry that slimy git got invited in to give us all the third degree. And as soon as I get the chance, I'm going to find out if Sean was responsible."

Another reason to see Cullen? Claire didn't say it out loud. "D'you think our man's coming?"

Dave looked at his watch. Dale was five minutes late. "I think so." He scanned the tables around them in the supermarket café. It had taken all his people skills to get Dale to agree to meet with them and then to arrange a time and a place. He wouldn't give any information about himself over the phone, not what he looked like or even how old he was. Dave checked out the faces of the men sitting around them. In his notebook, open in front of him, was an A3 photocopy of the picture their station's artist had made of the man Tom Adams had seen twice, once when meeting Victor and then again outside the Halo Centre. As he let his eyes travel over the faces around them, trying to look as if he wasn't, Dave couldn't see anyone remotely like the picture. Besides, every man already there was part of a pair or a group, and none of them looked as scared and unhappy as Dale had sounded on the phone.

Claire was toying with the café menu. "Kids' size meal," she scoffed. "Have any of them actually got a kid? Even Sam eats more than this at a go."

"I think he's here."

Claire looked up. A youngish man, certainly no older than thirty, was standing uncertainly in the café entrance, looking out across the tables. He quickly spotted them, the smartly dressed police officers standing out amongst the more casually dressed café clientele, as well as being the only couple without children. When he registered them, the man half raised his hand as if going to wave, dropped it awkwardly, looked for a second as if he was going to turn and walk away, then put his head down, stepped fully into the café, and walked towards their table.

"He doesn't look anything like that bloody picture," Claire said under her breath.

The man stopped at their table. "Inspector Summerskill?" he said uncertainly, looking at Dave.

"I'm Inspector Summerskill," said Claire. "This is Sergeant Lyon."

"Dave." Dave held out his hand which, after a brief hesitation, Dale took.

"Oh yes, of course. I'm sorry. I got a bit confused there."

"It happens," Claire said drily. She held up her own hand which he shook. "Mr…?"

"Forrest. My name's Dale Forrest."

No, it's not, Claire thought. "Won't you sit down?"

The two officers only relaxed when Dale finally pulled up a chair and sat down, and they knew that, for the moment at least, he wasn't going to do a runner. Close to, Dale could still have been anywhere between twenty-five and forty, the age lines around his eyes and mouth at odds with his otherwise youthful appearance. A skinny man in jeans and a plain shirt, he sat looking from one to the other of them, occasionally darting glances up at the café entrance whenever anyone new came in.

"Coffee?" asked Dave. "Tea?"

Dale went to speak, cleared his throat, and tried again. "No, thank you."

"Thank you so much for coming, Mr. Forrest," Claire began. "We really do appreciate that this might not be easy for you."

His mouth twisted. She couldn't tell if it was meant to be a smile or not. "Call me Dale."

"Dale. Thank you. Could you tell us, Dale, when did you first call the Worcester and Hereford Switchboard?"

When he finally spoke, Dale's words were rushed, like something he'd rehearsed and now needed to get out of his system. "It was over nine months ago now."

"And in that time, you've spoken to six operators?" She glanced at Dave who nodded.

There was a flicker of panic in Dale's eyes. Already he was being asked a question he clearly hadn't anticipated. "I don't know. I never kept count. I suppose it could have been that many, yes."

"The exact number doesn't matter. Please don't worry about that for the moment." Dale's increased tension was obvious, and Claire was keen to keep him calm. "The fact is, you really only ever really talked to one, and that was Victor. Isn't that right?"

"Victor…understood me," Dale said. "I was lucky. He was the first person I spoke to."

"You say you spoke to him, Dale, but when we look at the records, very little seems to have been said, and the calls were very short."

Dale looked down at the sticky table. "That was Victor being kind," he said. "And, I guess, sort of covering his own back."

"You mean, there was more to your calls than Victor recorded?"

Dale nodded. "If he was on his own, we could talk properly. If there was someone else from Switchboard with him, then we worked out this system. We'd say a few words, and I'd ring off, then I'd ring again after ten when the other operator had gone, and we'd talk properly then."

"What did you talk about, Dale?"

Dale rubbed his hands on the tops of his legs. When he spoke, his voice was trembling, soft, so that they could hardly hear, but he looked at each of them in turn, almost defiantly. "Domestic abuse. I'm a victim of domestic abuse."

"Your boyfriend?" Claire asked.

"Husband?" said Dave.

"I told you on the phone. I'm not gay," Dale said.

There was a pause. "I'm sorry," Claire began, "but…"

"It's my wife. She can be… She… She loses her temper sometimes, all right?"

"Okay," said Dave, "I'm going to get you a drink. Tea or coffee?"

Dale looked at him gratefully "Tea, please."

Dave went to get the drink. Claire sat watching Dale, saying nothing, giving him time to collect himself. She could see his admission had cost him a lot.

Dave returned and Dale took the mug, holding it in both hands.

"Okay, Dale," Claire said, "you're telling us you're straight and you have a wife, but you called a gay phoneline about her violent behaviour."

Dale snorted, a sound midway between a sob and a laugh, and wiped his hand across his nose. "I know. How pathetic is that?"

"It's not pathetic," Dave said, "not at all, but we need to understand. Why a gay switchboard?"

"It's stupid, I know, but I'd seen this programme on telly. It was about gays getting married. Sal, that's my wife, was taking the piss, saying why on earth would you get married if you didn't have to, and that they were almost asking for it. And that's when it kind of came to me. I knew I needed to talk to someone, that I needed help. It was driving me crazy, but I didn't know where to go. There wasn't anyone I could think of who I'd want to know I was being abused by my wife. But, at the end of this programme, they gave information about lines that gay people could call for advice on a marriage and all kinds of other stuff, and I thought…if I could tell someone I was being abused by another man, they wouldn't think I was some kind of failure." He looked up at them again, with that odd defensive defiance, as if daring them to criticise him. "Not so much of a failure, anyway."

"Dale," Dave said, "being a victim of domestic abuse does not make you a failure. Yes, domestic abuse is largely committed by men against women, but by no means all of it. Believe me."

Dale nodded miserably. "That's what he said. Victor. I started by saying it was another man hitting me, but I couldn't keep it up, and somehow, I think he knew almost from the start. So, I told him the truth, and he said what you've just said, and he made me kind of believe it, but then I'd have to hang up and go back home and it was like…" He buried his head in his hands. A nearby waitress gave them a quizzical look. Claire shook her head. *It's fine,* she mouthed. They waited until Dale was ready to talk again.

"Victor helped me so much by being there and listening. He made me feel I didn't need to be ashamed, made me think that there could be some kind of future. He gave me the numbers of some organisations that are specifically for abused men, but I didn't call them. It was difficult enough for me to find chances to talk to him. And I wanted to talk to him. He was like a lifeline."

"Did he…did he ever say anything to upset or annoy you?" Claire asked carefully.

Dale looked at her in open astonishment. "No. Never. Like I said, he was amazing. He really understood. I think it was because he'd been there himself."

Claire frowned. "I'm sorry? Been there? What are you saying, that Victor told you he'd been in an abusive relationship?"

"That's all he told me. He said he couldn't go into details because it wasn't ethical, that Switchboard's operators weren't supposed to talk about themselves with callers. But, like I said, he told me it had been a long time ago, before he'd even come to Worcester, but he'd been there, and I could tell from the way he spoke and listened that he had. And now he's…" Dale took a gulp from his mug. "She's not a bad woman, Sal. Not really. She's got problems, you know? I knew that when we first got together. We were going to have a kid, but…we lost it. And that made her worse. Sometimes, she'll be fine, and afterwards she's always sorry. I don't…" He stopped, unable to continue, a picture of mute misery.

"Dale. Dale, I'm sorry to have to ask you this, but are you sure Victor didn't ever give you any details about this abusive relationship he'd been in?"

"No, I've told you. All he said was that it was a long time ago, and he wished he'd handled things differently."

"One last question. Did you ever meet Victor?" Claire asked.

Dale looked at her, his face blotchy, eyes red-rimmed. "Meet him? No, of course not. It was hard enough getting to speak to him, let alone meet him."

"Thank you." She wasn't sure she meant it. She wasn't sure what she had expected from this meeting, but what they had got definitely wasn't it.

Dave, who had been on his smartphone, scribbled something in his notebook. When he'd finished, he tore a page out and handed it across the table to Dale. "I've put down the number of an organisation you can contact. It's for men in your situation. You are not alone. Talk to them. They can help you. I've put my number on there too. It's Foregate Street police station but don't let that put you off. Call if you need to and ask for me, okay?"

Dale nodded dumbly, but Claire knew. *He won't call.*

Back in the car and returning to Foregate Street, Claire and Dave reviewed what they'd got from the meeting. "Bugger all," was Claire's summary. "In fact, less than bugger all because if Dale Forrest wasn't the man Tom Adams saw, then who was? You don't suppose it's just that Adams was useless at describing, do you?"

"I don't think even Tom could muddle a 'big, fifty-something' with Dale Forrest."

"I suppose we do know now that there has been at least one person in Victor's life who didn't think the sun shone out of him."

"This abusive former partner? Be more helpful if we actually had a name. I guess we have to check out those former boyfriends Roz told us about."

Claire braced herself. She knew Dave wouldn't be happy with what she was going to tell him. *Suck it up, Sergeant.* "Actually, I already have. Two of them, anyway. I don't think it was either of them."

Dave frowned. "When?"

"When you were making your small-screen debut. I had to do something to fill the hours while you were doing all those retakes." She could indeed see that Dave was not happy she had done these interviews without him. And she was pretty sure, too, he knew what she had been looking for. He said nothing but his expression was sour. Claire pressed on. "Roz gave me the addresses of the last two of Victor's former partners, and I'll say now that I don't think either of those guys had it in them to be abusive. She didn't give me any contact details for the one before that, so I guess she's out of touch. I don't think it matters, though, because Dale said Victor talked about his abuse having happened before he came to Worcester."

"Perhaps the reason he came here in the first place?" Despite his obvious annoyance with his boss, Dave considered what she was saying. "We're grabbing at straws, aren't we? I mean, we don't know the extent of the abuse Victor received, assuming that he wasn't just saying it to make Forrest feel better, and you don't really think some shitty ex from forty-odd years ago would suddenly turn up here not to abuse Victor but to actually kill him?"

"Perhaps that wasn't the intention." They drove on, mulling over what they had learned. "Y'know, I still don't get why Victor went to so much trouble to cover up the extent of his contact with Dale. You don't think the rest of Switchboard would have been bothered that Dale wasn't a card-carrying gay, do you?"

"No. I don't even think Clive at his strictest would have turned away someone in need like that. I don't think that was the reason. Look at how ashamed Dale is of what's happening to him. I think Victor understood because it had happened to him, and he'd been ashamed too. And still was—and didn't want to own up to it."

Claire shook her head. "That is so sad. To still feel that way after so many years. To end your life still feeling it."

"At least he was using the experience to help others."

Claire thought of all the people they had interviewed about Victor, of all the glowing, positive things they had said about him. Had it been a police officer's healthy scepticism that had made her suspicious no one could be that good? Or was the job starting to make her cynical? "Let's find the bastard who killed him, eh?"

Chapter Ten

"You're not really watching this, are you?"

"Yes, I am."

"So, why is the guy in the vest shooting all the other guys dressed in black?"

Dave, lying on his sofa, his head in Joe's lap, turned his head sideways to see the television and its pictures of gunfire, running around, and general mayhem. "Okay, I don't really know," he admitted. "I kind of stopped thinking when the muscly guy stripped to his vest." Joe reached for the remote. "Don't turn it off. I reckon the vest will come off in a minute too."

Joe muted the film, put the remote to one side, and began to massage Dave's shoulders. "You are tense."

Dave wriggled down to give Joe better access. "Not for much longer, if you keep doing that."

"Hard day at the office?"

"Kind of. Not so much following leads as walking down blind alleys and finding more blind alleys." He frowned. "Actually, that doesn't make any sense, does it? Tell me about your day. How was it? Caught any more crims trying to hide stolen things where the sun don't shine?"

Joe stopped massaging. "Oh, okay, I suppose. The usual."

Someone had once told Dave that you knew a relationship was going well when you could tell if your partner was lying or not. Dave had always thought that slightly contradictory advice. But he was pleased to note that he could tell Joe was being less than totally honest with him now. He sat up. "No, it wasn't."

Joe wavered and then spoke. "I had an odd conversation with Baz before I came out tonight."

"In what way odd?"

"He was being snarky. Lots of little digs about moving out."

"I thought you two got on well."

"We do. And it's not that he wants me to move out. Lord knows he needs help with the rent. No, he thinks I will be moving out. And moving up."

"I don't get you."

"Baz reckons my going out with you is like being put on a fast track to promotion."

"What! Young twat." Dave immediately regretted calling Baz that. *Twat* was fair but *young* was awkward. He was the same age as Joe. "What sort of influence does he think a sergeant has? I know he's still wet behind the ears, but come on." *Wet behind the ears* was a bad move too. Baz had exactly the same lack of experience as Joe. This conversation was proving tricky.

"Well, he says you're a bit of a star on the rise, a man on his way."

"Because I got shoved in front of a camera to make an idiot of myself."

"And interviewed by a national magazine. And I told you, I thought you looked great on the telly. Maybe Baz did too."

"If Baz wants to see how much power a sergeant has, let him see what shifts he gets for the next month. He'll be lucky if he sees the sun again before the New Year after I've had a word with Chris."

"God, you're hot when you're all aggressive and protective like that." Joe's grin faltered.

"What is it?"

"Nothing."

"Joe."

"I bumped into that reporter guy today, the one who came to do a piece on you."

"I think it's more about the problems that prick has with the police than about me, but anyway, go on. What did he say?"

"He suggested I was with you for some kind of protection."

"From what? DI Rudge?"

"Kind of. Institutionalised homophobia. He said he was quoting you."

"I never said… Hang on." Dave thought back to his interview with Simonson. "Okay, I used the words, but not in that way. I didn't say that was what was going on. Jesus, what the hell is this article going to read like when it comes out?" Dave rested his hands on either side of Joe's face. "Don't let sad fucks like Simonson get to you, Joe. We know what we're about, and it's not anything a hack like him could understand."

"You're beginning to sound like me."

"And you're beginning to worry like me."

"We must be rubbing off on each other."

"Now that sounds like a fun idea." Dave leaned in and kissed him.

"You know, you're very sexy when you go all caveman like that and swear to avenge my honour. But don't worry about it. Baz was being a bit of a tool, nothing worse. He'll be fine. Especially if I don't make inspector before Christmas."

"Have any of the other newbies said anything like that?"

"Not that I know."

"You'll tell me, won't you, if they do?"

"Yes, I will. Now, do you want to watch the rest of this film or"—Joe hooked a finger into the front of Dave's shirt—"can we talk some more about that rubbing off on each other stuff?"

Dave reached for the remote and turned the television off.

"Sorry I'm late."

"Funny. That's usually my line."

Ian dropped his bag of schoolwork on the living room table. "There was an unexpected…"

"Meeting?" Claire said. "Don't, Ian. Don't."

"Where are the kids?"

"Sam's in bed. It's an hour past his bedtime. I let Tony go and stay at his mate's house tonight."

"On a school night?"

"A reward. For the unexpected babysitting he'd done for you."

Ian sat himself at the living room table rather than join his wife on the sofa. "I thought you'd be later back."

"I hadn't said I would be."

"You never do. But you often are."

"And is that where you are, whenever I'm late at work? In a *meeting*?" Ian said nothing. "And are these meetings still with Cassie Grant or have you moved on to someone else?"

"For God's sake, Claire, I…"

"Don't come the injured party with me, Ian," Claire spat. "You were the one who went tom-catting around. Then you were the one who said he wanted to try again. Now you're the one who's creeping back in late, using one of his kids to cover up for him."

"Not my kid. Yours," Ian shouted. "And if he hadn't…"

"What?"

"Forget it."

"If he hadn't let slip that you and Grant were the talk of the school with your little meetings in her storeroom, then I'd never have found out, and you and I would still be blissfully happy?"

"We haven't been happy for years, Claire."

Ian's words hit her like ice water. "Why did you never say?" Her words were so quiet he almost didn't hear them.

"You were never here to tell."

"I was working."

"And I was supporting you. Being the modern man. Looking after the kids. Both of them. But then…"

"What?"

"I began to realise I didn't feel like a man at all anymore."

Claire sat, waiting for him to look up, to meet her eyes. When at last he did, she spoke. "I've had enough, Ian. It's over."

Chapter Eleven

Jenny Trent was not someone Summerskill and Lyon could agree about. Claire was determined still to see the good in her friend even though Jenny's increasing bitterness made that difficult. Dave thought she was a bitch.

She was, however, very good at research, with IT skills probably beyond Dave's, and definitely beyond Claire's. It was these she now brought to bear on the matter of Victor Whyte's history before he moved to Worcester.

"Robertston," she said, early the following afternoon, dropping a printout on Claire's desk.

Bleary from a poor night's sleep, Claire took the sheet. "What?"

"That's where Victor Whyte lived before he moved down to Worcester. He was in his very early twenties when he came here. Put himself through college. Went to work in a chemist's. Took over the chemist's shop in the late eighties. Retired. Died. But before all that, he spent the first part of his life in Robertston, not much more than a village in Yorkshire. Junior school, grammar school, and a brief stint in the offices of Barnsley colliery. Not exactly a life full of travel and adventure."

"If you pass over all the hundreds of people he helped by setting up and working for Switchboard," Dave said.

"Good work, Jen," Claire said, skimming the paper. "Seriously, really good work. I'm guessing there isn't any official record of a partner, though, is there? Gay relationships weren't exactly celebrated at that time and in that area."

"Oh, I think you'll be surprised," Jenny said. "In fact, I think you'll be very surprised."

"A woman? He was married to a *woman*?"

"It happens," said Dave. "You should try to be more broad-minded."

When Jen had broken the news, Claire had tried to look less surprised. There had been something a little gleeful about the way Jen had told them, and about the way she had looked to Dave in particular to gauge his reaction. As he'd say to Joe later, it had been as if she'd seen it as some kind of game, Straights v Gays, and the home team had scored a winning goal.

"I know it happens, but Victor? Educated. Proudly out. An activist you could say, in his own way."

"Founding an organisation to help and advise people isn't exactly abseiling into the BBC studios and hijacking a news programme."

"You know what I mean."

"You forget. *We* forget how much attitudes have changed in a relatively short space of time. Literally in a lifetime in Victor's case. And how far they haven't changed in some places. The early seventies was not a good time to be gay anywhere in Britain, but in some tiny northern village, it must have been hell. Lots of gay men would have hidden who they were, many of them denying it to themselves. And they'd have married because that's what you did."

"Fair enough," said Claire. "Looks like Victor wasn't fudging anything when he told Dale he knew what he was going through. He knew *exactly* what Dale was going through."

It took almost four hours for Summerskill and Lyon to reach Robertston, and when they did, they drove though it without realising. "Hardly worth a signpost," Dave grumbled, as he turned the car round. Getting out of the parked car in what had to be the town centre, they took in the small line of shops. A half dozen at most. Two were charity shops and one was closed and boarded up. "Not hard to see why you'd want to up sticks and leave," Claire said, turning up the collar of her coat.

"It would have been a different place fifty years ago. The colliery we passed a mile or two back would have been open. Jobs and money. It was where Victor worked for a while, remember. This wouldn't have seemed so bad back then. Maybe. I suppose anywhere looked good compared to working down a mine."

It was the work of barely a couple of minutes to locate the address Jenny had unearthed for them: a tiny, terraced house in a row of ten. "Not much privacy going on in there," Dave muttered.

The woman who answered the door was young and holding a baby that was probably no more than a few months old. She smiled openly, registering only mild surprise when the two officers showed her their identity cards. "What can I do for you?"

"We're looking for a Mrs. Whyte." As she spoke, Claire was trying to do the maths in her head. How could this young woman fit into Victor's family tree?

"Really?" the girl said in cheery surprise. "Well, that's a relief I suppose. I mean, you're not after me or Ed; that's my partner. Not that we've done anything wrong. Not really. I mean, they wouldn't send detectives after someone for speeding, would they? Not that we have done any speeding. Not really. Not lately." She hitched the baby up on her shoulder. "I should shut up now, shouldn't I?"

"Mrs. Whyte?" Claire prompted.

"Oh yeah. You've just missed her. When I say just missed her, I mean, by about eighteen months. She used to live here, but she sold up and we bought the house from her. Poor thing."

Claire swore inwardly. They'd been surprised not to have found a divorce certificate for Victor and his wife. They'd been even more surprised and a little relieved not to have found a death certificate for the woman. The odds of her still being in the same house after half a century had seemed long but then had come through— almost. Now it looked as if she might still elude them. Unless…

"Oh, she's not dead," the woman with the baby said. "She's at Brightholme. The nursing home up the road there." She lowered her voice and placed one hand over her baby's head as if protecting it from hearing something unpleasant. "Best place for her, if you know what I mean."

"I hope they shoot me before they send me to a place like this."

"I don't know. Yorkshire's not that bad."

Claire made a sour face and jerked a thumb at the granite building in front of them. "I mean a home like this."

"You've no need to worry. You've got Tony and Sam to look after you in your twilight years."

"Are you kidding? Tony thinks I'm ready for a place like this now and would put me in it tomorrow if he had the chance."

"Well, I'll visit you."

"Hopefully, I'll be too far gone by then to remember you. Ring the bell, Sergeant."

Dave did as he was told. "To be honest, I probably won't come that often. I had an Aunty Caroline they put in a place like this. Twice a year, me and my brother would be dragged across the country to visit her. Hours of trying to make small talk. I'm not sure who hated it more, Aunty Caroline or us. We did used to get an ice cream at the end though."

"You can get your own raspberry ripple when this is over."

The officers were buzzed into a small, light reception area where they presented their credentials to a startled girl behind the desk and asked to see Mrs. Whyte. "She's not been involved in anything, has she?" Her name tag identified her as Alice.

"Does she get out much?" Claire asked.

"No. Never."

"Then it doesn't seem likely, does it? We'd like to talk to her about matters related to a current investigation."

A middle-aged woman in something like a nurse's uniform appeared and took them into the house, along a couple of corridors to a large sunlit living room. Half a dozen or so elderly men and women were sitting in large armchairs arranged around the room, most with heavy blankets over their legs, angled to face a wide-screen television. The programme was a daytime special about a young couple turning an abandoned slaughterhouse into luxury apartments, but no one looked as if they were really watching. Claire wondered how they'd have been able to hear it anyway over the low-level muzak being played through the sitting room's large speakers. She shivered.

Their guide (name tag: Margaret) brought them to one of the ladies sitting hunched in her chair. At first, they thought she was dozing. A closer inspection revealed that her eyes were open but fixed on a point on the floor some three feet in front of her. "Della. Della. You've got a couple of visitors." The old woman didn't stir. Margaret looked up. "She can hear you, but sometimes, she doesn't like to talk." She stood up, speaking to Dave and Claire over Della Whyte's head. "And sometimes, she's not quite sure where she is any more. Would you like a cup of tea?"

They accepted the offer, glad of an excuse to have Margaret leave them for a while, and when she had gone, Claire pulled over a nearby armchair and sat down facing the old woman while Dave sat on a footstool to one side.

"Hello, Della," Claire said. The hunched figure in the chair gave no sign of being aware that anyone else was there, still less that anyone had spoken.

"Della," Claire said slowly, "we've come to talk to you about Victor. Your husband. Victor Whyte. Can you remember Victor?"

"Victor?"

Della's voice was so faint Claire almost missed it under the muzak. She twisted to face Dave. "Can't you get someone to turn that bloody music off?"

"I'll ask Margaret when she comes back."

Claire turned back to Della. "That's right. Victor? Do you remember him?"

Della's face creased into even deeper lines of anxiety, panic almost. "Is he here? Victor?" Her eyes, still fixed on the spot in front of her, widened.

Claire took the old lady's hand. It had no weight to it at all, and the skin was like paper. "No, Della. No. I'm sorry. Victor isn't here."

"Victor?" Della quavered. "Victor?"

Claire looked at Dave who shook his head.

"There, there, Della," said a brisk voice behind them. They turned to see Margaret had returned, without the tea but with an older lady, with the air and uniform of Somebody in Charge. She held her hand out to Dave who stood and shook it, before turning to Claire. "I'm Mrs. Lannigan, the matron at Brightholme. And you are…?" Again, she looked to Dave for the answer.

"I'm Inspector Summerskill," said Claire, "and this is my sergeant, Sergeant Lyon."

Mrs. Lannigan smoothly transferred the focus of her attention to Claire. "I'm afraid that's probably all you're going to get from Della today," she said. "Once she gets it in her head that someone from her past has come to see her, she tends to get, well, stuck with that idea, usually for the rest of the day."

Summerskill and Lyon looked down at the woman in the chair. She was rocking slightly, saying over and over, "Victor?" Her red-rimmed eyes were wide, and the mottled hands in her lap writhing. No one, Claire thought, deserved to end her life like that, even if what they suspected about Della Whyte was true. "Does she ever speak about her husband? I know they separated a long time ago but…"

Mrs. Lannigan looked about her as if worried that the old people there might be eavesdropping. Claire wasn't sure any of the other residents were even aware they were in the same room. "Perhaps we can go to my office," she said, "for a little chat. I'm Sarah by the way."

The matron's office was small but neat, a vase of local wildflowers on her desk and photos of a number of older people, presumably past and present residents, on the walls. All were smiling. *Well, you wouldn't put miserable ones on display, would you,* Claire thought. There was a tray with the makings of tea for three waiting for them. Mrs. Lannigan offered them biscuits, too, which Claire declined but Dave readily accepted.

"I hope you don't think I was intruding back there," Mrs. Lannigan began, "but honestly, once Della's in that frame of mind you might as well give up trying to get any further." Claire tried to suggest that it was fine, though the interruption had annoyed her. "You were asking about her husband." Mrs. Lannigan sat behind her desk, raised teacup in hand. It was clear she wanted to know why before going any further.

"I doubt if it made the news up here, but Mr. Whyte, Della's husband, was murdered earlier last week. We're currently investigating any leads, and that includes trying to build up as full and accurate a picture of the victim's past as possible." Claire stopped, wondering if this sounded as desperate to the matron as it was sounding to her. She could read Mrs. Lannigan's question in her raised eyebrows: *You think our seventy-something resident with advanced dementia is somehow involved?* She pressed on before the matron could put her question into words. "I don't suppose you know anything about Victor Whyte? I mean, I know he probably left Robertston before you were even born." *Just,* she thought, putting Mrs. Lannigan at late fifties, early sixties. She waited, fully expecting they'd shortly be on their way.

"Well, I might be able to help you a bit there, actually." The matron put her teacup down and folded her hands on the desk in front of her. "I know homes like ours tend to have a bit of a bad reputation. Dumping grounds for unwanted relatives, waiting rooms for God, that kind of thing." Claire knew Dave was thinking of Aunty Caroline. "But at Brightholme we pride ourselves on being a home in the full sense of the word. We are very much a family-run, local concern. My mother ran Brightholme before me, and my daughter will be carrying on long after I've gone. My family has lived in Robertston for generations, and, well"—she gave a small, rather self-satisfied smile—"we've known all the local families for generations too. Including the Whytes."

Claire waited.

"I'd have to say, I didn't know him personally, of course, but I was a small girl when they had their little moment of scandal, and I remember that as clearly as anything."

"Scandal?" Out of the corner of her eye, Claire saw Dave take out his notepad and pencil.

"Victor and Della were both very young when they got married. Very young." Mrs. Lannigan gave them what Claire believed was called a knowing look. "It was generally accepted that they'd tied the knot because, well, they had to."

"Della was pregnant, you mean?"

Mrs. Lannigan nodded slowly. "Very. By which I mean, she had twins. But it was also generally accepted that the marriage would never last. They had absolutely nothing in common. Victor's family wasn't anything special, but it was a cut above Della's, and by all accounts he was a bright lad who could have made something of himself if he hadn't tied himself down to a wife and kids. Della's was one of the tougher families in the area. She'd have been happier with a pit worker but, in those days, with kids on the way, you had no choice. Sad thing, of course, was in the end, he upped and left her anyway."

"You say, in the end. Do you know how long they were together?"

"About three years, I think. I suppose he gave it a go, but the kids were still only little when he left." Mrs. Lannigan sniffed disapprovingly. "All of a piece, I suppose."

"I'm sorry. What do you mean?"

"Well, I don't like to set myself up as judge, jury, and…" Mrs. Lannigan stopped, suddenly aware that what she had been about to say was not in the best taste given the circumstances. "Let's just say, I think the family, and the town for that matter, were better off without him. We don't need his sort around here."

Claire was stunned, not that someone could hold views like that, but that she should come out with them so openly to people she had only just met. People, it seemed, really did speak their minds up north. She darted a look at Dave. His face was set at its most stony. Never a good sign.

"Still," Mrs. Lannigan went on, oblivious to the effect she was having on her visitors, "shouldn't speak ill of the dead. Murdered, you say?"

Claire ignored the blatant angling for gruesome details. "You say they had children. Grown adults by now, of course. Do they still live around here?"

"Both left a long time ago. As soon as they could, to be honest. The work dried up, you see. Those as would have worked in the collieries had to move on to find work. Their houses have all been bought up by young executive types commuting to the city and starting their families."

Claire thought of the woman in Della's old home. "Do the children ever visit their mother?"

Mrs. Lannigan pursed her lips. "The son does sometimes. The daughter, never. Only to be expected, I suppose. Not very many happy childhood memories here for them." Mrs Lannigan paused, and Claire and Dave got the distinct impression that she was gathering her courage for something. "When they told me we had two policemen, sorry, a policeman and a policewoman, here, to see Della I got the queerest feeling. Do you know what I mean?" Dave shook his head. Claire bit the inside of her cheek. "And I know," Mrs. Lannigan went on, "that I shouldn't have done this, and I hope I can rely on your discretion, but I thought you might want to see it." She reached down into a desk drawer and pulled out a very old and very battered photograph album. "It is strictly against Brightholme policies to go through the possessions of our clients without permission, of course, but I'm assuming you could have made me do it by law, anyway?"

Claire nodded, the tone of the question obviously inviting it.

"Besides"—Mrs. Lannigan nodded in the direction of the residents' living room—"I don't think for a minute Della is going to miss it. I can't remember the last time she looked at it. And I don't suppose she can either." She opened the book. "Not many pictures," she said sadly. "Not a family for wanting to keep its memories. Most of them won't be of any interest to you at all but these"—she tapped a particular page—"will."

Claire and Dave leaned in to get a closer look. On the page Mrs. Lannigan was showing them was an old black-and-white photograph of a wedding. Very little of the fairy-tale nonsense of modern wedding photos, Claire noted. No misty backgrounds of castles, bride and groom looking coyly over their shoulders as if they'd been caught by surprise while wandering through their country estate. This was a lineup, as regimented as any identity parade Summerskill and Lyon had organised at Foregate Street, bride and groom in the centre, families stretched out on either side. Only the bridesmaids, three small girls, looked like they were enjoying themselves. The photographer must have been standing about a mile away to get everyone in, there being more of the church's cold granite in the picture than there was of people. But there were Victor and Della.

"Handsome chap," said Dave.

"Hmph," said Mrs. Lannigan.

"So sad," Claire murmured. She was looking at Della on the first day that she was Mrs. Della Whyte. She wasn't exactly smiling, but she was standing tall, her rm in Victor's, the future ahead of her. Claire looked up and across to the residents' living room, which they could see through a window in Mrs. Lannigan's office. She couldn't see Della from here, and she was glad. The contrast, particularly in her present state of mind, would have been too great. Maybe, she thought, films and books were right after all, and the high point of anybody's life was the wedding. No point in bothering to find out what happened after that. It was bound to be shit. *Work and home, Claire. Keep them separate.* She shook her head and brought her attention back to what Mrs. Lannigan was saying.

"And these are the children." Mrs. Lannigan had turned the page to show a scene from a seaside holiday. Two children—Claire estimated them to be no more than two years old—were staring at the camera. The boy was holding a bucket and spade; the girl was holding her mother's hand. The mother, looking rather cross about something, was pointing out of the picture, obviously encouraging the children to look into the camera. The photographer, she assumed, was Victor. Both kids were frowning. It could have been amusing. Catch kids the wrong way, particularly little kids, and they all looked like miniature Churchills. But Claire thought that wasn't what had happened here. She suspected that neither of these kids had done a great deal of smiling when they were little.

"Not really many photographs after that," said Mrs. Lannigan. "It may have been the last time Victor went on holiday with them. May have been the last time they ever went on holiday, the poor little mites. There wouldn't have been a lot of money around when the breadwinner of the household ran off. Ah, here we are." She had turned to the last page and its solitary photograph. "Last year. We threw a surprise party for Della. Well, I say surprise. Almost every day is a surprise for her now, poor thing. She wouldn't have expected it if we'd told her about it the day before. Anyway, we had a bit of a party and Graham came along. That's him there."

There was no problem working out who was Graham in the picture. Only one man was under seventy and not in a dressing gown. Della was seated in the centre of the picture, a conical party hat on her head at a drunken angle. In the background there were residents and a beaming Mrs. Lannigan. Graham stood by the side of his mother's chair. He was holding her hand, pointing at the camera, possibly asking her to smile. Della was frowning. It was like a sad mirror image of that seaside picture from over fifty years before. Even in the poor-quality photograph, Claire could see how shabby Graham's donkey jacket looked, the sleeves too short, and that rip in his jeans probably had more to do with wear and tear than fashion.

Mrs. Lannigan tutted disapprovingly. "No daughter, you see? You expect a girl to be closer to her mother, don't you? That's why I'm glad I've got girls. Have you got children, Officers?"

"No," said Dave.

"Two. Boys," said Claire. "Both very loving."

"Well, it's to be hoped the boy doesn't take after his father."

"I'm sorry?" Dave sounded aghast.

"I think," Claire said carefully, "that's not really the sort of thing people say these days, is it?"

"Isn't it?" Mrs. Lannigan looked surprised. "Well? Maybe we speak our minds more up north."

"There's honest and there's…" Dave began.

"But an abusive man is an abusive man, no matter how you want to dress it up and excuse it away," Mrs. Lannigan said over him.

Dave stopped. "What?"

"An abusive man?" Claire said. "Victor Whyte?"

"Well, yes. I assumed you knew. To be honest, I thought that might have had something to do with why he'd been killed. You know, his nasty ways catching up with him." She folded her arms and spoke each word very clearly. "Victor Whyte was a wife-beater."

★

"The son?"

"We've got nothing else."

Driving them back from their visit to Brightholme House, Dave looked dubious. "These straws we're grabbing at are getting…strawier and strawier."

Claire snorted. "And they say it's the Welsh who are supposed to have a way with language."

"You're thinking that the son waited all this time to avenge his mother? Why?"

Claire shrugged. "You said yourself: Victor's shame was still with him years later. Perhaps the son's resentment at being abandoned so young was too. Or perhaps something in the son's own life triggered him."

"And how would he know where his father was? As far as we can tell, Victor completely cut all ties with his family and that town."

"Maybe Victor junior grew up to be a detective."

"Well in that case, we don't want to arrest him; we want to offer him a job 'cause he's making a better fist of this than we are."

They drove on, the winding rounds around Robertston giving way to major roads and then motorways.

"Are we sure we believe Mrs. Lannigan? About Victor abusing his wife?" Dave said.

"What reason would she have to lie?"

"She'd only have been young at the time. Kids often get the wrong end of the stick."

Claire thought about Sam, her youngest, and what he might, in years to come, make of his parents' marriage. *Work and home.* "Small communities have long memories. Trust me. I could tell you things about neighbours in Pontypridd who've been dead for fifty years."

"Victor was a man walking out on his family. That wouldn't have made him popular with a small, tightknit community like Robertstown. His wife-beating may have been a tale that grew in the telling." Dave paused. "And Della Whyte can't have been the easiest woman to live with."

"Don't even go there, Sergeant."

"All right. But imagine this. You're a young, gay man, growing up in a small, remote place like Robertston."

"I'd get out, as soon as I could."

"Like you did from Pontypridd?"

"That had been the plan. I…kind of got caught. Not about Victor. Move on."

"Okay, but I say again: this was fifty years ago. Back then, a lad like Victor wouldn't have thought there was anything wrong with Robertston. He would have thought there was something wrong with him. He would have tried desperately hard to fit in."

"So, he sleeps with women?"

"One woman. And from what Mrs. Lannigan was suggesting about Della and her family, I'm guessing Della didn't play hard to get. There's Victor, all his mates bragging about the girls they're shagging, and along comes Della who's only too happy to make him a man. Help him become one of the lads. And then to confirm his feelings that the universe hates him, she falls pregnant first time. So, he has to marry her. Like I said, *expectations.* There's no way out, at least, none that a teenager can see. And he tries to make it work, he really tries, because he is a good man. But he can't. So…he lashes out."

"At Della."

"Who else?"

"I can see it, Dave. But it doesn't make it right."

"I'm not saying it does. And I don't think Victor thought it was right either. In fact, I'm thinking that's the real reason he left Robertston. Not to find some gay Nirvana—he ran away to Worcester, for God's sake—but to go somewhere where his misery wouldn't blight the lives of his wife and kids. He probably thought it was the end of his life whereas in fact it was the beginning. And maybe, all the good he did with his life from then on wasn't just gay activism—it was trying to make up for what he'd done to his wife and kids."

They drove on in silence for a few miles.

"Would you have married?" Claire asked.

"In that time and that place? Who knows? Probably. I may not have had it as bad as Victor, but I grew up in a family, in a world, expecting me to be straight too, and I dated for a while. A girl I mean. Trying to fit in, like Victor did."

"The girl with the kohl-rimmed eyes?" Claire said, recalling their conversation in the Switchboard office.

"Katherine. Kat, as she preferred. Laughable, looking back at it. She was a bit of a rebel, kicking out against society, conformity, all that sort of crap. I was the most conformist lad you could hope to meet, on the outside at least. Inside, though, a churning mass of confusion and uncertainty. We probably thought we saw something in each other that we needed."

Claire looked at her sergeant. She didn't know if it was Dave's opening up or her own emotional rawness caused by the previous night's showdown with Ian, but she found herself unexpectedly touched by what he had confided in her. "I can't imagine you…vulnerable," she said.

"It didn't last," said Dave bluntly. "And neither did the thing with Kat. Funny though." He smiled fondly, "I do still feel a bit guilty about it."

Claire's phone pinged. "Civilisation! Wi-Fi." She pulled out her mobile. "I've got messages."

When she came off the phone, her expression was grim. "Change of plan. Take us to Roz Joynson's place. You still got the address in the sat nav?"

"Yes." Dave reached forward to key it in. "What's up?"

"Tom Adams called the station. He says she's been attacked. By the same man he saw at that befriending."

★

"Oh, it's you."

"Is that what you say to everyone when they ring on your door?" snapped Claire. "Didn't your mam teach you any manners?"

"He's comforting me, darlin'," came Roz's voice from within her flat. "Come in and comfort me too."

With bad grace, Tom stepped aside to let Summerskill and Lyon in.

"Lovely to see you, sweethearts." Roz came out into her hallway. "Come in, come in. Let me get you a cup of tea. Nothing like that muck we get at Switchboard either."

They followed her into her living room, which was tiny, or at least, that was the first impression it gave. Looking closer, Dave could see that it was actually a fair-sized room but was packed to the gunnels with books and… Well, he wasn't sure how he would have described the rest of what it was packed with. Art pieces? Museum pieces? Junk? On shelves he saw cases containing stuffed animals, although one of them seemed to contain a wellington boot and a flute. A gorgeous old phonogram was complete with a large metal trumpet out of which a sunflower poked. On the walls hung pictures ranging from apparently traditional watercolours to the most baffling of abstract pieces. And one large black-and-white photograph in a gold frame was frankly pornographic. Dave suspected it might also be illegal and determined not to look at it. There was also the smell: an undeniable and instantly recognisable, earthy smell, masked, though not very successfully by something else. He caught Claire's eye. *Patchouli,* he mouthed.

"Sit yourselves down," Roz fussed, plumping up two enormous, hand-crocheted cushions on her settee. "Tom, be a love and bring in the tea. I've laid the tray out ready."

Rather to the officers' surprise, Tom did as he was bid immediately.

"He is an angel," Roz murmured. "I'll admit, I was in a bit of a tizz so it was lovely having him here. It was he who insisted I call you. I wasn't sure I should bother you. And what can you do anyway?"

"Roz," said Claire. "What has happened? The message said you'd been attacked."

"Oh dear." Roz put her hand to her heart. "I think that may have been Tom being a little overdramatic. He is inclined that way you know." Claire's expression made it clear that she knew this about Tom. "I was walking home from the Hive.

I got this feeling, you know the kind of thing, when you sense that someone is looking at you. There's actually a lot of scientific evidence now to show that humans…"

"Roz," said Claire. "Please."

"Sorry, sweetheart. Anyway, the feeling grew as I got nearer to home even though there were fewer people about. I kept looking over my shoulder and that's when I knew. I wasn't imagining it. I was being followed. By a man. I sped up a bit and he sped up too. By this time, I was in the park, and it was getting dark. There was no one else around except for him, So I sped up again and he did too. I started running and he ran too. He caught up to me outside the flat. I was trying to open the door, but I couldn't get the key out fast enough. He came right up to me. I really didn't know what to do. He reached for me as if he was going to grab me…" With a storyteller's instincts, Roz paused. Claire frowned in annoyance but waited. "And then Tom turned up. I saw him coming round the corner and called out to him. The man took one look at him and ran."

"It was the man who attacked me." Roz's unlikely rescuer came back in bearing a tea tray. He set it down on a small table.

"Not those brownies, dear." Roz rose and removed a biscuit tin. "They're for…other occasions."

"You weren't attacked, Tom," said Claire. "And I don't mean to downplay what happened to you, Roz, but technically, neither were you."

"I know. I completely agree," said Roz. "I wasn't sure even whether or not to bother you with it. But when Tom said it was the same man who had…whom he had seen, we thought it best. So here we are. Shall I be mother?"

"Are you all right, Roz?" Dave asked as Roz set about pouring the tea.

She gave him a grateful smile. "I'm fine, thank you."

"Here you go…Claire." Tom handed out a cup.

"Thank you. And you can call me Inspector Summerskill. Roz, can you describe the man?" She held up a warning hand. "Succinctly, please. Police speak, no poetry."

"Oh, sweetheart. You crush the lily in my soul." But Roz obliged.

"You see," said Tom. "It's the same guy. The guy from the befriending and the guy who was stalking me."

"Hardly stalking, Tom," said Claire.

"You saw him clearly, then?" Dave asked.

"Not clearly as such. But well enough to know it was him. And Roz's description matches the one I gave you, doesn't it?"

Claire reached into her coat pocket and pulled out the photos that Mrs. Lanigan, after only a little persuasion, had let them take away. She chose the most recent, the one from Della's birthday party, and held it up. "Did he look something like this, Roz?"

Roz jammed on the thick glasses hanging on a chain round her neck and inspected the picture. "No, sweetheart. He didn't look something like this." She took off her glasses and beamed at Summerskill and Lyon with childlike pleasure. "He looked *exactly* like this."

"Let me see," said Tom. "Yes! That's him. That's the guy who…I saw."

"Straws getting a bit less strawy?" Claire asked Dave.

"Will we get some sort of police protection now, then?" Tom said.

"What?"

"Come on. There's a guy running around out there with a grudge against switchboard. It's obvious, isn't it? He's a serial…"

"Don't say it!" Claire snapped.

Tom looked put out by her rebuff.

"Not wanting to downplay what's happened," Dave said, "but technically you can't be a serial killer if you've only killed one person. And it's much more realistic to look for a proper motive than jump to the assumption he's a psychopath."

"Well, even so. Don't you think we deserve some sort of protection?"

"We don't even know yet that the man you and Roz have seen, who, let me remind you, has not actually laid a finger on either of you, is the man who murdered Victor Whyte. Although," Dave said, holding up a hand to stop Tom butting in, "we obviously need to find him and talk to him to find out what is going on. Besides, no way have we got the manpower to post an officer to look after every switchboard operator, even if you have got fewer now than in the past."

"Well, all right then," Tom said with a grumpy face. "But at least put one on Roz."

"Sweet boy," Roz said, placing her hand on his arm.

"We'll make sure someone checks in regularly. On both of you. And if you like," Dave went on, making sure he wasn't facing Claire as he said it, "we'll give you a lift back to your flat."

"'S all right." Tom sounded somewhat appeased. "Thanks, but I'm going to hang on here for a bit. Roz said she's going to dig out a book for me."

"Oh, that's right, isn't it?" Roz exclaimed. "I'm so sorry. What with all the excitement, I nearly forgot. You wanted that second volume of my poetry, didn't you? Hang on here a moment, darlin', and I'll go and fetch it."

"What?" Tom demanded, once Roz had gone out of the room and he was left with the smiling police officers. "It's for an essay I'm writing, okay?"

★

"Okay," said Claire, as she and Dave walked back into their office at Foregate Street. "We are not going to post armed guards on all the members of Switchboard, but we do need to do a ring round and let them all know that they need to be careful, without actually scaring the shit out of them. And we need to get this copied and circulated. Jen."

"Photocopying bitch at your beck and call." Jenny Trent came over from where she had been depositing paperwork on DS Cortez's desk, took the photo from Claire, and headed out of the office.

"All right. We get that on the local telly news and in the papers and social media. Fancy doing another interview?" Dave's reaction to that suggestion was clear. "We'll get some posters printed out and put up round the Halo Centre and near Roz and Tom's places too. 'Have you seen this man?' That kind of thing."

"Hive might be an idea too?"

"Good one. Can't hurt. And by the same token, we could put up a load around the university lecture halls, specifically any that Tom is likely to go to, in case our man has been stalking him there."

"With all due respect, though, it's still pissing into the wind, isn't it? I mean the chances of finding this guy this way are…"

"I think I know your man."

All eyes turned to new recruit Baz South who was striding through the office doorway, the picture Claire had given Jenny in his hand. Aware that he was suddenly the centre of attention, he stopped. "I mean, sorry, Inspector. Ma'am. Sir. I didn't mean to barge…"

Claire waved the flustered young man's apology to one side. "You know him?"

"Well, I've met him. Seen him, I mean. He didn't look as good as this though." Baz began to wilt under the pressure of so many high-ranking eyes on him. "At least I think I saw him."

"When, Constable? And where?"

Baz collected himself. "It was a few days ago. Three days," he said hastily when he saw Claire's irritated expression. "Late night beat, Monday. I was with PC Jones." He smiled at Dave as if expecting some praise for this unexceptional detail. "Yes, well, he was down and out in a shop doorway."

"Down and out? What do you mean, Constable? Was he drunk? Stoned?"

"Probably. I mean, I don't know which. I thought drunk. Whatever, he wasn't really with it. If you know what I mean?"

Claire made a mental note to have a word with Chris McNeil, the lad's mentor. If this rookie was ever let loose on a witness stand before being taught how to give a proper statement, any half-decent lawyer would rip him to shreds. "Tell us what happened."

"Joe—PC Jones—and me, we came across him getting on for midnight. I can check the exact times in my logs."

"Yes, yes. Go on."

"He was asleep in a shop doorway. Poole's. We explained he had to move on. It took a bit of getting through to him, but he got the message in the end, and got to his feet. We told him about the night shelter at St. Thad's, pointed him in the right direction, and off he went."

"Did he have a sleeping bag?" Dave asked.

"No."

"Cardboard boxes? Newspapers for sheets?"

"No, none of that."

Dave looked to Claire. "Doesn't sound like he was set up for it."

"What was his mood like?" Claire asked. "Was he argumentative? Aggressive?"

"No, ma'am. Biddable, I suppose you'd say. Didn't complain. Didn't say much of anything, really. Wouldn't give his name or say what he was doing there, but he did say he'd go to St. Thad's when we told him about it. He was last seen heading in that direction."

"St. Thad's?" Dave looked thoughtful. He turned quickly to the computer on his desk.

"All right," said Claire. "Thank you, Constable. Good work. Go and get your logs and send us the exact details. Dave, you and I can go and check on…"

"St. Thad's." Dave looked up from his screen. "I'm on it. But I've got a feeling our man's not there any more."

"Well no. But we might be able to find out where he's gone from there. Any thing's better than…"

"I think I know where he's gone. You remember Wednesday morning's inci dent log?"

Dave was referring to the summary sheets of the previous night's activity that were given to each officer at the start of their shift. Claire had a neat pile of the recent ones on one corner of her desk and was quite pleased at how organised they looked. She hadn't read any of them. "Let's say some of the details may have slipped my memory," she said. "Go on."

"Yesterday's morning sheet referenced St. Thad's. I couldn't remember ex actly what it said—"

"Memory going?"

"—so, I've looked it up. At half one the previous night, they had to call an ambulance to take a transient to the Worcester Royal Infirmary. Suspected over dose. Bit of a long shot but…"

"Send a copy of Graham Whyte's picture to the infirmary."

"And they say only woman have intuition," Jenny said, as Dave was leaving the room with the photograph. She was facing Terry Cortez with her back to the rest of the office, but her remark was easily loud enough to be heard by everyone there.

"Intuition my arse," snapped Claire. "Good policing is what."

Jenny Trent flushed and hurried from the office.

Dave was back in ten minutes. "Confirmation. Provisionally, anyway. The Royal says that they may indeed have the man in our picture."

"Right. Grab your coat and let's…"

"That was the good news. The bad news is, he's dead."

"Yes, that's our man. Thank you."

The young woman pulled the sheet up over the face of the dead man and pushed his gurney back into the storage unit.

"Cause of death?" Claire asked.

"We've not had time to do the full autopsy yet, of course, but initial indicators suggest some kind of drug overdose. Plus, there was a half-empty bottle of prescription painkillers next to a nearly empty bottle of whisky."

"Prescription painkillers? Nothing illegal, then?" Dave asked.

"Well, we'll know for sure when we do the blood, but if he'd taken only half of the pills in the one bottle on top of half the whisky in the other bottle, then that would have been more than enough to kill him." The doctor smiled, more like some perky shop assistant than the person apparently in current charge of the Royal's morgue. "Sorry."

"No, no. We understand, Dr…Harris, did you say?"

"Jane Harris, yes." The young doctor stretched out a hand to shake Dave's but snatched it back when she remembered she was wearing latex gloves and where they had been.

"Nice to meet you. Our usual port of call in these matters is, shall we say, a little less easy to get along with."

Dr. Harris's face lit up. "Oh, do you mean Dr. Aldridge?"

"Er, yes," said Dave, aware that he may have been caught out being unprofessional. "Do you know him?"

"Only by reputation."

"Ah well, believe me, everything you've heard is probably true."

"Wow. That good?"

"I'm sorry?"

"All I heard on the training course was about how great Worcester's Dr. Aldridge is. When I got this position here it was like, wow, I might get to meet him."

"You know what they say about meeting your heroes?" Claire said. "Never mind. How long till you can get us a toxicology report?"

Dr. Harris consulted a clipboard attached to the freezer cabinet. "Not until the middle of next week I'm afraid," she said cheerily.

"Make it tomorrow." Claire gave her a mirthless smile. "Sorry, but this is now a murder investigation. It bumps things up the list. Hope you enjoy your new job. C'mon, you," she said to Dave.

Dave gave Dr. Harris a more sympathetic smile as they left.

★

St Thad's, a row of former workers' cottages a stone's throw from the city centre, had survived the wholesale destruction of Worcester's medieval heart in the sixties by dint of its proximity to the cathedral. Ten years previously, after a succession of different uses over the decades, the ramshackle collection of small buildings had been appropriated by a charity for rough sleepers. Now, it was very often the place to which bobbies on the night beats would direct the down-and-outs they came across in shop doorways, bus shelters, and the like.

Summerskill and Lyon were met by a young man in jeans and an overlarge badly knitted jumper who looked ready, there and then, to confess to any crime the two might have chosen to accuse him of. He introduced himself as Paul and showed them to the room Graham Whyte had been given when he had arrived at their door three nights previously. It was tiny, the walls whitewashed and bare of any decoration, two trestle beds on either side taking up almost all the available space. As he took it in, Dave was reminded of the almost equally cramped Switchboard office. He felt an unexpected pang of pity that father and son had both ended their lives in such humble places. And then he reminded himself that, quite possibly, Graham Whyte was the man who had strangled his own father,

"And you hadn't met Mr. Whyte before the night he came here?" Claire asked Paul.

"No. He turned up late, a couple of minutes before the eleven fifty-nine lockdown. I know," he said, "that a lockdown sounds a bit gothic and harsh, but we find it works. After midnight, we don't take anyone in. Usually, all our beds are taken by then anyway, especially at this time of year. Graham was lucky." Paul bit his lip, his eyes moving nervously from one to the other of them. If he'd been behaving like this in an interview room, Dave would have sworn he was trying to keep something from them. "Me and Ethan, that's the guy I was on duty with, we were about to shut down for the night, so we cut corners a bit, made sure Graham had a room to sleep in, and let him get on with it. We thought we could do the usual processing in the morning. But the next day…" He let the sentence hang.

"Processing?" Claire asked.

"Sorry. Taking his details, as many as he would have been ready to give, checking his health, that kind of thing. Our main aim is to provide an emergency bed for the night, but if there's anything more long-term we can do, then we try our best."

"I see. And what kind of state was he in?"

And this, thought Dave, watching Paul's reactions, was the point where he would have cracked in an interview room and completely spilled his guts. "Okay," Paul burst out, "maybe I should have done more, maybe I should have said or done omething, but I never thought…" And he threw himself down onto one of the beds, shoved his head into a pillow, and began to cry, great, heaving sobs.

Claire turned to Dave and rolled her eyes. *Over to you,* she mouthed.

Thank you very much, he mouthed back. He knelt to one side of the bed, ducking his head, trying to see the lad's face. "Paul? We're not here to accuse anybody of anything. We're just trying to find out what happened."

Paul lifted his head from the pillow, hiccoughed, and sniffed. "Really? It's… You see, there was something wrong with Graham when he turned up. I could tell there was. He was slurring, didn't really seem that sure where he was, you know?"

"Do you think he was drunk or under the influence of drugs?"

Paul had yanked a handkerchief from his jeans pocket and was busy blowing his nose. "I thought he was drunk. I should have tried harder to find out if that's what it was; I know I should. We've got all these questions we're supposed to ask to make sure about things like that. But it was late, and…I didn't. I told myself he was drunk and that he'd be fine in the morning. That the worst that could happen would be he'd wake up with a hangover. But he… But he…"

"It's okay," Dave said gently.

Claire indicated the second bed in the room. "Was there anybody else in here with Mr. Whyte that night?"

Paul wiped his nose with his handkerchief and shoved it back into his pocket. "Ken. One of our regulars. When you rang to say you were coming, Ethan went into town to see if he could find him. He's in the office now."

"Now that," said Dave, "is very useful. Thank you, Paul."

Paul gave him a wobbly, grateful smile.

Waiting for them in the office was another earnest young man in a slightly better-fitting jumper, with a much older, much less well-scrubbed man. From under his beanie, a profusion of grey hair erupted, to merge with the wildness of his equally grey beard. Even though they were indoors, and the office was pleasantly warm, this man kept his raincoat on. The bulk of it suggested he had several other layers on underneath. After a quick glance at the police officers when they came in, he dropped his head and sat, staring at the floor. Dave thanked Ethan who scuttled from the room to join Paul, and Summerskill and Lyon focused their attention on the man siting morosely in front of them.

"Hello, Ken," Claire said.

The bearded man mumbled something neither of the detectives could make out.

"We understand that you were in this room last night with Graham Whyte."

More mumbling.

"Did you talk at all during the night?"

Ken shoved a hand into one of the pockets of his raincoat and pulled out handkerchief. It was considerably grimier than the one Paul had used. He hawked something up into it, peered closely to see what it was, shrugged, and shoved th handkerchief back. "Might have done."

"Work with us here, Ken," Claire said. Dave readied himself to step in.

Ken darted her a hostile look. "He cried a lot. Fuckin' nuisance. Kept m awake for ages."

"He was upset? Did he say anything?"

Ken's expression changed, became craftier. "Anything in this for me? Any like, reward for information, that kind of thing?"

"Yeah, next time a constable finds you on the street at night, you get sent her again, and not to one of our cells." Claire gave him a thin smile. "Reward enough?

Ken grunted. "Nah. He didn't say much. He didn't!" he insisted in the face o Claire's evident disbelief. "Just…odd words."

"What odd words, Ken?"

"'Dad.' He said, 'Dad,' a lot. And, 'Sorry.' And once he said, 'Didn't mea to.'"

"Did you see him take any pills, Ken?"

"There was no drugs!" Ken jerked back in alarm. "No drugs."

"Not drugs. Not drugs in that sense, anyway. Listen, please, this is importan Did you see him take any pills while he was in here with you?"

Ken looked at Claire distrustfully. "No." He appeared pleased that he coul give an unhelpful answer. "He curled up on that bed there, in his coat, and moane and complained and cried until he fell asleep. Least, I thought he fell asleep."

Claire looked at Dave and shook her head. They'd got as much useful infor mation out of this man as they were going to. "Thank you for your help, Mr…?"

"Ken."

"Right. Ken. Stay out of trouble."

Ken grinned at her. Most of his teeth were missing.

★

"So, is that it?"

"Looks like it."

Dave pulled a face. "But all we have is a dead suspect with a pretty shaky motive."

"Identified as the man who was harassing both Tom Adams and Roz Joynson." Claire opened the car door and got in.

"So," said Dave after he'd joined her in the car, "a man with unresolved daddy issues who waits nearly fifty years before he does something about them, strangles his father in an office where other people might see him, rather than in his home away from prying eyes. He then spends the next few days wandering around Worcester, bumping into Switchboard operatives and scaring the shit out of them before taking an overdose of prescription pills and booking himself into a hostel to die."

"You see any problems with that?"

"Only if you tell me you don't."

Claire threw her head back and ran her fingers through her hair. "Of course I do. It's got more holes than one of Sam's jumpers. All right!" She sat up in the car seat with renewed determination. "One last shot. You've got Clive Grover's number?"

"Of course."

"Find out where he is. Roz, Tom, and him seem to have been the closest to Victor. Roz and Tom were threatened by Graham Whyte." She made air quotes round the word "threatened". "We've presumed Clive wasn't because he hasn't told us anything, but maybe he was approached. Seeing Graham's photo might jog his memory and give us some more information about what's been going on."

"We're clutching at straws again, aren't we?"

"It's what the little pig made his house from."

"What?"

"Sam's favourite bedtime story."

"You do know what happened to that little pig's house?"

Claire shrugged. "Sold and turned into flats? I don't know. Sam always falls asleep before the end."

"I worry about your children sometimes." Dave reached for his phone. "Goo luck," he said after a short call. "Grover's working from home today." He starte up the car.

"And that's lucky because…?"

"We get another piece of Trevor's cake."

Claire waved a finger at him. "Only if you've been a good boy."

"Oh, it's you," Tom said to the unexpected visitor on his front doorstep. H leaned forward to see if there was anyone else. There wasn't. "Bit of a surprise. Ca I help you?"

A surprisingly strong arm reached up and out and shoved him backwards int his hallway, the figure on the doorstep following through and closing the door o Tom's muffled cry of surprise and alarm.

"May I offer you some tea, Inspector?"

"That's very kind, Mr. Grover, but I'm afraid this is only a flying visit." Clair outlined the reason for their visit and held out the photograph of Graham Whyt on his last visit to his mother at Brightholme.

Grover took it, polished his glasses, and looked closely. "No. No, I'm sorry but I don't think I have seen this man."

"You're sure? If you've not actually met him, might you have seen him, mayb hanging around the Halo Centre for instance? Or even near your house."

Grover looked at the picture again, studying it carefully, but, at the end handed it back with a shake of his head. "No, I'm afraid I honestly don't think have ever seen this man."

"I have."

Claire jumped slightly. Trevor, as softly spoken as before, had been standin so quietly in the background that she had forgotten he was there. He stepped for ward now. Grover's face twitched with irritation, and it looked like he was abou to reprimand his partner, but Claire pre-empted him. "Really? Could you have proper look at this, please?"

Trevor took the picture from the inspector and studied it. He nodded deter-
minedly. "Yes. I thought I recognised him. I've seen him around Switchboard when
I've gone to pick Clive up."

"Well, I've never seen him there," Clive said with a touch of pique.

"It's only been in the last month or so," Trevor said, almost apologetically.
"It's when I've been waiting for you outside the office." Trevor gave Summerskill
and Lyon a happy smile. "I'm not allowed into the office. I have to wait outside."

Like a naughty schoolboy, Claire thought. She pushed the faintly disturbing image
from her mind.

"Confidentiality," Clive said. "Wouldn't do to have non-Switchboard people
seeing or hearing things they shouldn't."

"Quite." Claire didn't look at him. All her attention was on Trevor. "Did you
ever talk to him? Did he give you his name?"

Trevor shook his head. "No, I'm not allowed... I mean, I don't talk to
strangers very much. It was only two or three times. I think he came to pick up his
wife."

"His wife?"

Trevor nodded happily. "Yes. At least, I assumed they're married. They could
just be living together I suppose."

Claire tried to fit this new and unexpected information into the picture. "Is
his wife another Switchboard operative, then?"

Trevor laughed. "No. She's one of the cleaners."

"Hang on a minute!" Dave opened his notebook and pulled out of it the other
pictures that Mrs Lannigan had given them. He picked one out and studied it for a
moment. "Oh my God!" he breathed. He held up the picture of Graham Whyte,
his mother, and his sister at the seaside. "Recognise anyone here?"

Trevor and Clive both leaned in to see better. "Good lord," said Clive. "That
little girl."

Claire snatched the picture off Dave. Fifty years brought a lot of changes to a
person, especially if her life had been one of hardship and disappointment. But
even so, some things didn't change: the line of the jaw, the look in the eyes. It had
been there all along in plain sight, but they hadn't seen it simply because they hadn't
been looking for it. All their attention had been on the boy and not on the girl.

Scowling out of the photograph was Karen Haines. Not Graham's wife—his
sister, and Victor Whyte's other abandoned child.

★

"What d'you think you're…?"

"Is anybody else here?"

Tom stared in confusion at Karen Haines, standing in his hallway, blockin his exit through the front door. He still couldn't believe she'd pushed him like tha What was she playing at? "Yes," he lied.

Karen's face didn't change. "Call them."

"No."

She took a step towards him. "Call them," she repeated.

This is ridiculous. She's a woman. She's one of the cleaners. I'm in my own home. She can order me around. This is crazy. But even as the thoughts crashed around his head, Tor took in Karen's stolid build, her hunched, tensed stance, and the implacable ex pression on her face. He did not want to cross this woman. He was beginning to be afraid of her. "All right. All right. There's nobody else here. What do you want?"

"What did he tell you?"

Tom blinked in confusion. "Who? Who are you talking about?"

"Victor Whyte." The woman practically spat the name out. "What did he te you?"

"About what?"

"About Graham. About me?"

Tom shook his head. "I don't understand. Who's Graham? And why woul Victor have told me anything about you?"

"He liked you, didn't he? Victor?"

Tom licked his lips. He had no idea what this woman wanted, but he had n doubt that she was crazy. Desperately, he wondered if he could make a break fo it, not try to run past her but run back into the house and out through the bac door. But there were two closed doors between him and the outside. Haines woul be sure to catch him before he got very far at all. "Yes. Yes, I think he did." H prayed he'd given her the answer she wanted.

"Did you fuck?"

"What?"

"Did he fuck you?"

"Right, that's…" Outrage momentarily overcoming his fear, Tom took a step towards the woman. Karen reached into her coat and pulled out a kitchen knife.

With a small, inarticulate cry, Tom fell back, almost stumbling, only keeping his balance by flailing his hands against the wall, knocking a mirror askew as he did.

The doorbell rang.

Karen stood, watching Tom. Tom's mouth was dry. With everything he had in him, he wanted to call out to whoever it was on the other side of the door, beg them to break in and rescue him. But whoever it was obviously didn't have a key, and if he did call out there would be no way they could get in before Haines sliced into him with her knife.

The doorbell rang again, and a voice called out. "Tom? Come on, Tom. I know you're in. Seb told me. Open up, please." It was Emily.

Tom opened his mouth, but nothing came out.

Karen Haines raised her knife and began to walk towards him.

★

"That was Emily Tufton." Dave replaced his mobile in his pocket. "She says she's worried about Tom."

"What's new?"

"No, seriously worried. She says she's called on Tom, but he was leaving the house with someone and didn't want to talk to her."

Still working through the ramifications of Karen Haines's involvement with Victor's murder, Claire was short. "So, they've had a tiff. I don't…"

"The other someone was a woman. In Emily's words, big, grim, not another student. She thought Tom looked frightened."

"Haines?"

"Could be."

Claire assessed the situation. "Okay. We're what, two, three minutes from Tom's flat here? They can't get far from it by foot. C'mon."

★

They were met outside Tom's flat by a frantic Emily and another young man they didn't recognise. "Oh, thank heavens you're here," she said as soon as she saw

Dave. "I wasn't sure you'd come. I mean, perhaps I'm overreacting. But with everything that's been going on, I thought perhaps…"

"You did the right thing," Dave said.

"Can you tell us what's happened, please, Miss Tufton?" Claire said.

"I always call in on Tom about this time of day," Emily said, still addressing most of her comments to Dave. "But at first he wouldn't answer the door. Then when he did come out, he hadn't got his coat or scarf on and, I mean, it's freezing. And there was this woman with him, big, older, but she looked…hard, you know what I mean?"

"I think we do," said Dave grimly.

"I couldn't understand what she was doing coming out of the flat. At first, thought she wasn't with Tom, but then they walked away, and she was right behind him, I mean, really close behind him, almost touching."

"Did he say anything?"

"He said, 'I'm fine. Go away. Don't follow us.' But he looked so frightened. don't think that's what he wanted to say. I didn't know what to do. I didn't… Overcome finally by her fears, Emily threw herself forward onto Dave and sobbed uncontrollably on his shoulder.

"You did the right thing," Dave said again, patting her awkwardly on the shoulder before gently pushing her back from him.

"Did you see any weapon?"

Emily gave Claire a horrified look but shook her head.

"I think we've got to assume she has something," Claire said to Dave. "Which way did they go?" she asked Emily. She looked in the direction Emily pointed. "Why down there? The only thing that way is…"

"The river," said Dave.

"C'mon. They've got a good five, ten minutes on us. If we take the car, we might be able to head them off before they actually reach it."

"Don't worry," Dave called back to Emily as he ran after Summerskill. "He'll be okay. Go home and we'll call you when it's all over."

★

He didn't have time to question Claire's jumping into the driver's seat. He only just had time to wonder why, given that every other time she made him drive efore they were off, and he was scrambling to fasten his seat belt as they careered alarming speed along the narrow roads between Tom's flat and the river. "Lights nd siren?" he shouted, partly to take his mind off the near collision with another r as they shot through a red light.

"No. I don't want her spooked. Get on the radio for backup and tell them I ant them coming in silent too."

"O-whoa-kay!" Dave exclaimed as a sharp left turn left a fuming cyclist in eir wake, shaking his fist.

Dave put in the terse call for backup, keeping his voice as level as he could hen a sudden spurt of speed and a swerve right put them briefly in the path of a rry before Claire pulled back left in front of a dawdling Ford Fiesta that had been owing them down. "You're...you're actually very good at this, aren't you?"

"Why surprised?" Claire snapped, eyes fixed fiercely on the road.

"Because you always get me to do the driving."

"Why keep a dog and bark yourself?"

With a spray of gravel, they pulled into a small parking space by the side of e river, leaped out, and quickly scanned the area.

"What's she up to?"

"It's November," Claire said. "You know what happens this time of year, reg- ar as bloody clockwork. Dead student in the river. Moody started calling it the Curse of the Severn'. Didn't stop to think about kids new to the city, away from ome for the first time, out on the lash and walking home along the riverbank blind runk. I'm only amazed we don't get more."

"You think...?"

"I don't know what to think. And I don't think Haines does either. But I don't ink she was taking him for a walk for his health. There!" Claire stabbed a finger a path about a hundred yards away, and the two figures moving to the end of it wards the riverbank.

"All right," said Claire. "You go up that way and come back down behind em. I'll meet her head on. Move it!" She waited until Dave had made a start and en picked up her own pace, fast enough to meet up with Tom and Karen before ey got to the side of the water, but hopefully not so fast as to frighten the woman to doing something rash. She was about thirty yards away from them before Tom gistered her. *Don't say anything*, she prayed, hoping for at least a few more seconds fore Haines clocked her. She had three before Haines's head snapped up, and aire knew she had been recognised. "Hello, Karen," she called out.

Tom gasped with relief and made a move towards Claire, but Claire saw Haines lean into him, say something, and nudge him in the back with one of her hands which was thrust into her long coat. Tom stopped moving, staring helplessly at Claire.

"Go away!" Haines shouted.

"You know I can't, Karen." Claire took a step towards them.

"Keep back." Haines pulled her hand out of her pocket, and a kitchen knife caught the pale afternoon sunlight.

"Okay. Okay." Claire stopped and held up her hands. The two women stood warily regarding each other. Haines was breathing heavily. "Let Tom walk over to me, Karen. Then we can have a proper talk."

"No."

"All right. What do you want to do now, then? Where do you see this going?"

"Shut up!"

Claire watched Haines's hand on the knife—tightening and relaxing, tightening and relaxing. She counted to five in her head and then spoke again. "Seriously? You know there isn't anywhere you can go from here. It would make things a lot easier for everyone if you put the knife down now and…"

"I said, shut up." Karen raised the knife. Tom whimpered.

Trying not to give away what she was doing, Claire glanced at the path behind Haines and Tom. Still no sign of Dave. And where the bloody hell was that backup? "I don't understand, Karen," she said, playing for time. "Why are you doing this?"

"He was my dad."

"Victor? We know."

"Did you know he left me? Left us?" Her words sounded choked, as if it was an effort to get them out. "When we was kids."

"We know, Karen." And there he was! At last, Dave, a hundred yards behind Haines and her hostage, moving very, very slowly towards them, wary of making the slightest sound. "But that was years ago," Claire went on, intent on keeping Haines's attention on her.

"Don't matter."

"So, what happened? It's been fifty years, Karen. Were you looking for him all that time?"

"Don't be fucking stupid! I never wanted to see him again. I wouldn't have ssed on him if he'd been on fire."

Fifty yards. "I don't…"

"It were fate. It were meant to be."

Forty yards. "What was?"

"It were fate I ended up here, in Worcester. Looking for a job, that's all. So's could keep a roof over our head, food on the table. That's all I've ever done."

"Our head? You mean for you and your brother, Graham?"

"Course I do. He could never look after himself. Soft in the head he was. It as always me and Mum looking after him, and then just me. So that's why I ended ɔ here. And there *he* was." Her tone became viciously scornful. "My dad. I didn't ven know it was him at first. It sort of crept up on me each time I saw him, heard ɪm. It was when he…when he smiled at me one day. He smiled and he said sum-at stupid and he laughed. And I knew. It were him." Her voice hardened. "And ɛ didn't even recognise me. Not once. Not until the end. When we told him."

Thirty yards. "I'm sorry, Karen," Claire said. "That must have been hard."

Haines barked a laugh. "I didn't care."

"I think you did, Karen. What daughter wouldn't? You could have left. You ɪid you didn't want to see him again, so why didn't you leave, just go away?"

"I told *him*, didn't I? Graham. I should have kept my mouth shut and my head ɔwn, but no, I had to go and tell him."

"And Graham killed Victor. But then why was he going after other Switch-ɔard operators? And why are you…?"

"Are you daft or summat?" Haines yelled. "He wanted to tell him, didn't he? raham wanted to tell *Daddy* who we were, have the big family reunion, lots of ars and hugs and apologies and everything fine again. So, I told him. No way."

Twenty yards. "But then what…?" Suddenly she saw it. "He called Switchboard, dn't he? Started talking to Victor that way." *And that's why Haines had tried to get the lder of records out of the building. She didn't want there to be anything to link Victor with her other.* Not that she and Dave had seen anything, focused as they'd been on the issing records of Dale's calls. The arrival of Clive Grover and the police must ave prevented her getting away with the folder, only leaving her time to shove it ɛhind a noticeboard, perhaps hoping she could come back and get it later. And ɛen there was the befriending. Claire turned her attention to the boy. "Did he ɪow, Tom? Did he know he was going to meet his son?"

Tom's eyes were wide with fright. "I don't know. I don't understand any of this," he shouted.

"I don't think he did, you know. Maybe Graham dropped hints, said things that made him wonder, enough that he chose you, Tom, as his partner on that befriending. Someone he could rely on to be…discreet." She was thinking "biddable". "And then when he saw Graham for the first time, he knew. He knew who Graham was."

"Yeah," said Karen. "He recognised his son."

Ten yards. "And then what?" Claire knew the unhappy truth. All too often children who found the parents who had abandoned them were then rejected a second time. "Did Victor send Graham away?"

Karen snorted. "He were the prodigal son, weren't he? The apple of his eye, his daddy's darlin'. And he loved it, Graham did. It was like everything I'd done for him had been for nothing, swept right away."

"What do you mean, everything you'd done?"

"He was never able to look after himself. Thicker than you, he was. Always had been. Mum said it was because Dad had left us when we were so little. I reckon it was 'cause she took it out on him, being the only man she could hold on to. Whatever. It was me who looked after him, kept him out of trouble. Me who gave up any chance I might have had of a decent life. And what does he do as soon as Daddy walks back onto the scene? Drops me, that's what he does."

Five yards. And now she could see Dave's face, tight with the effort of creeping forward slowly and quietly. "Then why would he…?" And finally, standing in front of a woman so crazed with grief and rage she was holding a young man at knife point, Claire saw it all. "You're right, you know," she breathed. "I have been thick."

"I wanted him to see, to see what our loving dad was really like. So, I told him to come that night, to the Halo Centre, when I knew he was on duty. Swapped my own rota to make sure I was there and on my own too. Thought we could have it out, right and proper, and Graham would see what a bastard our old man really was."

"But he wasn't, was he?"

"Yes, he was!" Karen screamed. "He lied! He told Graham how he was so glad to have him back in his life, and how he loved him, and how he was so sorry for what had happened in the past, but he'd been a different person then. He even said he was glad to see me and how he hoped we could be as close as we always should have been. And he was going to take Graham away from me."

"Take him away?"

"Let him live in his house, set him up in a proper job, look after him. Do all the things I'd done for him all my life because he hadn't been there, but better cause he was older and wiser and he was our dad. But he didn't offer to take me , did he? Oh no. I'd have been on my own. Chucked on the scrapheap again like ears ago. And I couldn't take that," she screamed, tears running down her face, not again. So, I… So, I…"

"You killed him, didn't you? It was you."

"It…it weren't planned. I just lost it. Never happened like that to me before. unny really. Used to happen to Graham all the time. Main reason he was never ole to hold down a job. But this time it were me. I didn't know I'd done it, not till were over and he was there…not moving."

Haines stood, and Claire could see her eyes unfocused on reality as, in her ead, she relived that moment. *Now, Dave!* she thought. *Now!* But her sergeant was ill that bit too far away, and within a couple of seconds, Haines had recovered her ocus on her immediate surroundings and the moment had been lost. "His fault, ally," she said dully. "He deserved it."

"And when Clive Grover turned up, Graham ran and left you to pick up the eces."

"'S what he does. 'S what he's always done." She gave a ghastly smile. "It's hat the men in my family do, isn't it?"

"But he came back. He kept coming back. To the Halo Centre. To Tom there, id Roz Joynson."

"He wanted to tell. Said he couldn't live with it. He'd wanted to go to the olice after he'd had time to get over the shock of it all, tell them everything. I had keep my eye on him that night, and the nights afterwards."

Claire glanced at the meaty hand still holding the knife tight. She had a fair ea how Haines had kept her brother by her side.

"But you couldn't keep him with you forever, could you? He went to the Halo entre, to the last place he'd seen his father alive, and he saw Tom there, the lad 's'd seen at the befriending. He tried to tell him what had happened."

"But he didn't!" Tom yelled. "He didn't tell me anything."

"And he tried to tell Roz, but Tom came along again, and he took fright."

"He was soft in the head," Karen said, almost now as if she was talking to erself. "He'd have shopped me if I'd let him. I had to stop him."

"The pills," Claire said. "You gave them to him, didn't you?"

"He was hysterical. I'd had 'em when I…when I had hard times. I knew they' calm him down."

"If he took enough of them. With alcohol. And was then turned out to wal the streets alone in November."

"He was streetwise."

Claire looked to Tom. "But you didn't know what he'd said to Victor's friend did you? Couldn't be sure they didn't know what you'd done. A couple of loos ends to tie up, Tom, then Roz, and then you'd have been in the clear. My God, wa that why you turned up at Switchboard the other night when Dave and I wer there?"

Haines shook her head. "Not Roz. I…I knew he hadn't told her. But the one—" She gave Tom a punch in the back with the empty hand. "He liked th one. I reckon he was fucking this one. Disgusting old man."

In front of her Tom was shaking his head and weeping miserably.

Almost there. "What's the plan, then, Karen? A quick push into the river an all your problems are swept away? The current's pretty fierce at this time of yea Just another dumb student falling for the Curse of the Severn. Or were you goin to help matters along by a quick bash with a rock, make it look like he'd slippe and banged his head on the way down? We know it happens. We've all seen th news." She forced herself to ignore the look of mute horror in Tom's eyes as sh outlined his murder. "But it can't happen that way now, can it? Not a good plai But then, I don't think it was a plan, really, was it? It's all spur of the moment wit you, isn't it? That'll count for something. If you can say that none of this was pre meditated." Claire held out her hand. "Give me the knife, Karen."

Just for a second, Claire thought she might get away with it.

"No!" Karen raised the knife high.

Tom screamed.

Dave leaped on Karen from behind. He wrapped his two arms around he raised arm and twisted hard. "Drop it!"

Karen Haines struggled and screamed, but the outcome was inevitable. Th knife fell to the muddy earth, and Tom ran to Claire, sobbing with relief. He wer to throw himself on her, but she shoved him to one side and ran to her sergean reaching for the cuffs in her coat pocket.

"She was going to kill me," Tom yelled, jabbing an accusatory finger at Kare "She was going to fucking kill me."

"Yeah, well, no one's all bad," Claire muttered as Dave brought Haines's arm und and she cuffed first one wrist and then the other. "You have the right to main silent…" she began.

"Looks like you've got everything in hand here, Inspector," Chris McNeil said, ghtly out of breath after a dash from the carpark, PC Baz South at his side.

"Oh, so you've made it, have you?" Dave grinned. "Come to steal the show?"

"Talking of shows." McNeil pointed back to the parking space. Alongside his ɔlice car and Summerskill and Lyon's there was now another vehicle and picking ːr way through the mud in the impractical shoes she favoured, followed as ever ʳ her cameraman, was *Midlands Now* reporter Sarah Moody.

"Shit," said Claire, as she joined them after having read Haines her rights and aving her in the charge of Constable South. "How did she find out?"

"Doesn't matter. We can't get to the car without going past her."

"You're the one she likes. You go get another fifteen minutes of fame. I'll eet you back at the station."

"Aw no. This must be your turn now. You know the deal. The grunts do all e work, and the boss steps in at the end and takes all the…hey! No! What're you ʲing? Stop!"

Claire's first thought was that her sergeant had flipped and was taking out his ɛnt-up frustrations on the approaching reporter. Too late, she saw he was looking ʳer her shoulder to Constable South. He was sprawled on the floor. Karen Haines as trying to run away, hands still handcuffed behind her back. "What the…?" It as almost comical, except it was happening in front of a reporter and her camer- ɲan. And then Claire saw where Haines was heading. "South, you prat, get up! ɪe's heading for the river."

It was too late. Haines had reached the edge of the riverbank. Before anyone ʲuld move more than a couple of steps, she had thrown herself into the swirling rrent. Strong dark currents swept the handcuffed woman away in an instant.

"Fuck!" yelled Dave, pulling off his coat and diving headfirst into the freezing ater.

Chapter Twelve

"I thought you'd be in bed."

"You mean you *hoped* I would be. And what the hell is that?"

Sean Cullen looked at the preposterously large bouquet of flowers in his hand with mannered surprise as if he were seeing it for the first time. "I thought it might be something to brighten the sick room of a man convalescing after a dip in the clear from fresh and undoubtedly icy waters of the River Severn. But given your state of obvious rude health, let's say they're a reward for your act of heroism." He gave his characteristic lopsided smile. "Well, the first part of your reward anyway."

Dave looked at his visitor and at the flowers. He took them with ill grace. "You'd better come in," he said.

"Indeed. Wouldn't do for the neighbours to see me, would it?"

"Not with half a florist's shop in your hands."

Dave led Sean into his living room, where he dropped the flowers on the dining table. He did not invite Sean to sit down.

"I had thought you'd be in the Royal. Quite probably being shot up with all manner of antibiotics. I was rather looking forward to playing the part of concerned local MP."

"Sorry to spoil your photo opportunity. They wanted me to go to the hospital for a check-up, but I told them I felt fine and would let them know if anything changed. How did you know about this anyway? It only happened a couple of hours ago."

"Connections, David. It's always connections. In this case, my very good sources from *Midlands Now*."

"Don't tell me you're sleeping with that reporter, Moody."

"God, no. Sexual preferences aside, I don't think there's a bed big enough for both of our egos."

Dave pulled a wry face. "Okay, Sean, what are you really here for?" He braced himself for another flip answer.

"I wanted to make sure you were okay."

"Oh. Right. Well, I am. Thank you."

Sean took a step towards him and then stopped. "May I congratulate you properly?"

Dave closed his eyes. The scent of that ridiculous bunch of flowers mingled with the smell of Cullen's cologne. God, he loved that smell. When he opened his eyes again, he was wearing his poker face. "Joe's coming round. He could be here any minute."

For the first time since had had met him, Dave saw Cullen look uncertain. "Ah. I don't suppose he'd be interested in helping me congratulate you? Sorry," he said quickly with a smile. "You know that's a little fantasy of mine." He hesitated. "And sometimes I can't help going for the comic line. Classic defence mechanism."

"Defence…?"

"Later, then?" Sean said, cutting Dave off.

Dave looked him in the eye. "No, Sean."

Cullen looked at him as he might have looked at someone quoting an unexpectedly high price for some antique he wanted to buy. "And is that no as in never?"

"Yes, it is."

"I see." Sean stood there, weighing up what Dave had said, much as Dave imagined he would weigh up the pros and cons of some bill in the House of Commons. "Interesting."

As he'd said to Claire that night in the Switchboard office, Sean Cullen was completely unlike any man he had ever known. Dave was reminded of that now as he stood there, not having a clue how he was going to react. "What is?" he said finally.

"Would you think it very arrogant of me if I said that I've never actually been dumped before?"

"I'm not dumping you, Sean. We were never in that kind of relationship."

"If you say so." Sean continued to stand, looking thoughtful. "And if it had been that kind of relationship? I mean, if I'd fudged matters a little, been a little less honest, trotted out all the little white lies lovers do to keep the other man sweet instead of showing you the respect of being honest about my feelings and what

anted, would that have made a difference? Would you still have chosen Constable
nes over me?"

"You're trying to make everything too black and white."

"How apposite."

"Oh please."

"Sorry, there it is again. Comical knee-jerk reaction. You're saying, then, that
isn't that clear cut? Not binary? Yes or no? Black or white? Joseph or me?"

"Nothing's ever that clear cut, is it? But no one can keep having the best of
both worlds all the time. Sooner or later, a choice has to be made."

"I see. Very well." Cullen drew himself up. "If there's one thing I've learned
a politician, it's not to devote your energies to a cause you can't hope to win."
e leaned in, and before Dave could say or do anything to stop him, he kissed him
the mouth. "Although, if there's one thing I've learned as an elite sportsman,
s never to give up the game before it's over." He stepped back. "Beneath that
thlessly pragmatic exterior of yours, Sergeant Lyon, there beats a surprisingly na-
e heart. Dare I say, it's part of your fatal attraction. I wish you well of Joseph, I
ally do. He seems a sweet boy. But *youth's a stuff will not endure*. I still think we could
ake a very effective team, you and I. So, *au revoir*, David. Not *adieu*."

"Goodbye, Sean."

Joe arrived ten minutes later. "Quick! Quick! Television!" Bemused, Dave
ached for the remote and turned the television on. "Local news."

The screen flickered on to show the riverside carpark Dave had come from
ly hours previously. Over a caption that read "Breaking: Star Cop Saves Escaping
isoner," Dave caught shaky shots of himself being wrapped in a silver foil blanket
Sergeant McNeil, while in the background a similarly wrapped Karen Haines
s being bundled into a police car. In the background he saw PC Baz South, his
ad hanging while Inspector Summerskill harangued him at length. He had a feel-
g it was just as well her words couldn't be picked up by the microphone.

The camera suddenly shifted and steadied on a head and shoulders shot of
rah Moody. "Extraordinary scenes here of heroism and some haplessness as local
lice arrest, then lose, then save a suspected murderer. We understand the hero
the day is Inspector Dave Lyons. We are unable to speak to him at this moment,
t in the background, you can see his number two, Inspector Summerby. I'm
ing to go over now and try to get an interview with her."

The camera swung round to focus on Claire, zooming in, and wobbling mad as the cameraman moved rapidly towards her, while from the reporter came cri of "Inspector Summerby. Inspector Summerby. Sarah Moody of *Midlands No* Can you tell me, how do you feel?"

Dave turned it off. "I can't look. I really can't look. Tell me Claire didn't h her."

"It was a close thing, but I think she was too mad at Baz to have anything le for the media. She gave a no comment." Joe held up his mobile. "And you're a over social media again. Hashtag *wetshirtcop*. Got to say you looked well hot wi your shirt all clinging to you like that."

"Trust me," said Dave, shivering at the memory, "I was not hot."

Joe's eyes narrowed with concern. "You okay? You should be in hospital, yc know, getting them to look you over."

"So I've been told."

"Come here, you." Joe went to put his phone down on the table so that h could hug Dave. As he did so, he finally noticed the flowers that Sean Cullen ha left. "Wow. Someone rob a flower shop?"

"An admirer."

"DI Summerskill?" Joe ventured, semiseriously.

Dave snorted. "No."

"Who then?" He grinned. "Anyone I should know about?"

"Yes actually. Sean Cullen."

"What? The MP?"

"Our local member of Parliament. Yes."

Joe's liveliness faded a little, replaced by bemusement. "What, so they gi flowers now? That was the guy we met in Gallery 48 that time, right?"

Dave winced at the memory. "That's the one."

"He…"

"We had a thing, Joe. For a while."

"Oh. Right. Wow. You and an MP." Dave waited. He knew what Joe wa thinking: about that hellishly awkward meeting, about what Dave had been lik what Cullen had been like; about Dave's frantic request to him afterwards not t tell anyone; about Cullen's recent visit to the station; about the flowers on the tab. And now he came to think about it, could Joe smell the lingering mark of Cullen logne? He'd be thinking about timescales. Where had Cullen ended and Joe be-n? Had it been that simple? Joe stepped back from him. "Wow."

"It's over."

Joe looked at the flowers and then back to Dave. "Is it?"

"Yes. Completely over." Dave reached out and took both Joe's hands in his. oe Jones, I love you and want to be your boyfriend. Will you move in with me?"

Chapter Thirteen

"And did he say yes?"

Dave took a sip from his coffee mug, keeping Claire hanging for a few seconds fore answering. "Yes."

"Good."

"Good? Is that it? After all the manipulating and cajoling you put into this, all u can say now is good?"

Claire affected a thoughtful look. "Well, of course, I am disappointed."

"What?"

"Well, most of the fun is in the manipulating and cajoling, and that's all done w, but I suppose I'll get over it." She laughed. "Seriously, though, I am pleased. e'll be good for you."

"*He'll* be good for *me*?"

"He'll help you lighten up. At least I hope he will. You need someone to re- ind you there's life beyond these four walls." She gestured at the none-too-well inted surrounds of their Foregate Street office. "It's what you deserve."

"Thanks." Dave finished off the last of his coffee. "And what about you?"

"What do you mean?"

Dave said nothing and waited.

"I'm good."

Dave waited some more.

"No, really. I'm good."

Dave gave her another couple of seconds.

"We're separating," she said. "Ian and Me. Living apart. For a while at least."

"I'm sorry."

"It wasn't working. If something isn't working you need to…move on."

"Right."

They sat for a moment, both pretending they were interested in their empty coffee mugs.

"You all right?" Dave asked.

Claire shook her head. "But I will be. That's the way it goes, isn't it?"

"Can I help?"

Claire gave herself a shake and ran her fingers through her hair. "Well, you could begin by getting this bloody paperwork on the Whyte case sorted."

"Yes, well, you did make that just a little bit more complicated at the end."

"*I* made it complicated?"

"I believe the word 'prat' was used, quite loudly, with reference to Police Constable South?"

"He *was* a prat! A suspect in handcuffs and he lets her go for a splashabout the river!"

"To be fair, pound for pound, I think Haines had the advantage. And while accurate, 'prat' is frowned upon as a designation for a junior officer."

"I'm going to be put on a course, aren't I?"

"You might get off with a light reprimand from Madden. If you apologise to PC South."

"I'd rather poke my own eyes out with my well-manicured nails," Claire said with quiet venom.

"Well maybe I can use my…connections with a certain young friend of South's to see if we can skip over the apology."

"And do you still have any connections with a friend of Madden's that you can use to get me off the tongue-lashing?"

"No," said Dave.

Claire nodded. "Good." She reached for the first of that day's batch of paperwork. "By the way, you'll notice the absence of a certain detective inspector."

"Rudge? I assumed he was out eating children."

"I hear he's with Madden now. And not for a dressing down either." Claire gave him a smile. It was the one he had come to distrust weeks ago. It was the smile e'd given when she'd first started to try fixing him up with Joe. "I hear our Jim finally thinking of retiring."

"I thought being undead meant you kept working forever."

"We'll be an inspector down."

"Until Cortez gets his feet under the table."

"Terry? C'mon. You'd be twice the inspector he could ever be. What's the atter with you? I thought you'd be all over this like a shark scenting blood in the ter."

Dave smiled. "Thanks for the comparison. And for the vote of confidence. t no. I won't be putting myself forward."

"You think you wouldn't get it?"

"I think I might. And now isn't the time."

"Because of Cullen?"

"Yeah. Sean muddied the waters. If I got promoted now, people wouldn't ow if I'd got it on my own merits or because of his influence. I couldn't work th that. Besides"—he adopted a deliberate air of breeziness—"I've got a new ationship going on. We'll probably have to start looking for a house, shortly. od knows how we're going to manage in my small flat on top of each other all e time." He held up his hand. "Don't!"

"And the cats. Don't forget the cats."

"That's lesbians, ma'am." Dave looked dreamy for a moment. "Though I uld like a dog. We always had dogs growing up. "

"Enough already," Claire said. "Paperwork. You know you love it."

"You know me too well." Dave pulled over his keyboard and went to enter s password.

"One thing."

Dave paused, hands over the keys.

"That last boyfriend of Victor Whyte's. The first one, really, the one he had on after moving to Worcester but the last one I got to investigate. Roz didn't e me any contact details for him. I thought that was her being a bit flaky or even ing cross with me for barking up the wrong tree. Turns out, she had good enough son. Jen did the research and got this." Claire passed across to Dave's desk a gle sheet of paper.

Dave scanned the few lines of print. "He's dead."

"A long time ago. He and Victor were together for seventeen years. On sixty-two when he died."

"Which means…"

"He was forty-five when he and Victor met. And Victor was twenty-one. I' sorry."

"What for?"

"I had this feeling that Victor…liked younger men. That it might have ha something to do with the case. I was wrong."

"You had a feeling, and you went with it. It's what we do."

"Thanks." Claire took back the piece of paper from Dave. "Ray Jordan," sl said, reading the name on it. "I hope he made Victor happy. He must have been mess when he first came down here."

"He made mistakes, and I think in some ways, he spent the rest of his li trying to make up for them, especially at the end, but he was a man with a lot give." Dave raised his coffee mug. "Here's to Victor."

Claire raised her mug. "To Victor."

About Steve Burford

eve Burford lives close to Worcester but rarely risks walking its streets. He has
ded conveyor belts in a factory, disassembled aeroplane seats, picked fruit on
ms, and taught drama to teenagers but now spends his time writing in a variety
genres under a variety of names. He finds poverty an effective muse, and since
last book has once again been in trouble with the police. (He would like to thank
e inventor of the speed camera.)

E-mail
Summerskilllyon@gmail.com

Website
www.summerskillandlyon.com

Other NineStar books by this author

Summerskill and Lyon series

It's A Sin

Bodies Beautiful

Sticks and Stones

Also from NineStar Press

Good Boys by Keelan Ellis

aving risen through the ranks of the Baltimore City Police Department to the te Homicide unit as an out gay man, Paul Solomon has always prided himself on integrity and self-reliance. As the last vestiges of his failed eight-year-long rela-nship fall away, Paul finds himself adrift, forced to rely on others to help him d his footing again.

hen Paul and his partner, Tim Cullen, are called to the scene of a double murder two high school students on the city's west side, Paul finds the lives and deaths the two boys hitting closer to home than he'd expected. With his personal life upheaval, he struggles with the perspective needed to untangle the web of secrets d lies that led to their demise.

hile working his way through the complicated case, Paul starts getting his life ck together. After a date with an enigmatic young man takes a dark turn, he

reaches out to an old flame who brings some much-needed lightness to his life. B
Paul finds that relationships, like murder investigations, are never as simple as he
like.

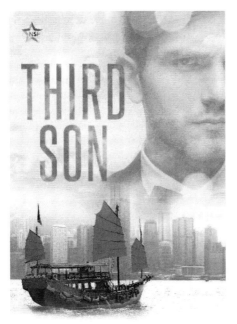

Third Son by Mickie B. Ashling

nerican Niall Monroe returns to Hong Kong—a city he calls home—after being
~ay for eight years. He hopes to finally find happiness with Peter Wei, his closeted
~er of fourteen years, but is disappointed to find Peter has been put in an unten-
le position. He must marry and produce the long-awaited grandchild or get cut
f by his millionaire father.

~rard Sun, a talented artist, bursts back into Niall's life after a one-night stand in
s Vegas. Circumstances force the men to deal with their attraction, especially
~en Niall's firm considers Gerard to help promote tourism in the People's Re-
blic of China.

~nes, Peter's younger brother, has been Niall's best friend since they were school-
ites. He encourages Niall to ditch his brother and move on. He encourages Niall
 ditch his brother until he finds out Niall is thinking of dating Gerard Sun, a
ented artist.

Coming home seemed like a great idea until it wasn't. Niall finds himself a strange in a familiar landscape, slammed on multiple fronts by broken promises, jealous intrigue, unimaginable deceit, and undercurrents of evil. As his dreams quickly turn into nightmares, Niall reaches out to new allies for support.

Connect with NineStar Press

www.ninestarpress.com

www.facebook.com/ninestarpress

www.facebook.com/groups/NineStarNiche

www.twitter.com/ninestarpress

www.instagram.com/ninestarpress

Printed in Great Britain
by Amazon

87813965R00121